The Sirena Quest

Books by Michael A. Kahn

The Sirena Quest

The Rachel Gold Mysteries
Grave Designs
Death Benefits
Firm Ambitions
Due Diligence
Sheer Gall
Bearing Witness
Trophy Widow
The Flinch Factor
Face Value

Writing as Michael Baron
The Mourning Sexton

The Sirena Quest

A Novel

Michael A. Kahn

Poisoned Pen Press

Poisoned Pen Press
6962 E. First Ave., Ste. 103
Scottsdale, AZ 85251
www.poisonedpenpress.com
info@poisonedpenpress.com

Printed in the United States of America

For Sophie, Madeline, Oliver, Charlie,
Phoebe, and others to come.
Love, Grandpa Mike.

Acknowledgments

As with my other books, this one would not have been possible without the inspiration, love, and support of Margi, my editor-in-chief and soulmate for life.

Oh, to live on Sugar Mountain,
With the barkers and the colored balloons.

—Neil Young

Prologue

In the beginning there was the pink slip.

At least that was the conclusion of the college's archivist, who had compelling reasons to get it right. When he and the others tried to piece it all together afterward—to gather the key documents, interview the main players, get the facts set down in proper sequence—most of them would focus on the message slip.

Here, they would declare, holding the pink phone message slip aloft.

Here is where our story begins.

Perhaps.

Where do you begin a narrative?

Not an easy call.

There's always a backstory. Every tale is a tale already in progress.

Always.

Think of Act I of *Hamlet*.

Or the attack on Fort Sumter in 1861.

Or the opening paragraphs of *Moby Dick*.

Or that scratchy announcement at 4:18 p.m. on July 20, 1969: "Houston, Tranquility Base here. The Eagle has landed."

And then think of each of those backstories.

Thus our challenge: where in the stream of these remarkable events do we wade in?

The origins of our story predate the pink message slip by more than a century. Many who read this account already know the backstory. They know when Sirena first arrived. They know that she'd been loved and that she'd been kidnapped and rescued and kidnapped again and rescued again.

And that she'd disappeared.

And then years passed.

And then decades.

Until we reach June 6, 1994—a date hitherto known, if at all, as a slow news day following a busy month. During May of 1994, Jacqueline Kennedy Onassis died of cancer, Nelson Mandela won South Africa's first democratic elections, Michael Jordan swapped his Air Jordans for baseball spikes, and President Bill Clinton beamed as Israeli Prime Minister Yitzhak Rabin and PLO leader Yasser Arafat signed what the pundits declared "an historic accord" on Palestinian autonomy.

June sixth. No big headlines. Not much on the sports page. Nothing special at the movies, either. Release dates for *Forest Gump* and *Pulp Fiction* are later that summer. Ace of Base's "The Sign" sits atop the rock chart. For a little more perspective: the first iPhone is still thirteen years away.

All we have for that day is the pink message slip—stuck in the middle of a pile of pink message slips on the desk of Lou Solomon, Class of 1974. The handwriting on that slip states that the call came in at 10:48.

That would be 10:48 a.m., Central Daylight Time.

On Monday, June 6, 1994.

As good a place as any to wade in.

Part 1:
The Call

She has pouting lips and high round breasts. Thousands of men have dreamt of her. Hundreds have chased after her. Two have died in pursuit.

Her name is Sirena, she weighs 193 pounds, and she vanished in 1959.

Without a trace.

"The Lady Vanished:
Pining for the Eternal Prom Queen of Barrett College,"
NEW YORK TIMES SUNDAY MAGAZINE (Dec. 10, 1972)

Chapter One

At 10:48 on the morning of June 6, 1994, Lou Solomon was in his law firm's library. That in itself was noteworthy. The law library of Rosen & O'Malley, as with the libraries of most large law firms, is not a likely place to find a partner. Although one may occasionally poke his head in looking for an associate or to scan that day's *Wall Street Journal*, the library is—as its name suggests—a place for research. Within the law firm hierarchy, associates do the research. They are, in the jargon of the profession, the mind mules.

Even more unusual, by 10:48 that morning Lou Solomon had already been in the library for nearly three hours. And there he would remain for several more. There hadn't been a partner in the Rosen & O'Malley library for that long since old Mr. Caruthers spent the night back in the spring of 1982, and that didn't really count. After all, when the assistant librarian found the seventy-four-year-old tax attorney the following morning slumped against the side of a carrel, his right arm clutching volume four of *Scott on Trusts*, he was already in an advanced stage of rigor mortis.

When Lou finally gathered his research materials at three that afternoon, two male junior associates peered over their library carrels to watch him leave. As the door swung closed behind him, they exchanged glances.

"Almost seven hours," one said.

The other shook his head. "That's incredible, dude."

He said it with affection.

Lou Solomon was a favorite of the associates. The younger litigators tried to emulate his unassuming style in front of judges and juries, and he was often the topic of firm lore when associates gathered for lunch during the week or over pitchers of beer at Dooley's after work on Fridays.

As the older associates occasionally reminded the younger ones, Lou Solomon had been a different guy back when they joined the firm.

"Remember when he played on the softball team?" one would reminisce between sips of beer.

"Lou played?" a younger associate would ask.

"Oh, yeah. He was good, too. Damn good. Played ball in college, didn't he, Dave?"

And then Dave would lean back with a smile. "He ran the summer program when I was a law clerk."

"My summer, too. Remember those float trips?"

"What float trips?" a younger associate would ask.

"He organized this annual float trip down the Meramec. It was a real hoot."

Invariably, one of the senior associates would add, "She used to go on the float trips with us."

"She?"

"Andi."

And then there'd be silence. They all knew about Andi, even the ones who'd never met her. Especially the women.

"Yeah," one of the senior associates would eventually say. "He was a different guy back then."

Standing at the library carrels, the two associates watched as Lou disappeared down the hall.

"What's he working on?"

"I think it's that Donohue appeal."

"Donohue? Isn't Brenda on that with him?"

"She says Lou's obsessed."

And he was. Obsessed and haunted.

The brief was due tomorrow, and he still couldn't let go. He'd promised Brenda his final changes by six that night. That would still leave her enough time to proof and cite-check the brief, shepherd the final version through the word processing department, and arrange to have the correct number of copies bound and filed in the court of appeals by the close of business tomorrow afternoon.

The Donohue appeal.

Its grip on Lou was all the more unusual because of the type of case it was. Lou's specialty was complex commercial litigation—or, as those cases are known among law firms, elephant orgies: massive disputes featuring lots of parties, warehouses of documents, Dickensian plots, hordes of witnesses, squadrons of attorneys, and millions and millions of dollars at stake. His growing reputation in the field had placed him on the short lists of most general counsels in the region, which made him, at the age of forty-one, one of the firm's top rainmakers.

But the Donohue appeal was no elephant orgy. The case arose out of a traffic accident, that hoary staple of the personal injury bar. Nevertheless, it possessed him like none he'd ever worked on. He found himself thinking about it in bed at night and on his morning jog and off and on during the day while listening to a long-winded client on the phone or waiting in court for a motion to be called. Although he was hardly the introspective type, Lou wondered about his devotion to this lost cause.

His office was one floor above the library. As he reached the interior stairway between the two floors, he was flipping through his research notes. He scanned one of the pages as he bounded up the stairs two at a time. The human shape registered in his peripheral vision at the last possible instant.

Roger Madison ducked back to avoid the collision.

"Whoops," Madison said. "That was close."

"I'm sorry, Roger."

The older man chuckled. "No harm, no foul, Louis."

Roger Madison, a litigation partner who specialized in condemnation matters, was sixty-three, bald, slightly hunched over, and recently divorced. His only son, Roger Jr., had died of AIDS a year earlier. Lou was close enough to Madison to pick up the tang of alcohol beneath the Polo cologne.

Lou gave him an apologetic smile as he started back up the stairs. "I'm a little out of it today, Roger."

"No problem, Iceman."

Lou paused and looked back, but Madison was already heading down the stairs.

Iceman.

He started up the stairs again, shaking his head.

He was scanning the headnotes of the next case in the pile as he strolled into his office. Taking a seat on the front edge of his desk, he began reading the court opinion.

The Donohue appeal.

It was a tale any fiction editor would reject as forced and overwrought and far too dependent upon coincidence. Thing was, God seemed to like them that way. The law books were filled with Donohue appeals—fact patterns served up with heavy platters of melodrama, seasoned with pure happenstance, and smothered in a thick gravy of pathos.

The Donohue of *Donohue v. Henderson Construction Co.* was Jane Donohue—attorney, widow, quadriplegic, mother of two little girls. The Henderson Construction Company had been her client. When old man Henderson died a few years back, Jane advised his adult sons to restructure the company into three separate corporations, one responsible for finances, one for marketing, and one for operations. Her legal strategy was to limit the liability exposure of the operations end of the business. The sons agreed, Jane drew up the new corporate papers, and six weeks later a Henderson dump truck loaded with eight tons of hot asphalt ran a stop sign in her subdivision and plowed into the driver's side of her station wagon, leaving her paralyzed from the neck down.

Jane was a widow at the time of the accident, her husband having died of cancer a year earlier. She hired Lou to represent her and her daughters in the lawsuit, and he'd grown close to all three over the course of the fourteen months of pre-trial proceedings. He'd even taken the two little girls—Emma and Abby—on several outings with his children to the zoo, the science museum, and elsewhere.

He tried the case earlier that year. Forty-five minutes after closing arguments, the jury returned a verdict in Jane's favor for $3.2 million. That was the good news. The bad news was that the judgment was against the operations corporation, which had total assets of $384,000. Jane Donohue's medical bills alone had long since exceeded that amount.

Lou had been struggling with the appellate brief for weeks. The court had granted him three extensions of time as he searched for a loose brick in the legal fortress that Jane had built around the assets of the business. With no support from Missouri precedents, he had spent the last seven hours scouring the legal countryside for aid, reviewing dozens of court opinions from other states and law review articles from across the nation in what seemed an increasingly doomed effort to get some money to a paralyzed woman and her little girls. He'd even turned to California cases—a true sign of desperation. Asking a panel of Missouri appellate judges to follow a Left Coast precedent was akin to asking them to join you in a rousing evening of pansexual bondage. You might get lucky, but the odds were against you.

But even with California in the mix, there wasn't much help out there. He set the court opinion down and with a sigh of fatigue reached for the latest draft of the appellate brief.

And that's when he saw the pink Phono-O-Gram slip.

Actually, he saw several. They were in a neat stack on top of the latest draft of the brief. He picked up the slips and started flipping through them. He stopped when he came upon the one from 10:48 that morning:

> Mr. Gorman of San Diego called re "fame and fortune" (His words) "Change of plans." Arrives @5 PM tomorrow: TWA Flight 432. Said you should "clear your calendar and fasten your seat belt."

Lou smiled as he leaned back.

What was Gorman up to now?

Their twentieth college reunion was less than two weeks away. Three months earlier, Ray Gorman had put Lou, Gordie, and Bronco Billy together on a conference call and made them take a pledge to meet him at Barrett College two days before the reunion. It would be the first gathering of the James Gang since the end of freshman year.

Lou read the message again.

Change of plans?

He checked his watch. Twenty minutes after three. He'd promised Brenda the brief by six. San Diego was two hours behind St. Louis time. He'd call Ray later.

He flipped through the other messages. Nothing urgent. He folded Ray's message slip and put it in the pocket of his white dress shirt.

Chapter Two

Two hours later, Lou handed Brenda Harris his marked-up final draft of the Donohue brief.

"If you have any questions," he told her, "call me at home. I'm coaching a Little League game tonight, but I'll be home by nine. If you need me before then, you can try my cell phone. I'll have it with me at the game."

She nodded solemnly and reached for the draft. Brenda was a second-year associate from the University of Chicago—frizzy red hair, wire-rim glasses, thin, intense. Like many younger associates at Rosen & O'Malley, she worked late most nights and was down at the office at least one full day each weekend.

She looked up from the draft as Lou turned to leave. A moment later, she leaned back in her chair with a wistful expression.

It was an expression Lou tended to evoke in women, and not just those who knew about his situation. He was a tall, good-looking guy who kept in shape by running four miles each morning and playing basketball in the bar association league. During a rowdy secretaries-only gathering after the firm's Christmas party last year, they voted his the best butt in the firm.

Butts aside, women loved his boyish smile and his intelligent brown eyes and the way his thick dark hair was tousled from a habit of running his fingers through it as he concentrated. But what charmed many of them the most was the vulnerability they sensed beneath that superlawyer persona.

As Lou reached the main reception area, he heard the unmistakable chortle of Ben Schwartz. The silver-haired partner was standing by the elevator with Cindi Shields, one of the firm's paralegals. She was giggling at something Ben had told her.

"Ah, Louis." Schwartz gave him a wink. "I was just imparting the wisdom of the ages to our lovely young Cynthia."

With his white handlebar mustache and bronze tan, Ben had the look of a well-groomed satyr.

"What's Ben's gem tonight?" Lou asked her.

She giggled again. "He is *so* bad."

Cindi had permed blonde hair, blue eyes, a perpetual tan, and a wardrobe selected to highlight her full breasts and long legs. Tonight she had on a short black skirt, a silky white blouse, black suspenders, and spike heels. The suspenders ran directly over the center of each breast.

Ben was grinning. "A riddle worthy of the Sphinx, Louis. Why do you need one million sperm to fertilize just one egg?"

Lou shrugged. "No idea."

Ben looked at Cindi. "Enlighten him, my dear."

She leaned toward Lou, brushing her right breast against his upper arm as she put her hand on his elbow. "Because none of them will ask for directions."

Lou smiled. Yet another from Ben's anthology of cornball dirty jokes.

Ben Schwartz had been at Rosen & O'Malley for almost fifty years. Now the firm's oldest partner, he was the polar opposite of Sidney Rosen, the founding partner.

Sidney Rosen, a brilliant Russian immigrant, arrived in St. Louis penniless in 1916 and worked his way through college and night law school. From the Depression years until a heart attack felled him in his office in 1967, Rosen had crafted corporate structures and estate plans of Byzantine complexity for his Jewish merchant clients. In the photographic portrait of him hanging in the firm's large conference room, Rosen stares into the camera, a thick cigar clenched between his teeth, his scowl amplified by the dark bushy eyebrows that joined above a tomahawk nose. The

Sidney Rosen you saw was the Sidney Rosen you got: a shrewd and fiercely puritanical man who married late in life, never had children, and devoted his evenings and weekends to work on behalf of numerous Jewish philanthropic organizations.

By contrast, Ben Schwartz's principal "community service" was his term as president of Briarcliff Country Club back in the 1960s—back when it was *the* exclusive Jewish country club. Back before, as he once told Lou, "we shamelessly lined our coffers with initiation gelt from real estate developers, shoe peddlers, and other *Galitzianers*."

Though brilliant by even Sidney Rosen standards—between his Yale undergraduate days and his law degree from Columbia University, Ben Schwartz had spent two years at Oxford as a Rhodes Scholar—he had long since decided that having the law as your mistress was far less appealing than having a mistress as your mistress. He entertained clients at the horse tracks and casinos, kept a stocked bar in his office, had been named co-respondent in the celebrated Singer divorce, and had *shtupped* Judge Milton Abrams' wife Peggy every Wednesday afternoon in Room 402 at the Chase Park Plaza while handling a lengthy will dispute before His Honor.

Even in his self-described dotage, suffering from bourbon-induced impotence, Schwartz continued to escort the lovelier young paralegals and secretaries up to his secret "bachelor pad" at the Mansion House apartment complex overlooking the Mississippi River.

His erectile problems had not dampened his ardor. "I may not always have a hot dog," he once told Lou, "but I can still lick the mustard jar."

His wife Beatrice—a plump regal presence at charity balls around town—affected ignorance of her husband's philandering.

As Lou and the other two stepped onto the elevator, Schwartz explained that Cindi was joining him for dinner at Faust's in the Adam's Mark, just down the block.

And just across the street from your place at the Mansion House, Lou added to himself, remembering the weight of Cindi's breast against his arm. The younger lawyers hung around her office like dogs in heat, jostling for position and getting nowhere, failing to grasp that her target demographic was at least ten years older and several hundred thousand dollars a year beyond them.

Schwartz checked his wristwatch. "Louis, my boy, you calling it a night so soon?"

"Got a game in a half-hour."

"Ah, yes." Schwartz turned to Cindi. "Coach Solomon. The Connie Mack of the Little Leagues. Did you know that Louis named his son after his boyhood hero, Ken Boyer?"

Cindi flashed her 200-watt smile at Lou. "Really?"

Lou shrugged, willing to bet his next mortgage payment that she'd never heard of Ken Boyer.

They said their good-byes on the first floor. Lou headed toward the front exit while Schwartz and Cindi headed toward the side entrance. Her giggle made him turn back. She was leaning against Schwartz as they walked, her high heels clicking on the marble floor. Schwartz placed his arm around her, and his hand came to rest on her swaying hips. As she passed through the revolving door into the sunlight, her breasts were silhouetted through her blouse.

Lou walked south along Broadway past the Old Courthouse and Tony's restaurant. The Arch shimmered in the early-evening sun. Ahead to his right stood Busch Stadium. The Cardinals were in town tonight, and most in the arriving crowd wore something red—red shorts, a red baseball cap, a shirt with the birds-on-the-bat logo.

He walked up several flights of stairs at the Stadium East Garage, brushing past the fans coming down, mostly families.

Lots of mothers.

Mothers with kids. Mothers with husbands.

Everywhere, mothers.

He paused on the stairs, leaning against the rail, vaguely aware of people moving past him. It was as if a locked vault somewhere in his mind had sprung open. He started up the stairs again, forcing the vault closed.

Five minutes later, he was turning onto the entrance ramp to Highway 40. He checked his watch. The Little League game started in thirty minutes. Kenny would be there already. Another parent was bringing him.

Lou smiled as he loosened his tie. No time to change, but that was okay. He could feel the day's tensions ease as he began putting together the starting lineup in his head. He unconsciously reached for a pen in his shirt pocket, and when he did he felt the crinkle of the folded message slip. He pulled it out of his pocket, unfolded it, and reread Ray's message. Glancing at the telephone number, he punched it up on his Motorola cell phone, hoping he had reception, which tended to be iffy with these portable phones. Ray's secretary answered and put him on hold.

Just as Lou passed under the Science Center walkway that spanned the highway, Ray came on the line.

"Hey, Solomon, you got any trials the next two weeks?"

Lou squinted as he tried to remember his calendar. Two Little League games, a deposition, several client meetings, no trials.

"Nope."

"Excellent. We got a slight change of plans, buddy."

"Oh?"

"I'll fill you in tomorrow night. We're catching the morning flight to St. Louis. It gets in around five."

"Who's we?"

"I'm bringing Brandi along. We're staying at the Marriott downtown. She's going to go spend some time with her family in Peoria after we're through."

Lou changed lanes as he approached the I-170 exit.

He asked, "What's happening in St. Louis?"

"Got to meet some money boys about refinancing one of the shopping malls, but that's just a tax excuse for Uncle Sam." Ray paused, and when he spoke again his voice was low. "I may have a lead."

"On what?"

"Sirena."

Lou drove on in silence for several seconds.

"Really?"

"Maybe."

Ray said something more, but his voice broke up in static.

"Say that again," Lou said.

"Been sitting on it for about a year. Then I saw that thing in the alumni magazine. About all that money. You see it?"

"Yep."

"Two mill for the finders. And then *People* magazine put up another mill for the story rights. Got me thinking. Had one of my people do some calling around. Could be just a wild goose chase, but I figure what the hell? It's worth a shot."

Lou asked, "What did you find?"

"I'll tell you tomorrow. Meet you in the hotel bar around six-thirty. Gotta go, buddy."

Chapter Three

Lou let the cat out around midnight and made his final rounds. Kenny was scrunched against the wall, the bed sheets tangled around his feet, a Calvin and Hobbes book on the bed near his pillow. Lou straightened the sheets, put the book on the nightstand, and kissed his son gently on the forehead.

"Beautiful catch tonight, champ," he whispered.

Kenny shifted in his sleep and scowled.

Lou glanced around the darkened room. Kenny's backpack hung from the closet doorknob. He carried it to the hallway and searched through it for school announcements and Kenny's work papers. He found some of each, stepped back in the bedroom, re-hung the backpack, and moved back in the hallway to see what Kenny had brought home:

There was a permission slip for a field trip to the Missouri Botanical Gardens next week, along with a note from Kenny's teacher seeking parent volunteers. Lou had helped chaperon Kenny's field trip to the zoo—the only father among a group of mothers—but Kenny had been pleased.

Next was a lunch card reminder:

Your child has only $2.35 on his/her lunch account. Please send a check for $20.00.

Lou folded the reminder slip and put it in his pocket.

There were three math work papers, each with a happy face and a 100 at the top. A spelling test. Kenny had missed two words:

Europe (Europ) and Portugal (Portugle). He hadn't mentioned the test results to Lou, but he must have been disappointed. He was so excited when he got a perfect score. Lou felt a pang of guilt. They usually practiced Kenny's spelling list the night before the test, but Lou had been working late on the Donohue appeal and hadn't gotten home until after Kenny was asleep.

Next stop: Katie's room.

She was asleep on her back, her arms folded neatly over her stomach. Lou looked closer in the dim light. Her arms were actually folded over a large book, which was open and face down on her stomach. Lou carefully slid the book out from beneath her hands and held it so that the cover would catch the light from the hall.

He smiled.

One of his high school yearbooks. He closed it, using his index finger to keep her place until he could find a bookmark. He kissed her softly on the bridge of her nose.

On the floor by her door was her social studies textbook, open to what appeared to be a unit on France. He could make out a photograph of the Eiffel Tower and another of an elderly man in a beret carrying two baguettes under his arm. Lou picked up the textbook and slipped it into her backpack, which was resting against the back of her desk chair.

He paused in the doorway for a moment to look at his daughter. As he did, he remembered back to when Katie was an infant, back to that night he awoke in the wee hours for no particular reason. Unable to fall back asleep, he'd gone into Katie's bedroom to stand over her cradle. As he watched his tiny baby girl sleep, he'd had a sudden vision of her as an old woman, bent with age, standing at a busy street corner as traffic whizzed by, confused and afraid. When Andi came into the room looking for him, he was still standing at the crib, tears streaming down his face, grieving over the vision of his baby girl grown old and helpless and without a father to protect her.

She was in fifth grade now, her final year of elementary school. Last Tuesday night he'd gone to parent orientation for the middle school. As he listened to the principal, he'd suddenly realized that this phase of Katie's years was coming to an end. Life in middle school would be much closer to life in high school—changing classes every hour, hall lockers, homeroom. He'd left the orientation session gloomy. His baby daughter was growing up.

As Lou walked down the hall toward the master bedroom his mind drifted from the Eiffel Tower in Katie's textbook to French cooking to Julia Child to Faust's restaurant to the elevator ride with Ben Schwartz and Cindi Shields. Schwartz's licking-the-mustard-jar joke metamorphosed into a steamy image of Cindi naked on Schwartz's bed, knees raised, hands cupping her full breasts, nipples taut, back arched, as Schwartz, leering in anticipation, placed his hands on her knees and lowered his head between those firm tanned thighs.

He shook his head, trying to clear the image as he sat on the edge of his bed. More than once since she'd joined the firm, Cindi had given him an obvious hint that she was his for the asking. He'd passed. His life was complicated enough without adding sport fucking to the schedule, especially with a coworker.

There were women, of course, including two—an in-house counsel at Monsanto and an anesthesiologist at Barnes Hospital. Both were at an age (twenty-eight for the lawyer; thirty for the doctor) and stage of life where they were interested in dinner, a movie, and sex—especially sex—but not commitment, which was okay with Lou, at least for now.

As he sat in the dark, his thoughts drifted to Ray's arrival tomorrow night.

He smiled.

A welcome complication. Although Ray's lead was probably a dead end, that was okay. It was a good excuse for them to see each other. After all those years, any excuse was good enough. Last fall they'd ended more than twenty years of silence, dating all the way back to their sophomore year.

Lou looked forward to spending time again with his freshman roommate—even if it was for some dead-end clue.

Then again, he reminded himself, it was always possible that Ray had stumbled onto a real lead. Just because hundreds of others had searched in vain for Sirena didn't mean that she'd never be found. Presumably, she was still out there somewhere.

He glanced over at his nightstand, where the special issue of the Barrett College alumni magazine laid face up. That was the issue Ray had mentioned in the phone call. The cover was the last known photograph of Sirena—the famous black-and-white shot taken at the senior class banquet in June of 1956. Sirena is seated in front of the upperclassmen, all of whom are dressed in black tie and standing at attention, staring solemnly at the unseen camera. She is, as always, seated and gazing into the distance.

As Lou stared at that photograph, he realized that he was still holding the yearbook with his finger saving Katie's place. Last year Katie had found a box in the basement filled with his high school memorabilia: yearbooks, student newspapers, clippings, varsity letters that had once been sewn to his letter jacket, report cards, photographs, SAT scores, programs from various high school sporting events—all stuff his mother had meticulously packed and stored when he left for college. When his parents sold their house eight years ago and moved to Florida, his mother made him take that box (and, to Kenny's delight when he discovered them last year, a shoebox filled with his old baseball cards). Although Katie was still years from high school, she loved looking through his high school mementos. Every few weeks or so she'd scavenge through the box and return from the basement with a new treasure.

He clicked on the reading light on his nightstand and looked at the black cover of the yearbook. The University City High School *Dial.* 1970. His senior year. He smiled. Probably hadn't looked at it since graduation, almost a quarter of a century ago.

In his nightstand drawer he found a bookmark and opened the yearbook to Katie's place. The first thing he saw was the white dress. He took a breath. His vision blurred for a moment before the rest of the photograph came into focus: the girl in the white dress, her escort in the white tuxedo and black bow tie. The girl's dark hair gathered on top of her head. Not even the institutional quality of the photograph could dull her Mediterranean beauty. She had a white corsage on one wrist. Her escort's dark hair flared out into wide sideburns that ended at his jawline. He wore a MAKE LOVE, NOT WAR button on the wide lapel of his tuxedo. They stood side by side, his arm around her waist, both of them smiling into the camera. Behind the couple was a large hand-painted banner: THE JUNIOR PROM COMMITTEE WELCOMES YOU TO "THE LOOK OF LOVE"! Lou read the caption under the photograph:

> Junior Prom Queen Andrea Kaplan and her escort, senior class president Louis Solomon.

At the bottom of the page, beneath the caption and the description of the prom, was a handwritten message in blue ink:

> Dear Lou - I'm so glad I got to know you this year!! You're such a groovy guy.
>
> 2 Good
>
> 2 Be
>
> 4 Gotten!
>
> Love ya forever,
>
> Andi XOXOXOXOXOXOX!!!!!

The "i" in Andi was dotted with a daisy.

◇◇◇

When Lou finally looked up, it was raining. Coming down hard. He placed the bookmark on the page, closed the yearbook, and placed it on the floor next to his nightstand.

He lay awake, listening to the sound of the rain, a steady drumroll against the roof.

It had rained that first night, too. He'd arrived in a thunderstorm, located James Hall on a campus map, slogged across the quad, lugged his footlocker and suitcase up the stairs, and, after a moment's hesitation, knocked on the door to Room 305. No answer. He'd unlocked the door, flipped on the light, and peered around. The outer room consisted of four bare desks and chairs on a scratched linoleum floor. On the far wall were two windows overlooking the quad. A door to the right opened into the bedroom, which consisted of two bunk beds and four banged-up dressers. There were four bare mattresses and no sign of anyone else's luggage. He was the first arrival.

He'd spent that first night alone, turning off the light after he finally finished the letter to Andi that he'd started on the Allegheny Airlines three-stopper from St. Louis to Bradley Airport. He'd lain in bed in the dark, the raindrops thrumming against the window, the muffled sounds of people in the hallway. The room had suddenly been illuminated by a bolt of lightning followed by a crash of thunder that rattled the window panes.

He'd squeezed back tears that first night. *Who was he kidding?* he'd asked himself. A Jewish kid from Missouri? A public school graduate from the Midwest in this New England enclave of preppies? *What was he doing there?*

Chapter Four

Shortly after six the following evening, Lou headed down the hallway toward the main reception area. They'd filed the Donohue brief in the Court of Appeals a little over an hour ago.

At last, he told himself with a mixture of relief and unease.

Coming down the hall in the opposite direction was Ron Perlow, one of the senior associates.

Lou smiled. "How'd the Carson deposition go?"

Perlow gave him the thumbs-up as he passed. "Pretty good, Iceman."

Iceman.

Lou shook his head with resignation.

He'd earned the nickname during his second year at the firm. Earned it on the final day of the Cunningham Industries trial—although "earned" might be too strong a word. The Lou Solomon at the end of that insane day thirteen years ago more closely resembled the stunned army private who receives a medal of honor for stumbling through the smoke and explosions on a blood-spattered battlefield.

He'd been the junior associate on the case—the grunt that spent the trial days on a hard bench in the back of the courtroom taking copious notes and then headed back to the office to work until the wee hours getting his superiors ready for the next day. But two weeks into trial, on the night before the long-awaited cross-examination of the defendant's founder and CEO, the lead trial lawyer was rushed to the hospital with a bleeding ulcer. The next morning, the high-strung junior partner freaked out and locked himself in a men's room stall after the judge denied his plea for a continuance. When the jury filed into the courtroom a few minutes later, there was only one attorney at defense counsel's table. A new face. The jurors eyed him curiously, as did the reporters for the *Wall Street Journal* and the other national publications that had been tracking the case.

"Ladies and gentlemen," the judge had said, "Mr. Reynolds has taken ill and can't be with us this morning. The young man at counsel's table is Louis Solomon. He'll be pinch-hitting this morning." He turned to Lou, eyebrows raised. "Do you have any questions for the witness, son?"

Lou glanced up at the witness box as he stood and walked to the podium. The imperious Jeremiah Cunningham gazed back with a look that seemed to say, *If you just sit back down, boy, you won't get hurt.*

Lou leaned forward so that his hands rested flat on the podium. That way Cunningham wouldn't see them shaking. He cleared his throat.

"I do have some questions, Your Honor."

Word spread back at the firm. When Lou's cross-examination resumed after the lunch recess, there were at least a dozen Rosen & O'Malley lawyers in the gallery. And Andi, too. She'd been called by one of the attorneys and rushed down to court. By noon the next day, shortly after Cunningham Industries had dismissed its lawsuit, he'd been given the nickname Iceman.

Iceman, he thought as he waited for the elevator.

He glanced down at his shoes and smiled. Awfully macho handle for a guy wearing loafers with tassels.

Even so, he'd never forget walking through the front door that night—the first time in a month that he'd been home before midnight. Andi came out of the kitchen wearing nothing but a red teddy and matching string bikini panties.

She'd placed her hands on her hips, given him an impish grin, and said, "Let's go upstairs and see if we can make the Iceman cometh."

Chapter Five

Lou entered the lobby of the Marriott and checked his watch.

6:32 p.m.

He smiled as he stepped into the bar, thinking back to all those late nights freshman year, stumbling down into the basement bar of one of the fraternities in search of Ray. He'd usually find him seated on a barstool, a sixteen-ounce plastic cup of beer in his hand, sometimes singing rugby songs with rowdy upperclassmen, sometimes staring vacantly at the wall above the bar, sometimes listening to the rambling words of wisdom from a boozy, melancholy senior. ("Never underestimate a fat girl after midnight," one drunken philosopher had advised them after they'd returned, alone again, from a mixer at Hampton College.)

Lou scanned the barstools.

"Yo, Lou!"

Ray was standing at a back booth. Lou waved and headed toward him. They gave each other a hearty handshake. A waitress appeared as Lou sat down. He ordered a beer, as did Ray.

"Where's Brandi?" Lou asked.

"Fucking TWA. Plane was late. Got to the hotel only fifteen minutes ago. She's in the room unpacking. She'll be down soon."

"So how's the shopping center czar of San Diego?"

Ray chuckled. "Up to my neck in Old Navy. Thank God for the American consumer. How're your kids?"

"Doing well."

"You still dating that sexy doctor—what's her name?"

"Robyn. Sort of."

"What the hell does 'sort of' mean?"

"We see each other about once a week."

"And?"

Lou shrugged. "Whatever it is, it isn't love."

Ray studied him a moment. "To quote that great American philosopher, 'What's love got to do with it?'"

"Ah, yes, Professor Tina Turner."

Ray grinned and leaned back in his chair. "Remember that concert? Freshman year?"

Lou nodded. "Remember the Ikettes?"

"Those chicks were wearing the shortest dresses I'd ever seen." Ray leaned back, smiling. "Ol' Ike Turner in the back with those shades? Jesus, what a badass he turned out to be."

"Shot his newspaper delivery boy, right?"

"Claimed the kid was throwing his paper in the bushes on purpose. Been reading all that crap in the papers about the twenty-fifth anniversary of Woodstock this summer. Bunch of nostalgic bullshit—summer of love, Age of Aquarius, and how Altamont sounded the death knell for the sixties. Altamont?" Ray shook his head. "Nope. Death knell was Ike Turner shooting his paperboy in the ass."

The waitress arrived with their beers and a bowl of roasted nuts. Although she was at least sixty years old and sixty pounds overweight, neither fact deterred Ray, the consummate waitress-schmoozer. He promptly got her into an animated discussion over the racetrack across the river.

As Lou watched them banter, he thought back to his first encounter with Ray—all the way back to that morning after his rainy night in the dorm room. Ray had been the first of the others to arrive. Lou had been expecting preppies. He hadn't been expecting a hood, which is what they called guys like Ray back in high school. Close-cropped black hair, long sideburns, an Iron City Beer T-shirt with a pack of Camels rolled up in one of the short sleeves. Sears-label dungarees, black wraparound sunglasses, paint-splattered construction boots. An army duffel bag in one hand, a leather bowling ball bag in the other.

After they'd introduced themselves, Ray set the bowling ball bag onto one of the desks and unzipped it. "Check it out, man." He pulled out the bleached white skull of an adult gorilla.

Two decades later, Lou noted, Ray had gone upscale in the clothing department. He wore a khaki safari shirt, navy-blue pleated chinos, a braided leather belt, and penny loafers sans socks. Brandi, or perhaps a clothing consultant from one of his upmarket shopping centers, must have steered Ray away from Sears and toward Lands' End.

He'd also put on at least twenty pounds since college, and there were touches of gray in his black hair. But the weight and the gray looked good on him. Ray had never been Hollywood handsome. Not even close. More like a nightclub bouncer or junkyard owner. He'd had plenty of rough edges back in college, and plenty of fistfights to back them up—in crowded bars, on the intramural football fields, and once at a candlepin bowling alley in Belchertown. But the extra weight and sprinkling of gray hair helped smooth some of those rough edges.

Made him almost look contented.

Almost.

Ray Gorman was the youngest of six sons of a Pittsburgh steelworker and the only one to go to college. Although his brain landed him at a prestigious liberal arts college in New England, he didn't concede an inch his freshman year. Went candlepin bowling on the weekends, chewed Red Man, and tacked above his desk posters of his two heroes: John Wayne and Joe Frazier. To celebrate Joe Frazier's pummeling of Muhammad Ali that year, Ray put on a keg for the floor. Schaefer's, of course.

When the waitress left, Lou asked, "So when's your meeting on the refinancing?"

"Tomorrow morning at nine." He gave a dismissive wave. "A couple of jarheads from Mercantile Bank. The whole thing'll last less than an hour." He leaned forward with a grin. "We got more important stuff to do in this town. You're on board, right?"

Lou gave him a noncommittal shrug. "I don't even know what I'm supposed to be boarding."

"The Sirena Express, dude."

"You really think you have a lead?"

"Maybe."

"Maybe?"

Ray raised his eyebrows. "Enough of a maybe to get in a goddamned plane and fly out to this shit-ass town."

"What about the others?"

Ray took a sip of beer. "I tried to reach Gordie yesterday, but he was out of the office. I'll try him again tomorrow."

"And Billy?"

"I reached Bronco. Told him I was meeting you today. Told him we'd check it out down here. Told him if it panned out, he and Gordie better be ready to shit and split."

"Can Billy get away?"

"Hard to say." Ray shook his head. "Poor guy. You ever met Dorothy?"

"She's a tough woman."

"A beast," Ray said. "Runs some sort of New Age nursery school—one of those cult outfits where the kids can only play with wooden toys and can't watch TV and can only wear clothes that are one-hundred-percent cotton. Poor Bronco. Talk about pussy-whipped."

Ray took a big sip of beer and reached for a handful of peanuts. "Worse comes to worse, we'll just have to liberate that sorry bastard." He popped the peanuts in his mouth and chewed. He took another sip of beer. "But, first we've got to make some progress down here."

"Speaking of which," Lou said, "what exactly is supposed to be down here?"

Ray was looking past Lou's shoulder. "Here she comes."

Lou turned as Brandi approached. He was not alone. Every pair of male eyes in the room followed her to the booth.

She gave Lou a big smile and bent over to kiss him. "Hello, Louis."

Brandi looked and smelled terrific. Her straight platinum hair was cut in a pageboy, which accented her hazel eyes, pug nose, and Southern California tan. Gordie Cohen had described her as a cross between Doris Day and the porn star Seka. Tonight she was wearing a simple cotton twill shirtdress with flap breast pockets, a wide olive belt, and white sandals. She could have stepped off the pages of *Vogue*.

She scooted into the booth next to Ray.

"How are you, Louis?"

"Doing okay. You?"

"Couldn't be better."

"Still swimming?"

"Of course." She paused to give the waitress her order. "Stoli and tonic water, twist of lime." She turned back to Lou. "Four nights a week. Girl's gotta make a living."

"Not really," Ray said.

"Yes, really." She gave Lou a wink.

"Still Queen of the Nile?" he asked her.

"Nah. They may bring that Egyptian shtick back for the summer, but this month—" she paused, giggled "—this month we're doing the French revolution."

"And it's truly revolting," Ray added. "You haven't seen dreck until you've seen 'The Love Slaves of Robespierre.' Worse yet, she plays Marie Antoinette in the 'Let Them Eat Cake' number."

"That one does sort of suck," Brandi said. "I wear these round cakes over my boobs. I pull them off at the end—the cakes, that is."

Ray said, "Hard to believe Meryl Streep got her start that way, isn't it?"

Brandi poked him in the side with her elbow. "Very funny, Raymond. Just wait. Someday, when Steven Spielberg decides to go aquatic on a remake of *Peter Pan*, I'll be ready."

When Lou visited Ray last fall—the first time they'd seen one another in more than twenty years—Ray had taken him to see Brandi's show. The huge neon sign out front proclaimed the Seahorse Saloon as "Home of the Topless Mermaids—Featuring

San Diego's Favorite Little Mermaid, Brandi Wine." The high wall behind the bar at the Seahorse Saloon was thick glass. It had taken Lou a moment to realize that it was actually the front side of an enormous tank of water. Except for a pair of red underwater lights and an occasional wiggle of bubbles, the water was dark and opaque.

At the hour, the lights had dimmed, and a tinny version of "The Theme from Rocky" came over the sound system. The underwater floodlights came on. An unctuous voice welcomed them to "the Seahorse Saloon's Special Salute to Ancient Egypt."

And some salute it was. Depending upon the scene, anywhere from two to five "mermaids" entered the water from an unseen platform above the bar and, with bare breasts bobbing and brightly colored G-strings flashing, enacted ninety-second routines, including such timeless masterpieces as "The Slave Girls of Tutankhamen," "A Romp with Ramses," and "An Afternoon With the Vestal Virgins of the Temple of Amon." Brandi played Cleopatra in the finale, wearing nothing but a pink spangled G-string and a rhinestone-studded headdress. She was flanked by four topless handmaidens, all wearing King Tut masks and treading water while the announcer offered a solemn tribute to "the glory that was Egypt."

The lights had come back on as the last stanzas of M.C. Hammer's "Can't Touch This" faded.

Ray Gorman had looked over at Lou and shook his head. "That's the kind of crap that gives kitsch a bad name."

But Lou came to appreciate Brandi, and mostly for reasons that weren't on display in that tank of water. She had a feisty, no-nonsense personality and a generous, sympathetic heart. Moreover, despite her cynical airs and Ray's gruff demeanor, they were clearly crazy about each another.

Brandi downed the rest of her drink and stood up. "Come on, guys, I'm starving. Let's get some chow."

"Where to?" Ray asked Lou.

Lou thought a moment. "Broadway Oyster Bar. Good food, good beer, good blues."

"Sounds like heaven," Brandi said.

As they walked south on Broadway past Busch Stadium, Brandi hooked an arm through each of their arms.

"It's awesome having you guys together again," she said. "You make a great pair."

Lou smiled. Once upon a time they'd been a great pair—in the dorm, in those freshman intro classes, at parties. Even at work in the dining hall, where the two of them—both on financial aid—had been assigned campus jobs as bussers. Wearing their white cotton jackets, they'd work the evening meal as a two-man team, pushing that cart up and down the dining hall, clearing the tables one by one—scraping and stacking the plates and trays, emptying and racking the glasses, sorting and standing the silverware in the baskets.

A long time ago.

Chapter Six

They were at a table in the outdoor courtyard listening to the Soulard Blues Band, which had just finished a rousing rendition of Muddy Waters' "Mannish Boy." The waitress cleared away their dinner plates. As she was setting down another round of beers, the band's drummer announced they were taking a fifteen-minute break.

"Okay, Ray." Lou set his beer mug down. "Tell me about this lead."

"More a hunch than a lead." Ray took another pull on his longneck Bud and leaned forward, lowering his voice. "About a year ago, I was in the library in Orange County. I'd been looking at some commercial properties in Newport Beach—trying to get a handle on the real estate values. So I spent an afternoon going through real estate listings. I began with current values and then started going back five, six, seven years, trying to find some patterns in the area. Well, in a lot of the issues, the real estate listings were back near the obituaries. Guess whose obituary was in one of those issues? Henry Washburn's."

Lou turned to Brandi. "Washburn used to be the president of Barrett College."

"Well, duh." She laughed. "Trust me, Louis, living with this guy means learning all about Henry Washburn."

Ray pulled out his wallet and removed a folded piece of paper. He handed it to Lou. "Check it out."

Lou unfolded the paper. It was a photocopy of Henry Washburn's obituary. He read it. Then he read it again, slower this time.

He looked up at Ray and frowned. "There's a clue in there?"

"More like a wild-ass hunch." Ray took another sip of beer. "I checked out Washburn. Dude never married. No wife, no kids. No gay lover, as far as anyone can tell."

Lou scanned the obituary again.

"'Survived by his sister Abigail,'" he read aloud.

"Exactly," Ray said.

Lou frowned. "Go on."

"Here's how I see it." Ray leaned forward again. "Guy spent more than half a century at Barrett College. First as a student, then as a geology professor, and finally as president. We're talking Mr. Barrett College. It's his whole fucking life. Then he retires."

Lou nodded. "Okay."

Ray glanced around and then raised his eyebrows. "Think about it. There he is, puttering around the house, carrying in his head the answer to the biggest mystery in the history of his college. What's the fun of a secret like that if you can't share it with at least one other person? But who? He's got no wife. He's got no kids. He's got no lover. Who's left?"

Lou pursed his lips and nodded. "It's possible."

"Good a guess as any."

"Was he close with his sister?"

"Don't know. But she was his nearest living relative."

Lou thought it over. Henry Washburn had not merely been *a* president of Barrett College. He was *the* president on May 29, 1959, which is when Sirena made her final appearance. That was the night of the senior banquet for the Class of 1959. Midway through the evening's festivities, a team of freshmen, accompanied by several armed Pinkertons, burst into the banquet hall and abducted her. During the ensuing automobile chase through the hills of western Massachusetts, one of the cars overturned. Its two occupants—both seniors—were killed, instantly, and gruesomely. One was decapitated. His head was never found— presumably carried off in the night by a wild animal.

The police brought Sirena back to the college the next morning, and there she remained, under heavy guard, until the wee hours of June 17, 1959. Out on the quad the following day, Henry Washburn opened his commencement address by announcing Sirena's departure. She had not been destroyed, he assured the buzzing audience. Instead, she was in transit at that very moment, heading toward her final resting place. She was gone, he declared, and she never would return.

After a heated debate at a special meeting later that day, the board of trustees affirmed Washburn's actions in a resolution that now hangs in the foyer of the Plympton Administration Building. It decrees that Sirena *shall be and is hereby removed from the premises of the College to her final destination, her location known only to President Henry Emerson Washburn and, upon his death, to none other.*

Lou asked, "When did Washburn die?"

Ray pointed to the date above the obituary. "Six years ago this July."

Lou began to smile. "So Abigail lives in St. Louis?"

"In Lemay Gardens."

"Which is?"

"A nursing home. In the south suburbs."

"How'd you track her down?"

"Easier than you'd think. Took one of my guys just two hours."

Lou finished his beer and set the mug on the table. "And she's willing to talk to us?"

Ray shrugged. "Don't know. Haven't asked. Visiting hours are one to four tomorrow. I thought maybe we'd just kind of show up and introduce ourselves to the little lady."

"Just like that?"

"Sure." Ray smiled. "We're talking mega-bucks for the school, dude."

"And don't forget the money for the finders," Brandi said.

Lou sat back in his chair and stared at Ray. "Henry Washburn's sister, eh?"

Ray gave him a wink. "I got a good feeling about this one."

Chapter Seven

By the time the Soulard Blues Band took their second break, Brandi was yawning. Big gasping yawns. She was entitled. The night before she'd done her three regular shows at the Seahorse plus a night-owl special for a San Diego Padres bachelor party. She didn't get to bed until after four in the morning. They flagged the waitress and paid the bill.

In the hotel lobby, Brandi gave Lou a big hug.

"It's so wonderful to see you, Louis."

Ray turned to Lou. "Wait here a sec."

Lou watched them walk toward the elevators. They were a wonderful pair, he thought, and wonderfully improbable. They'd met at a United Jewish Appeal Young Leadership event in San Diego. Ray was there because he'd heard that the UJA program was a good place to meet nice Jewish girls. After a series of miserable relationships with shiksas, he'd decided it was time to find a nice Jewish girl and settle down. Brandi was there in search of a nice Jewish man, having just walked out of a grisly two-year affair with a Vegas pit boss. She'd heard from one of her girlfriends that the UJA was filled with eligible, housebroken Jewish attorneys, doctors, and CPAs.

And thus two lapsed Catholics—Ray from St. Joseph's parish in Pittsburgh, Brandi from Sacred Heart in Peoria—found themselves seated next to each other during the UJA Young Leadership main event that night: a talk by the Israeli consul on

West Bank settlements. Both affected keen interest in the speech while sizing each other up. Ray fit Brandi's stereotype of a nice Jewish boy: black curly hair, broad nose, dark eyes, platinum Rolex. As for Brandi, although her blonde hair and blue eyes didn't quite fit Ray's stereotype, her nametag (B. Wine) assuaged his doubts. After all, he reminded himself, wasn't Goldie Hawn Jewish? It wasn't until their third date that they discovered their unexpected kinship. It was not until their sixth date that Brandi revealed the precise nature and venue of the "modern interpretive dance" that she performed for a living.

Over by the elevators, Ray said something to Brandi. She glanced over at Lou, back at Ray, and nodded. The elevator doors slid open, and Ray gave her a quick kiss before she got on. She waved good-night to Lou as the doors closed.

Ray came back to Lou. "Where's your car?"

"In the garage down the street," Lou said.

"Come on. I'll keep you company."

They walked to the end of the block. Busch Stadium was directly ahead. To their left was a multi-story concrete parking garage. The wind had picked up—a warm summer breeze that rattled the flagpoles in the plaza in front of stadium. The huge bronze statue of Cardinals legend Stan Musial—Stan the Man—shimmered in the moonlight. Lou looked up into a clear night sky. A crescent moon hung just above the ridge of the stadium. They crossed the street and stopped when they reached the parking garage.

Ray said, "Do me a favor."

"What?"

Ray was studying Busch Stadium.

"I was out of the loop all those years," he said. "First I heard was last year when you came to San Diego." He turned to Lou. "I want to say good-bye to her."

"What do you mean?"

"Tonight."

Lou looked away. "It's probably closed."

"Maybe not."

Lou stared at Stan Musial—bat cocked, head tilted at that trademark angle. Stan the Man appeared to be staring back, studying Lou, waiting for his response.

"Come on," Ray said. "I haven't been to St. Louis in more than twenty years, and with any luck I'll never come back to this shithole."

◇◇◇

They parked near the main entrance. The front gate was closed but Ray found an open service entrance around the side.

The moon and stars illuminated the pathways, although Lou could have found his way blindfolded. The first year he'd come here every Saturday morning after saying *Kaddish* at the synagogue. He'd tell her things—about the kids, her parents, her girlfriends. Sometimes he'd try to tell her about himself—his cases, crazy stuff at the firm, a book he was reading. Sometimes he'd try to apologize. Often, though, it was just too hard to talk.

As they approached her grave, Lou slowed his pace to scan the ground. He spotted a white stone about the size of a walnut and bent to pick it up. He straightened and pointed down the aisle.

"This way," he said.

They walked along the grass between the headstones. The wind was stronger now, the trees swaying and rustling, casting moon shadows over the graves.

Lou gestured toward the headstone.

The two of them stood side by side at the foot of the grave, facing the headstone. Lou tried to focus on the rustling of the leaves and the shifting shadows of the trees. In the moonlight, the engraved words were clearly visible:

ANDREA KAPLAN SOLOMON

1953 – 1990

Beloved Daughter, Wife, Mother, Friend

Lou stepped around the grave toward the marble headstone and placed the stone on the level top surface. He laid it near the one he'd placed there two weeks ago. He studied the new stone for a moment, and then slid it across the marble surface until it was touching the other one. He took a step back. His moon shadow fell at an angle across the headstone. He stared at his shadow as he listened to the rhythmic grinding of the crickets.

The past year he'd been to her grave about twice a month—several times with his children, once with her parents, other times alone, usually on his way home after work. He still talked to her. Not as much as before, but he made sure she knew about her kids, how they were doing, how they were growing up, how so much of her was in each of them. And, always, how much he missed her.

But tonight was the first time he'd brought an outsider. Lou glanced back. Ray was still at the foot of the grave, staring at the headstone.

Ray met Andi freshman year when he came home with Lou for winter break. Andi and Ray hit it off immediately and stayed in touch even after Ray had drifted away from the rest of them. They had a special simpatico—as if they had been siblings in another lifetime. During Ray's junior and senior years—when he was living off campus and completely out of touch with his freshman year roommates—he visited Andi at Wellesley whenever he went to Boston. They remained pals throughout.

Ray looked up. The branches overhead rustled and swayed in the moonlight, sweeping shadows back and forth across the plot.

"She was a helluva gal," Ray said.

Lou nodded.

Ray took a last look at her gravestone and turned to Lou. "Let's go."

Part 2:
Picking Up The Scent

$25 million. That's the ransom for Sirena, Barrett College's infamous kidnap victim. $23 million for the college plus $2 million for her rescuers, but only if they are alumni. This is strictly a Barrett College affair.

The two checks will be waiting inside an armored car on the fifty-yard line at the college's graduation ceremonies next week on June 17th. Sirena will turn 100 that day, Barrett College will turn 150, and the Class of 1959—the last class to hold her—will celebrate their 35th reunion. The alignment of those numbers caught the attention of Silicon Valley billionaire Robert Godwin, the wealthiest member of the Class of '59. His foundation has pledged $23 million to the college—to be known as the Sirena Endowment—and another $2 million reward to her rescuers, but only if she returns in time for the June 17 celebration.

No Sirena on June 17, no $25 million.

"The Ransom of the Century"
NEWSWEEK MAGAZINE (June 10, 1994)

Chapter Eight

Abigail Washburn, spinster sister of the late Henry Washburn, became a time traveler during her ninth decade on the planet. Although her body continued its journey down the narrowing rails of time, her mind occasionally jumped the track. Some days it was terrifying—lost in the woods, stumbling through the underbrush, strange voices in the shadows, searching for a gap in the thicket, a way back to the rails. But on days when she came upon a clearing—oh, that was almost too marvelous. Emerging into sunlight, eyes blinking, watching in wonder as a rerun of a favorite episode of *The Life and Times of Abigail Washburn* began unreeling. And always with her in the lead role.

Yesterday, for example. Oh, yesterday had been almost too grand for words. To be eighteen again, shopping at Stix, Baer & Fuller with her mother for that lovely white formal she would wear to the Veiled Prophet Ball.

Today was almost as splendid: planning her parents' fortieth wedding anniversary. Oh, what a simply marvelous party it would be. Top notch. Everything perfect, if only she could firm up the details with these two dim-witted caterers.

She gave them a stern look. "Good veal is the secret to Swedish meatballs," she repeated. "You do appreciate that, do you not?"

Ray turned to Lou, his eyes narrowing. The vein throbbing over his right temple eliminated any doubt that Ray's patience was about to run out. Lou stared at him with a barely perceptible but clearly translatable frown that said, *Cool it.*

After a moment, Ray looked down and shook his head.

Lou turned to her with a comforting smile. "I can personally assure you, ma'am, that we use *only* prime cuts of veal in our meatballs. That's what makes ours so special."

She wagged a crooked index finger at him. "And only *lean* pork, young man. I will not tolerate fatty meatballs." She closed her eyes and shuddered. "I absolutely loathe fatty meatballs."

Lou glanced at Ray. "We trim all the fat, don't we, Mr. Gorman?"

Ray was still staring at the floor.

"Don't we, *Mr. Gorman?*" Lou repeated.

"Yeah, yeah, yeah. Trim the Fat. That's our slogan."

Abigail leaned back against her pillows and nodded in satisfaction. With her unkempt white hair, gnarled fingers, and fierce brown eyes, she reminded Lou of a fairy-tale crone.

"Now that we finally have that item settled, gentlemen, shall we go over the canapés again?"

"Lord deliver me," Ray mumbled.

Brandi had dropped them off at the nursing home with a promise to pick them up in an hour. Lou checked his watch. Just twenty minutes to go. Thank God.

Although he didn't know the proper medical terminology, Abigail Washburn was batty. For the past forty minutes they'd been going over a menu for an imaginary anniversary party, apparently for the poor woman's parents. When their initial efforts to convince her that they weren't caterers sent her into a rage, Lou decided to play along, partly out of pity, but mostly in the hope that she might return to the present long enough for them to raise the subject of Sirena. After the first twenty minutes, Lou tried to nudge her in the right direction by asking whether her brother Henry would be attending the party. Abigail had sighed, shaken her head, and explained that his teaching commitments at Barrett College prevented it. When Lou tried to follow up, she refused to discuss the subject any further.

"Oh, yes," she continued, raising her index finger in the air, "you must make your oyster Roquefort canapés. Father absolutely adores them. I want three dozen. No, make that four.

Yes, four dozen of the little darlings would be perfect, don't you agree?"

"Yep." Ray checked his watch. "We'll make sure you got oysters out the ol' wazoo."

"Oh, how could I forget?" She clasped her hands over the front of her faded robe. "Shrimp vegetable kebabs. With tomato wedges and bacon. They are simply divine."

And so it went. Like some bad Monty Python routine, the appetizer list grew to include cocktail frankfurters with barbecue sauce, deviled ham pastry snails, asparagus cheese fingers, stuffed mushrooms, salmon mousse, egg salad triangles, and so on. By the time Abigail Washburn reached the desserts, Lou and Ray were both slumped forward in their chairs.

"Mother adores meringue. But you must be careful to beat the eggs until…until…"

The pause stretched into silence.

Lou looked up.

At first he thought she'd had a stroke. The old woman was sitting rigid in bed, eyes wide, mouth open, staring beyond them toward the door.

Lou turned.

Brandi Wine stood in the doorway, dressed in a flowery peasant dress and sandals.

She smiled at Abigail. "Hello, Miss Washburn."

Abigail was still gawking at Brandi, dumbfounded. Finally, she whispered, "Melinda Bennington."

Another long pause. Abigail shook her head in wonder. "My heavens, dear, we all thought you were dead."

Brandi glanced over at Ray, who rolled his eyes.

"No, ma'am," Lou said. "Miss Bennington is alive and well."

Abigail looked sharply at Lou. "And just who in Sam Hill are you, buster?"

Lou gave her a friendly smile. "A friend of Miss Bennington's."

Abigail frowned at Lou, but after a moment her attention shifted back to Brandi.

"My dear," she said to Brandi, her voice gentle, "everyone

thought you were on that train with your parents. It said so in the newspaper. We thought you perished with them. My heavens, there is even a gravestone for you in the family plot. I have been there. I have seen it myself."

Brandi smiled and curtsied. "But here I am."

Abigail nodded, pensive. "Henry thought you were killed. Oh, my, the poor boy has been so distraught, Melinda. So brokenhearted. But you are alive, dear!" She clasped her hands and pressed them against her chest. "Thank goodness."

Her eyes widened and she put her hand against her mouth. "Oh, wait until I tell Henry this glorious news! I shall write him today. Oh, you must write him, too, Melinda. You must! My heavens, Henry will be so gratified."

Brandi sat down on the edge of the bed. "Does he ever mention me?"

"Oh, yes, in many of his letters." She took Brandi's hand in hers and patted it affectionately. "He still loves you, my dear. He loves you so much. Of that I am quite certain."

Brandi smiled. "I used to adore his letters. Do you still have any?"

"Do I still have them?" she asked with feigned irony. "Of course, dear. I saved them all." She leaned back in bed and gave Brandi an appraising look. "I declare, Melinda, you look marvelous. I am positively rapturous that you are still alive."

"You have all of his letters?" Brandi asked.

"Oh, yes. Every last one of them."

Lou watched in wonder as Brandi actually blushed. She moved close to Abigail. "Can I read what Henry says about me?"

"Certainly, dear. I have them all right—" She stopped and turned to glare at Lou and Ray. Leaning toward Brandi, she whispered into her ear as she eyed the two men.

Brandi nodded. "You're absolutely right." She turned to Lou and Ray with a severe look. "Gentlemen, you will have to leave us now. Miss Washburn and I have private matters to discuss."

"Certainly, ma'am." Lou stood up. "We were just on our way out. C'mon, Mr. Gorman."

Chapter Nine

"Think she ever has visitors?" Ray asked.

Lou looked up from a dog-eared issue of *Better Homes and Gardens*. They'd been waiting in the lobby for almost an hour. He shrugged. "Does she have any family left?"

"Nope. It was just her and her brother. Neither of them married."

"So, no nieces or nephews," Lou said. "Maybe cousins? Check the sign-in book."

Ray walked over to the narrow table in front of the reception desk and Lou returned to "The Man Next Door" column at the back of the magazine. His mother had subscribed to *Better Homes and Gardens* for as far back as he could remember. He hadn't actually looked through an issue since he left home for college, but most of the contents were exactly as he remembered them. Indeed, as he skimmed through the jokes in "The Man Next Door" column, he found himself asking the same question he'd asked back in high school: Are there readers out there who actually find these jokes funny? Presumably—fortunately—he was still outside the magazine's demographics.

Ray joined him on the couch. He held the sign-in book, his expression was grim. "You are not going to fucking believe this."

"Who?"

"Over the last six months, Abigail Washburn had a grand total of two visitors. Two. And they signed in together three weeks ago."

"Who?"

Ray handed him the book and pointed to the entry for April 3rd:

H. R. Pelham
F. Burke

Lou leaned back. "Reggie and Frank?"

Ray slammed his fist into the couch. "I can't believe those bastards beat us here."

"What bastards?" Brandi asked as she joined them. She had a triumphant expression.

"Well?" Ray asked. "Have fun with the social director of the Bates Motel?"

"Raymond, my darling," she said playfully, "remember that diamond pendant we saw at the shop in La Jolla?"

Ray frowned. "Sort of."

"I earned it today."

"Yeah, yeah. Let's hear your story first. Did you get beyond the appetizers with that crazy broad?"

"Way beyond the appetizers, my dear. I had the main course. Guess what she has under her bed?"

"A twelve-inch vibrating dildo?"

"A footlocker."

"Letters?" Lou asked her.

Brandi nodded. "Including close to a hundred from her brother. Organized in chronological order, with each letter still in its original envelope. We divided them up. She looked through the first half and I looked at every letter from 1955 through his death."

"And?" Lou asked.

Brandi smiled. "Bingo."

"No shit?" Ray looked around and then gestured toward the front door. "Outside."

When they were on the parking lot, Ray said, "He told her where?"

"Not where, but who."

"What do you mean?" Lou asked.

She turned to Lou. "Apparently, her brother wasn't the one who hid the statue."

"Why do you say that?" Ray asked.

"He sent her a letter on July 4, 1959—which was about two weeks after he had the statue removed from the college." Brandi pulled a folded sheet of paper out of her purse. "I wrote down the key paragraph from the letter. Here it is."

"I was determined," she read, "to forever rid my school of that accursed harridan. Fortunately, among the sons of Barrett on campus for their reunions was the mastermind of the Homecoming Heist. Alas, he must remain nameless, even to you, my beloved sister. Suffice it to say, I summoned the gentlemen to my home later that evening, explained my decision, and requested his clandestine assistance. He accepted with alacrity. Four days later, I received a pithy message via Western Union: SHE HAS REACHED HER FINAL DESTINATION. My hands trembled as I carried that telegram over to the fireplace in my study, struck a match, lit the corner, and placed the burning slip of yellow paper on the metal grate. As it curled and blackened, I softly uttered, 'May she rest in eternal peace.'"

Brandi looked up from the sheet of paper and smiled. "Well?"

"Fucking aye." Ray punched Lou in the shoulder. "We're in the hunt, dude. I've got that book on Sirena at the hotel. I'm sure it'll have something on the Homecoming Heist, whatever the hell that was. Let's go."

"Wait," Lou said, nodding toward the sign-in book, which was still in Ray's hands. "Perhaps Abigail's friend Melinda should ask her about Reggie and Frank."

"Oh, yeah. Good thinking."

Ray explained the entries to Brandi and described what Reggie Pelham and Frank Burke looked like.

After Brandi returned to Abigail Washburn's room, Ray turned to Lou. "You're on board, right?"

The question had been looming since Ray's original phone message. Lou had already ducked it once, and now his first thought was to beg off—to say he just couldn't get away, to apologize and wish his college buddy the best of luck. It was the responsible thing to do, and it was also true. He had plenty of responsibilities on his platter. A forty-two-year-old single parent with two children, a big mortgage, a stable of important clients, and several big lawsuits that needed attention didn't just drop everything to head off on what was likely a futile hunt for a missing statue that had eluded all pursuers for thirty-five years.

Right?

Ray put his arm around Lou's shoulder. "Your housekeeper can take care of your kids. Your partners can take care of your clients. We're talking one week of your life—ten days max. No one's indispensable. Trust me. Life goes on, man."

"I know, Ray, but—"

"But what? You're never gonna get a chance like this again. Again? Hell, man, most guys never get a chance like this once. And if we actually find her—" He paused, grinning. "Oh, man, it'll be incredible."

Lou studied Ray as he tried to consider his options rationally.

Ray said, "If you won't do it for yourself, you loser, then do it for me. I've already flown halfway across the goddamned country for this. If I have to haul around Gordie and Bronco all by myself, I'll go fucking nuts."

"Let's take it one step at a time," Lou said. "First let's see if we can identify this mastermind of the Homecoming Heist. Then let's see if he'll even talk to us. This whole thing could be a nonstarter."

Ray shook his head, amused. "You're so damn cautious. You've always been so damn cautious. For once in your life, dude, you gotta take a deep breath and say to yourself, 'What the fuck.' And it's not just the money. It's the glory."

Lou held up his index finger. "One step at a time."

Brandi returned.

"Well?" Ray asked.

She shrugged. "Hard to say. I told her their names. She claims they're catering some big party of hers. She started lecturing me on Swedish meatballs."

Ray groaned. "Not again with the lean pork."

Brandi smiled. "And plenty of prime veal."

Her smile faded, and she shook her head. "She told me no one else has seen those letters, but the poor thing is so confused. I doubt whether she'll remember tomorrow that she showed them to me."

Ray looked at Lou, who shrugged.

"The hell with them," Ray said. He put his arm around Brandi. "You done good, kid."

Brandi leaned against him. "You know what they say about diamonds, darling."

"Yeah, yeah."

She put her arm around him. "Lead on, Sir Lancelot."

Chapter Ten

The three of them were back in the hotel room at the Marriott.

Ray was on the king bed, his back cushioned against the headboard with two pillows, a hardbound copy of *The Legendary Sirena* open on his lap as he leafed through the pages. Brandi was clattering around in the bathroom packing her toiletry bag. She was leaving for Peoria that afternoon to spend a few days with her folks. Lou stood by the window looking down on the street below. Vendors outside Busch Stadium were setting up their wares for the crowd, which would start arriving in another hour or so.

Lou was holding Ray's copy of the special issue of the alumni magazine, the one with Sirena on the cover. He'd reread the article, looking for clues.

Nothing.

But there were other sources. Sirena had inspired an impressive bibliography over the years, including a cover story in the *New York Times Sunday Magazine*, "The Lady Vanishes: Pining for the Eternal Prom Queen of Barrett College," (Dec. 10, 1972); a segment on CBS' "60 Minutes" narrated by Morley Safer ("The Hunt for the Siren of Barrett," Nov. 6, 1989); an epic poem ("O Sirena," *Connecticut Valley Journal*, 1977); and a two-page tribute in *Esquire* magazine's annual women-we-love series (August 1992), which labeled her "the heartbreaker of Barrett College."

But now, with the twenty-three-million-dollar pledge to the school plus two million for the finders and another million from

People magazine for their story rights, the four of them would be just one of dozens of groups out there in the hunt. There was the so-called Bigfoot Crusade—a group from the Class of '84 who supposedly followed a clue into the Willamette National Forest near Tumalo Falls, Oregon. According to rumors, the group had "found something bigger than Bigfoot."

Then there was Buddy's Patrol. Ephraim "Buddy" Lagerfeld ('68) was supposedly leading an expedition down to Cabo San Lucas on the tip of Baja California, which happened to be the spot where Henry Washburn spent a month on a geological study during the summer of 1958, which also happened to be the summer before Sirena vanished.

And the Spelunking Sextet—a group of Delta Upsilons, headed by Kentucky Congressman Hank Fielding ('63). They were convinced that reasons other than geology had inspired President Washburn's three post-1959 trips to Mammoth Cave in central Kentucky. Reports had them inside the cave exploring nonpublic passageways, thanks in part to special arrangements made by Department of the Interior Undersecretary Daniel Maxwell ('52).

"Here we go," Ray said. "Chapter Twenty-one, 'The Homecoming Heist of 1956.'"

He skimmed the pages and gave them a quick summary: in the fall of 1956, the Class of '58, juniors at the time and the possessors of Sirena, decided to bring her out of hiding for a surprise appearance during halftime at homecoming game against Bowdoin. Word of their plan leaked, and before the end of the first quarter Sirena had been "liberated" by a group of masked students.

"Raymond, love," Brandi said as she came into the bedroom carrying a pair of jeans, "enough with the backstory." She folded the jeans and placed them into her suitcase. "Who is he?"

Ray glanced over at Brandi and then back down at the book. "Jeez, woman, cool your jets. I'm trying to set this up." He turned the page, and then another. "Here we go."

He read aloud: "'Although the mastermind of the Homecoming Heist has never stepped forward to acknowledge his achievement, few today question the conclusion reached by Professor Thatcher Hewitt in the article he authored in the fall 1966 issue of the *Barrett College Alumni News*. In that well-researched essay, Professor Hewitt concluded that the mastermind was Graham Anderson Marshall III, just a sophomore at the time of the heist.'"

"Graham Marshall," Brandi said. "So where is he now?"

Lou frowned. "That name sounds familiar."

"Let's see," Ray said, skimming the text. "Apparently, he was a young attorney with the Chicago firm of Abbott & Windsor when Professor Hewitt's article appeared." Ray looked up at Lou. "Abbott & Windsor. They're real big, right?"

Lou nodded. "Huge. Main office in Chicago, branches around the world. There's even a small office here in St. Louis"

"You know anyone in their Chicago office?" Ray asked.

Lou thought for a moment. "Gabe Pollack. He's from St. Louis."

"Give him a call," Ray said. "Maybe he can tell us the best way to approach this Marshall guy."

Ten minutes later, Lou hung up the telephone.

"Well?" Ray said. He'd just come out of the bathroom.

Lou shook his head. "He's dead."

"Your friend?" Brandi asked.

"No. Graham Marshall."

"Dead?" Ray groaned. "Fuck."

Brandi asked, "When did he die?"

"About two years ago. Gabe said he died of a heart attack at the office one night."

Brandi closed her suitcase and gave Lou a sympathetic smile. "Bummer."

"This Gabe guy," Ray said, "how well you know him?"

"Not that well. Same high school, but I was in eighth grade his senior year."

"You think he'd let you look at Marshall's stuff?"

"Depends."

"On what?"

"On what stuff we're talking about. I doubt whether his firm would let anyone look at Marshall's private papers. But there might be other stuff."

"Call him back. What is it—a five-hour drive to Chicago? See if your buddy can spare us an hour tomorrow."

Lou picked up the receiver and punched in the number.

Ray started pacing the room. "He's got to help us."

"Hey, Gabe," Lou said into the receiver, "it's Lou again."

Chapter Eleven

It was eight-thirty that night, and Lou was finally alone with his children. His son's bedroom was a sanctuary after a day of departure preparations—arranging for others to cover his cases, to do the car pools, to help with Kenny's baseball team and Katie's dance classes. But that was all behind him now. He was seated on the edge of Kenny's bed. His son was under the covers. Katie was on the bed, too, although not in her pajamas. She'd taken a break from homework to come listen. She was in her Rusted Root T-shirt, baggy shorts, and red Converse All-Stars.

Ever since they were toddlers Lou had been putting them to bed with fairy tales—all the popular ones, and dozens of obscure stories he'd found in the big Brothers Grimm collection that Andi had purchased the week before Katie was born (along with *Pat the Bunny*, *Goodnight Moon*, *Horton Hears A Who!* and at least a dozen other children's books she'd bought in a pre-delivery buying spree). Katie had loved the fairy tales from the start, and she and her brother still enjoyed them. For tonight he'd picked one of their favorites, and they were both wide-eyed as he neared the end.

"At last they reached the edge of the forest," Lou read, "and caught sight of their cottage in the clearing."

Kenny began to smile, his eyes shining.

"They ran as fast as they could and burst through the door, shouting 'Daddy, Daddy!'"

Katie was smiling, too.

"When their father saw his children, he jumped to his feet and scooped them into his big arms. Tears ran down his cheeks as he hugged them and kissed them and told them how much he loved them. He promised that they had nothing to fear anymore and that nothing would ever come between them again. Gretel opened her apron to show her father the beautiful pearls, and Hansel pulled all the gold coins out of his pocket. From that moment on, none of them was ever sad again, and they all lived together happily ever after."

Lou ran his fingers through Kenny's hair.

"Where are you and Mr. Gorman going?" Katie asked.

"Chicago."

"Why Chicago?" Kenny asked.

"We're going to try to find that statue."

"Sirena?" Kenny asked.

Lou nodded.

"Why?" Katie asked.

As Lou considered the question, Kenny turned to his sister. "It's like Sleeping Beauty. Daddy's the prince, and he's trying to find her."

Katie said, "Really, Daddy?"

He smiled and shrugged. "We'll see. It could all fizzle out in Chicago. I'll call you guys every night. I promise. Mrs. Walters will know how to reach me during the day if you need me." He placed his hand gently on Kenny's shoulder. "Jake's dad will coach the game on Sunday if I'm not back by then."

Kenny nodded. "Okay."

"No matter what happens," he said to them both, "we're all going to be at Barrett together for the reunion." He kissed Kenny and tucked in the covers. "I love you, pal."

He walked Katie to her bedroom.

"I'll be back soon, peanut," he said to her.

She gave him a fierce hug. "I love you, Daddy." She leaned back, eyes bright. "Go for it."

He kneeled down and kissed her on the bridge of her nose. "I'll try."

When he got downstairs, Mrs. Walters was in the foyer talking with Ray.

"I'll call tomorrow," Lou told her. He lifted his travel bag in one hand and the case of audio cassettes in the other. "I left the hotel phone number on the kitchen counter."

Lou got in the driver's side of his minivan and started the engine. He turned to Ray. "Ready?"

Ray was studying the titles on the cassettes. "Let's do it."

As Lou backed the van out of the driveway, Ray inserted a cassette into the tape player.

Lou shifted into drive and looked over at Ray. "What'd you pick?"

Ray gave him a wink. "Something to get us in the mood."

Soon the van was reverberating with the wailing feedback of the opening of Credence Clearwater Revival's "Run through the Jungle."

As with so much of the music from his youth, the initial chords triggered a flashback. All the way back to the last time Lou had seen Ray at college, just two days before graduation. Their paths hadn't crossed for more than a year, when Lou, strolling across the quad, came upon Ray seated beneath an oak tree, his back against the tree trunk, his unwashed black hair tied back in a ponytail, his skin pale, his T-shirt torn, his jeans filthy, his feet bare, his eyes dilated. Very dilated. Lou had said hello. Ray just grinned, his head lolling. Blaring from the speakers through an open window in one of the dorms facing the quad was "Run through the Jungle":

> *They told me, "Don't go walkin' slow*
> *'Cause the Devil's on the loose.*

Lou remembered the wave of sadness he'd felt as he walked past his freshman year roommate, so changed since then. Although Lou had wondered whether Ray would graduate, he did, and with honors in philosophy, earning an A+ on his senior thesis, a critique of William James' pragmatism that he apparently wrote, from scratch, without notes, in forty-eight hours, fueled by amphetamines, Wild Turkey, and two dozen Hostess Twinkies.

For the first decade after graduation, Lou kept track of Ray through the alumni gossip mill. Ray was in the philosophy graduate program at the University of Chicago, married a law student at Northwestern, spent a night in jail after a barroom brawl at Somebody Else's Troubles on Lincoln Avenue, dropped out of the graduate program, drifted into the drug trade, got divorced. Someone heard that Ray was in Colorado, a rumor confirmed when their goofball class secretary Bryce Wharton III wrote in his alumni magazine column that classmate Chip Reynolds (a Beverly Hills entertainment lawyer) had run into Ray at a film festival in Telluride.

"According to the Chipster," Wharton wrote, "Ray's present domicile is a commune on the outskirts of Telluride, where he shares space with a Brandeis grad named (I kid you not) Namas-te Abramovitz. *Ahh-ooom! Ahh-ooom!* A long way from the Pittsburgh steel mills, eh, Raymundo?"

The next time Ray's name appeared in Wharton's column, he was living in a bungalow near the beach in San Diego. Only someone as credulous as Wharton would have reported that Ray was "now an independent sales rep for several South American pharmaceutical houses."

Ray went legit eight years ago, shortly after one of his cocaine customers, a La Jolla plastic surgeon, complained to Ray about his limited partnership investment in a strip shopping center south of downtown San Diego. The doc said the bank was hassling the partnership—something about loan ratios out of whack. Ray sensed an opportunity, since the bank's loan officer happened to be another one of his customers. Ray gave him a nice discount on his next cocaine buy in return for a photocopy of the bank's entire loan file on the project. When the bank foreclosed, Ray was ready. He bought the shopping center, refinanced it a year later, sold his drug business, and used the proceeds to buy a controlling interest in another strip center.

He added his first mall two years later. His shopping center holdings expanded at the same pace as San Diego, which was then the fastest-growing city in America. By last fall, Ray was wealthy enough and respectable enough and Republican enough to be profiled in a cover story in *Forbes* magazine entitled: "The Shopping Center Czar of San Diego County."

Lou had seen that issue on an airport magazine rack. He'd stared at it, astounded. The Ray Gorman beaming at him from the magazine cover—clean-shaven, close-cropped, clear-eyed—was the Ray Gorman he hadn't seen since freshman year. Later that fall, Lou was in Orange County on a deposition and drove down to San Diego to meet up with Ray at his home in La Jolla. He was delighted to discover the Ray Gorman from their James Gang days, including the membership in a bowling league (instead of a country club) and the addiction to crossword puzzles—that odd corner of the language inhabited by strange birds (the Moa and the Erne), odd coins (the Avo and the Obol), Charlie Chaplin's daughter Oona, and an Oreo cookie in every puzzle. Of course, the effects of money were visible. Back at Barrett, Ray did the *Times* crossword in the back row of the lecture hall during Professor Barker's Econ 101 lectures. Now he did it in the backseat of his BMW while his driver took him to his office.

Lou pulled onto the highway just as the song reached the better-run-through-the-jungle chorus. He looked over at Ray, who was playing air guitar in the front seat and nodding his head to the beat. Ray grinned and gave him the thumbs-up.

Chapter Twelve

An hour north of Springfield, Illinois, Lou pulled off I-55 for gas. He was cleaning the windshield with the squeegee when Ray came back out carrying two cans of Coke. He handed one to Lou.

Lou popped the tab and took a sip. "Did you ever reach Gordie?"

Ray leaned back against the side of the van. "Tried again this afternoon. He was in a meeting. Had his secretary put me in his voice mail. Told him where to meet us tomorrow morning."

Lou dropped the squeegee back in the water bucket by the pump and turned to Ray. "When's the last time you saw Gordie?"

"Let's see…not for at least six years. He was still in California. Renting that crappy little studio apartment near the beach in Venice. Haven't seen him since he moved back. You?"

"About two years ago. I was up in Chicago for some depositions. We met for dinner."

"What about Bronco?"

Lou shook his head. "Not for a long time."

"Is he really a school teacher?"

"Middle school, I think. Spanish."

"Teaching Spanish to seventh graders." Ray shook his head. "Didn't he want to become Secretary of State?"

Lou smiled. "Yeah."

"Remember that humongous pile of *Foreign Affairs* stacked on his desk?"

Lou nodded.

Ray took another sip of his Coke. "A school teacher? After all he's been through?"

Lou said, "Nowhere near as wacky as you becoming the Mall Maven."

"Hey, I wasn't the guy with a poster of William Kunstler taped over my desk."

Lou shrugged. "Times change."

"Don't knock it. It's a living."

"I guess. But it ought to be more than that."

Ray groaned. "Oh, God. Not you, too."

"Not me what?"

"As in what's wrong with our generation? Who said your job is supposed to be your life? My old man worked in a steel mill. His whole life. Even died in there, for chrissakes. You think he ever wondered whether he was self-actualizing in there? 'Tapping into his inner child?' Shit, man, he was bringing home a paycheck, putting food on the table, paying the mortgage. That's what counts. Everything else is bullshit."

"You're not your father."

"That doesn't mean I'm looking for salvation in shopping malls, either. It's a job, Lou. A means to an end. Period."

The gas station was just off the highway overpass. A convoy of three trucks rumbled by heading north. Lou watched the red taillights fade into the distance.

"Still," Lou said, looking over at Ray, "shopping malls? You?"

"Pushing drugs, pushing merchandise." Ray shrugged. "Just trading one addiction for another. Profit margin is smaller, but there are upsides. The only government agents you have to worry about are those four-eyed fucks from the IRS."

Lou smiled. "I wasn't talking about your drug days. I meant before that. Back in college. We thought you were going to become one of the Philosopher Kings."

Ray laughed. "No way."

"So why'd you go?"

"Go?"

"To the University of Chicago. The graduate program in philosophy."

Ray considered the question. "Fame, I guess."

"In philosophy?"

Ray chuckled. "Sounds pretty lame now. But damn, Lou, I could pick that shit apart."

Lou thought back to the required humanities seminar freshman year, to the week they were assigned Plato's *Symposium*. Professor Milton Beckmann, chair of the department, came in that week to teach the class. For almost the entire hour, Ray went one-on-one with that arrogant old bastard and fought him to a draw.

"And that's how you'd become famous?"

Ray looked over at Lou with a sheepish grin. "Youth, eh? I was going to be a celebrity professor—one of those guys who packs the lecture halls, gets interviewed by Bill Moyers on PBS, gets called to Washington to advise the President."

"So what happened?" Lou asked.

Ray stared into the darkness.

"What happened," he finally said, "was a dead guy named Benjamin Clark."

"Who's he?"

Ray turned to Lou. "That's my point."

"What do you mean?"

"You never heard of him."

"What did he do?"

"He was a war hero."

"Which war?"

"Civil."

Lou frowned. "I'm not following you."

Ray turned toward the darkness again. "My ex-wife grew up in a small town in upper state New York. Near Lake George. Nice area. After my first year at the U of C, we drove up there to visit her folks."

He paused to take a sip of his Coke.

"I headed out for a drive one afternoon—just smoking a joint and cruising along this two-lane road that cut through the woods. Passed a sign for a hiking path. It was a pretty day and I had nothing better to do, so I decided what the fuck."

He finished the Coke and tossed the can into the trash bin.

The path meandered through the woods, he explained. A brook on the right, a hill rising on the left. About a mile down the path he came upon a half-rotted wooden sign that read, CIVIL WAR MEMORIAL. The arrow on the sign pointed to the left, where the main path branched off into an overgrown trail up the hill through the trees. Kind of curious and kind of stoned, he decided to check it out. The trail wound back and forth up the hill and leveled off in a small clearing.

"And there it was," Ray said. "The memorial for Lieutenant Benjamin Clark."

Your basic Civil War monument gone to ruin, he explained. Granite obelisk, twenty feet tall, leaning to one side, scraggly vines circling halfway up. Surrounded by rusted cannon balls and enclosed by a rusted iron picket fence, the black paint flaking off. A tarnished plaque near the base of the obelisk, barely legible, honored Lieutenant Benjamin Clark, a hometown hero who'd fought and died at Gettysburg at the age of twenty-three.

Ray paused and shook his head. "It blew me away."

"How so?"

"I was twenty-three, too. Here's this guy—fought in the most important battle in the most important war of his time. Maybe of all time. Died a hero. At my age. A real hero, too. Not some *People* magazine puffball."

Ray looked up at the night sky for a moment and then looked at Lou.

"I could picture the scene. Body brought home in a wagon draped in black crepe. Laid to rest with a hero's funeral. Brass band, patriotic eulogies, twenty-one gun salutes, pretty girls crying, grown men fighting back tears, women wringing their hands."

He paused, replaying the scene in his mind as he stared up at the stars. Lou waited.

Ray shook his head. "So they built that monument on the hill overlooking the town. I bet you could see that obelisk from miles away. And there I stood, a century later, and the town is gone, the memorial is overgrown with weeds, and the monument stands—or leans, if it hasn't fallen over by now—in the middle of the woods in the middle of nowhere. No one remembers the poor bastard. I mean no one. I've tried to find him in the books. Most of the stories on the Battle of Gettysburg don't even mention his name, and those that do don't say anything about him. Just list him as one of the dead Union officers."

Ray looked over at Lou and shook his head. "Anyway, there I was, staring at that forgotten monument to a forgotten hero, and it suddenly dawned on me: the whole fame thing is nothing but a meaningless crap shoot. Here's a guy who got famous for all the right reasons, and a hundred years later he's a nobody while yahoos like Sylvester Stallone and Pamela Anderson are living legends. Christ, Willard Scott is more famous than Thomas Hobbes."

He smiled, eyes distant.

"So I said to myself, 'Get real, douche bag.' I dropped out of school that fall. Never looked back."

Lou said, "And you became famous anyway."

"Isn't that a pisser?" Ray snorted. "Guy dies a hero at Gettysburg fighting to free the slaves and no one remembers his fucking name. I give the world another crappy Foot Locker opening onto another crappy food court with a piped-in Muzak version of 'Brown Sugar' and they put my face on the cover of a national magazine."

They stood side by side, leaning back against the van, staring in silence into the night sky beyond the halos of the arc lights. Lou thought of the image of that decaying monument in the middle of the dark forest.

A distant air horn caught his attention. The entrance ramp to I-55 sloped down as if it were a path along a river bank.

The passing headlights illuminated its surface. The river image held—as if the highway were a giant river cutting through the cornfields. He checked his watch. Time to get back on that river.

He turned to Ray. "Shall we?"

Ray winked at Lou. "She's out there waiting for us, Lou."

Lou smiled as he reached for the door handle. "Watch out, Willard Scott, here we come."

Chapter Thirteen

When Ray had called Gordie that afternoon, his secretary told him that Mr. Cohen was in conference and couldn't be disturbed. She was just following orders: hold all calls—no ifs, ands, or buts.

She attributed that instruction to the Klassy Kat Kitty Litter account. The entire Klassy Kat marketing team was flying in from Louisville next week for the big presentation, and thus she assumed that Gordie was holed up in his office working on storyboards for the new commercial—the so-called Black Pussy Special, a thirty-second spot built around two "singing" black cats, one with Aretha Franklin's voice and the other with Louis Armstrong's voice.

She was wrong. Although Gordie was definitely hard at work in there, his goal was somewhat higher than deodorized cat feces.

He was writing The Great American Screenplay.

He'd been working on it for fourteen years now.

He was up to page four.

The script had been longer, of course. Eleven years ago—back when he was still in Venice, California—Draft One of The Great American Screenplay had reached page 392 before Gordie junked it. Weighing in at close to five pounds, it made *The Sorrow and the Pity* seem like an episode of *The Young and the Restless*.

And it was with some sorrow and much pity that Gordie torched it in his backyard hibachi. But in typical Southern California style, what began as a funeral pyre morphed into something far more surreal. In his memory it played, complete with screenplay directions:

EXTERIOR—NIGHT—GORDIE'S TINY BACKYARD

Full moon overhead. Gordie has on just boxer shorts and sandals. He stands before the hibachi, smoking a joint as he watches 392 pages crackle and curl and blacken.

Gradually, he becomes aware of a strange mechanical FARTING NOISE. A car with a broken muffler? A motorcycle in need of a tune-up? The NOISE grows LOUDER. A large shadow glides across the backyard. Startled, Gordie looks up.

CUT TO:

EXTERIOR—NIGHT SKY

The Goodyear Blimp is directly overhead, cruising south along the shoreline. Its electronic advertising board flashes the Coca-Cola mantra: IT'S THE REAL THING!

CUT TO:

EXTERIOR—NIGHT—GORDIE'S TINY BACKYARD

Gordie stands there, head tilted back, spellbound, the screenplay CRACKLING at his feet, the advertising lights flashing on his face. A revelatory moment. The Goodyear Epiphany.

When he awoke the next morning, the Goodyear Epiphany had been shrink-wrapped into just another L.A. scene. That was the thing about L.A. The town generated one scene after another, each one weird and incandescent and unforgettable.

Such as **DEATH IN THE AFTERNOON:** waiting at a traffic light along Sunset Boulevard one brilliant October morning, glancing to his left and there, squatting in the shade, was an enormous emerald-green iguana tied to a palm tree, a diamond-studded leash around its neck, the lizard motionless, eyes inert, the only movement the thrashing brown legs of a toad clamped in its mouth.

Or **BONANZA IN OUTER SPACE:** peering out the window on a back-lot office at Universal, waiting for the assistant producer to get off the phone, when Lorne Green—yep, Pa Cartwright himself—strolls past, dressed in a space costume—black tights, green storm trooper boots, plastic ray gun in a rubber holster— puffing on a cigar and leafing through a Jacuzzi catalog.

And so on and so on. A slide show of the apocalypse, and Gordie struggling to crack the code, wondering whether there was a code, whether it was all just static. He'd stuck it out for fourteen years, but after the Jim Nabors debacle, he packed his bags and returned to Chicago and the world of advertising.

And to The Great American Screenplay.

Draft Two reached page 179 before he gave up. One late night last winter he'd fed it, page by page, into the mailroom paper shredder.

But Draft Three was off to a promising start. High school prom night. Seemed the perfect way to open a movie that would tell the story of four young men coming of age during their freshman year at Barrett College. The image of a white prom dress was a powerful opener, echoed several scenes later with that nameless girl in white from the Hampton College mixer—the one who'd haunted him ever since.

The new approach came to him that night last winter as he stood by the window in his condo watching the snowflakes float past. Maybe it was all that whiteness that triggered the memories, made him wonder whatever happened to Sherry Goldfarb, his prom date senior year at Niles East High School, the memories still vivid almost two decades later. White had been the color theme that night—her prom dress, his tuxedo jacket, her corsage, his starched shirt, her frilly panties and, alas, the spray of semen that ruined her dress, her evening, and their relationship, all in one shot, as it were.

He'd drafted the opening scene that same winter night, writing into the wee hours as the snow fell outside.

Four pages.

He'd been polishing it ever since. Best writing he'd done. The scene almost worked.

Almost.

It was that gap—between the experiences and the words—that obsessed him. He knew there was a story there, and a powerful one, and if he could tell it right, he might finally have something to point to in his life besides a thirty-second television commercial featuring a Siamese cat dressed in full opera gear (including breastplate and helmet) singing Wagner to a sack of kitty litter.

And thus, when Ray Gorman called that afternoon, Gordie was not there. Although seated behind a desk high above North Michigan Avenue on a sunny day in June of 1994, the window behind him displaying a dramatic view of Lake Michigan and the scalloped beaches on Chicago's north side, Gordie was back in Skokie on a moonless night in the spring of 1970. Specifically, according to the lines immediately below the words FADE IN, he was in the front seat of his father's Ford Fairlane, the Fifth Dimension's "Age of Aquarius" on the car radio, the windows fogged, receiving a clumsy but earnest hand-job from Sherry Goldfarb.

The moment was so vivid that when his secretary knocked on his office door, he realized that he had a throbbing erection—a predicament made all the more awkward by his glass-top desk. If she noticed, she didn't let on. She placed a stack of inter-office memos in his in-box and turned to leave.

"Any calls?" he asked, aiming for a calm tone.

"Mr. Richards wants to know if you can move tomorrow's meeting back to 3:30. Mr. Moran called about lunch. And a Mr. Gorman just called."

"*Ray* Gorman?"

She paused at the door and frowned. "I think that's his first name."

"What did he want?"

"I don't know. He told me to put him into your voice mail."

After she left, Gordie turned his chair toward the window, rapping a pencil against his knee.

Ray Gorman.

Other than that conference call last winter when Ray made them all take the reunion pledge, he hadn't heard from his freshman year roommate in years. His smile faded as he recalled reading in Bryce Wharton's goofy column in the alumni magazine that Ray was now a big-time real estate developer somewhere out west. Even got his face on the cover of some national magazine. No doubt a millionaire, life a bowl of cherries.

He glanced over at the phone, at the blinking red message light. After a moment, he lifted the receiver and pressed the message button.

"One new message," the automated female voice announced. "Received today at five-eleven p.m."

A pause, and then: "Hey, Cohen, it's Gorman. Your secretary claims you're busy. Yeah, right. Put your dick back in your pants and grab a pencil. Lou and I are driving up to Chicago tonight. We're staying at the Palmer House. We're in the hunt, dude. And so are you. Fill you in tomorrow morning. Meet us in the hotel restaurant at eight. No excuses. None. See you tomorrow."

Gordie placed the receiver back in the cradle.

After a moment, he turned toward his screenplay.

Draft Three.

The Great American Screenplay

Nearly twenty years in the making.

All four pages of it.

He sighed and shook his head.

Part 3:
The Hunt

In her last known photograph, Sirena is seated in front of the Class of '56 at their senior class banquet. If you study that black-and-white photo under a magnifying glass, as hundreds before you have done, you will see evidence of her more celebrated adventures. Most of the big toe on her right foot is missing, broken off in 1923 when her chaperones from the Class of '24 jammed her into the backseat of the waiting Model T in front of the Tremont Hotel in Boston after her evening at the senior class banquet. The uneven gash along her right arm is the scar from the cement used to reattach a chunk of marble that broke off when she was shoved out of a moving train during her third abduction from the college. The chips and nicks in the folds of her gown and the two deep grooves in the granite base were gouged when the heavy chains came loose during the notorious Homecoming Chase of 1937.

"The Siren of Barrett,"
NEW ENGLAND HERITAGE (Vol. 53, No. 2)

Chapter Fourteen

Ray downed the rest of his orange juice. "Advertising? Never would have guessed."

"I thought he'd be a comedian," Lou said.

"We all did. Gordie was the funniest guy I knew. I kept waiting for him to pop up on Johnny Carson, or in a movie, or on his own TV show." He shook his head. "What happened?"

"He told me there's more to life than making people laugh. He wanted to be a serious writer."

"So he picked advertising?"

Lou shrugged. "Pays the bills."

They were eating breakfast in the coffee shop at the Palmer House Hotel in Chicago's Loop.

Lou glanced at his watch. Gordie was running late.

"That's why he left Hollywood?" Ray asked.

"I think he'd had enough. He's from Chicago. An only child. His dad died a few years back, but his mom still lives here."

"Did he ever get a movie made?"

"He had scripts out on option—lots of them. But nothing got made." Lou shook his head. "Not even the talking monkey rewrite."

Ray frowned. "And what exactly is a talking monkey rewrite?"

Lou smiled. "Not quite *Citizen Kane*. The premise was that this nerdy accountant in Detroit inherits a squirrel monkey from his aunt. He's never had a pet in his life, has no idea what to do with it, decides to give it away. He's on his way to animal pound when he discovers that the monkey can talk."

"And?"

"The working title was Motown Monkey Business. Gordie got hired to do a rewrite. Gordie's agent heard it was going to be a comeback vehicle for Jim Nabors."

"And?"

Lou shrugged. "Nothing. Gordie heard Nabors backed out two days before filming was to start. Hollywood."

"Gomer Pyle and the talking monkey, eh?" Ray finished his scrambled eggs and took another sip of coffee. "How long was he out there?"

"Fourteen years."

"Never got married?"

Lou smiled. "I think he's still looking for Her, with a capital H."

"Oh, yeah. The hot chick from that mixer, right?"

Lou nodded, thinking back to the evening he spent with Gordie in his Venice apartment seven years ago. Gordie had three scripts out on options at the time, although his optimism sounded forced. As always, he was still searching for Her—or at least some reasonable facsimile thereof. All he had to show were dozens of receipts from the Boardwalk Florist (which he dutifully photocopied for his accountant) and a case of genital herpes.

Lou next saw him two years ago in Chicago. Gone were the Hawaiian shirts and baggy Army pants, replaced by Armani suits and antacid tablets. They'd met for dinner and gone back to Gordie's Gold Coast condo so that he could show Lou his TV commercials. All four were slick and clever. Each had impressive production values, but what struck Lou most were the missing ingredients: the zest and zaniness that had been Gordie's trademarks. His ads were retreads of other ads—clever retreads to be sure, but retreads nevertheless. Lou had returned to his hotel disheartened.

"There he is," Ray said.

Gordie was up by the cashier, peering around.

Ray stood and waved. "Gordie!"

Gordie came bounding over to their table, a big grin.

"How's it going, guys?"

Ray squinted at him. "Dude, where's your hair?"

Back in college Gordie wore his dark hair in a wild Jew-fro. Now he was almost completely bald.

"Where's my hair?" Gordie eyed Ray. "Hey, Slim, where's your waistline?"

"Fuck you, half pint."

Gordie turned to Lou as he took a seat. "I'm skipping a production meeting for this crap?"

"Crap?" Ray answered. "Listen, Mr. Huckster, we're here to inject some meaning into your existence. I'm about to give you a purpose in life beyond hawking laxatives to the AARP brigade."

Gordie looked at Lou with a bemused smile. "What the hell is he talking about?"

Lou smiled. "We're on a mission."

"Oh?" Gordie chuckled. "Which one of you is Elwood?"

"We're serious," Ray said.

Gordie formed his index fingers into a cross in front of him as if to scare off a vampire. "No more missions, boys. I went on a JUF Young Leadership Mission to Israel two years ago. Just outside Haifa they hauled me to the back of the bus with a pledge card. A Jewish gang bang." He groaned. "I'm still paying off that pledge."

"Serves you right," Ray said. "You probably went to Israel to get laid."

"Hey, I'd go to Afghanistan to get laid."

"And?"

Gordie shrugged. "Came back horny and poor. Story of my life."

The waitress took Gordie's order: a toasted plain bagel and a glass of milk.

"The old stomach's acting up," he told them when she left. "Doctor says no more coffee."

"Look at you," Ray said. "You look like an adult."

Gordie had on a gray pinstriped suit, a white shirt with a blue collar, and a red-and-blue striped tie with a matching red handkerchief in the breast pocket of his suit. With his neatly trimmed beard, bald head, and thick, wire-rim glasses, he looked like a cross between a Haight-Ashbury poet and a loan officer.

"Yeah, yeah," Gordie said. "So what's this sacred mission?"

"Sirena," Lou said.

Gordie frowned. "What about her?"

Ray said, "We're looking for her."

Gordie laughed. "You and half the alums. You see that piece in the *Wall Street Journal* last week? There must be guys on every continent looking for her. Like those goofy tax lawyers."

"Which ones are they?" Lou asked.

"Class of Sixty-four, I think." Gordie frowned as he tried to remember the article. "Three tax partners at Sullivan & Cromwell. Searching for her in Morocco, for chrissakes. Based on some obscure reference in a commencement address by Washburn."

Lou said, "Ray may have found something more significant."

Gordie turned to Ray with a skeptical look. "And what would that be?"

Ray glanced around and leaned forward, his voice low. "Washburn wasn't the one who hid her."

"Who did?"

Lou said, "A Chicago lawyer named Graham Marshall."

Gordie stared at Ray, and then Lou. "How do you know all this?"

The waitress arrived with Gordie's breakfast. After she left, Lou explained what they'd pieced together.

Gordie asked, "Have you talked to this Marshall guy?"

"He's dead," Ray said.

Gordie applied cream cheese to his bagel. "So why are you here?"

Ray said, "Marshall was a Chicago partner in Abbott & Windsor. Lou knows a guy over there. He agreed to see us this morning. You comin' with?"

Gordie glanced at Lou and then checked his watch. "When?"

"Twenty minutes," Lou said.

"Well, I have to be back by noon." Gordie took a bit of his bagel and gave them a sheepish grin. "Client lunch."

"We'll be done by then," Ray said. "You'll have plenty of time to strap on your kneepads."

Gordie checked his watch again, hesitant.

"Come on, Gordie," Lou said. "If I can do it, you can do it."

Gordie studied Lou a moment and then smiled. "What the hell, eh?"

Ray reached over and patted him on the back. "Welcome to the mission, Gordo."

"Please. No missions."

Chapter Fifteen

High school baseball made the meeting with Gabe Pollack possible. Although several years separated them, Lou and Gabe had both attended University City High School in St. Louis and had both pitched on the varsity team. As an eighth grader, Lou had watched from the stands as Gabe pitched his last high school game: a no-hitter against arch-rival Ladue—the single most dominating pitching performance he'd ever witnessed. Indeed, Gabe had a legitimate shot at the pros until he blew out his arm in college. Although Lou would be his team's ace pitcher senior year, comparing his skills to Gabe's seemed like comparing a Sopwith Camel to an F-16.

Lou, Gordie, and Ray were seated in Gabe's office, which was fifty-six stories above LaSalle Street in the Chicago Loop. The large window behind him framed a panorama of the skyline looking west from LaSalle Street, the view dominated by the Sear's Tower—or at least most of it. The top disappeared into a huge, dark cloud, which turned an otherwise picture postcard view into a post-modernist apparition—Jack and the Bladerunner.

Gabe was in his late forties—tall and trim, dark hair and a beard. He was a partner at Abbott & Windsor, one of the oldest and largest firms in the city, with branch offices around the nation and the world. He leaned back in his chair and listened to Lou explain the Graham Marshall connection.

Gabe scratched his beard pensively. "You really think Marshall was the one?"

"We do," Lou said.

Gabe nodded. "There's not much help I can offer. The firm doesn't have any of Marshall's personal papers. I checked yesterday."

"Who would?" Lou asked.

"His widow, but she's out of the country. She's traveling in the Far East with her new husband."

"Shit," Ray said.

Gabe pursed his lips as he studied the three of them. "You may not need his personal papers."

"Why not?" Lou asked.

"If you're right about this—if Graham Marshall was the one who hid that statue—then he left a clue where you can find it."

"Why do you say that?" Lou asked.

Gabe leaned back and crossed his arms over his chest. "How much do you guys know about Graham Marshall?"

Lou shrugged. "He was a senior partner in your firm. A fairly well-known antitrust lawyer. Found an article about him in *The American Lawyer*—the one they did after he died. Sounded like a strong personality."

Gabe smiled. "Colossal ego, too. But more pertinent for your purposes, he loved practical jokes. That's why I can believe he'd agree to hide that statue."

"Practical jokes?" Gordie asked.

"Not the hand buzzer variety," Gabe said. "He loved big, convoluted pranks, especially with plenty of intrigue. You ever hear what he did to Brendan Pritchard?"

They shook their heads.

"Or rather, what he *allegedly* did to Brendan Pritchard." Gabe smiled. "Pritchard eventually filed a claim against Marshall's estate. He sought damages for intentional infliction of emotional distress. I handled the matter, which is how I learned the details. *Vanity Fair* ran a piece on it. We got the claim dismissed for lack of evidence. Still, it's a remarkable story."

Brendan Pritchard was a senior partner in a major law firm in Washington, D.C., Gabe explained, and a mover and shaker within the Republican Party. Pritchard and Marshall had been rivals since college, where each played squash—Marshall for Barrett, Pritchard for Williams College. They played against each other in two New England college squash tournaments, each winning one. They stayed rivals at Yale Law School, where both were editors on the law journal. After law school, Pritchard took a job in the Justice Department in Washington, D.C., and Marshall came home to work at Abbott & Windsor. Both became antitrust lawyers, and fairly prominent ones, at that.

In 1978, they found themselves on a big case together—each representing a defendant in one of the uranium antitrust cases brought by the Justice Department. The pretrial preparations included an inspection of a classified government facility, which meant that all of the lawyers had to get security clearance for the inspection tour. All applied for clearance, and all received it—except Brendan Pritchard.

"What happened?" Gordie asked.

Gabe smiled. "That's precisely what Pritchard asked."

After all, Gabe explained, Brendan Pritchard had friends in high places, including the White House. He assumed that there'd been a clerical snafu. He applied again. A week passed, and then that application was denied as well.

The inspection tour had to be postponed because of Pritchard's problems. He appealed the denial, and that was rejected. He filed a Freedom of Information Act request with the FBI. A few weeks later a packet of documents arrived at his office from the FBI.

"His file?" Ray asked.

"Oh, yes." Gabe raised his eyebrows. "And what a file it was."

It contained more than a hundred documents, some dating all the way back to his college days. They ranged from photocopies of his personal correspondence to photographs of him at anti-American rallies.

"Guy was a commie?" Ray asked.

"According to the file." Gabe leaned forward, his eyes twinkling. "But everything in the file was fake. All forgeries—but done by a master counterfeiter, down to the tiniest details."

"Such as?" Gordie asked.

"There was an FBI surveillance report from 1964—an account of a clandestine meeting between Pritchard and members of some outfit on J. Edgar Hoover's lists of subversive organizations. Not only did the surveillance report look authentic, an analysis showed that it had been typed on a Royal portable manufactured in 1962. There was a photograph of the crowd at a 1950s Paul Robeson concert up near Glens Falls, New York. It was a benefit concert for the Rosenberg children. Right in the middle of the concert crowd, circled in red, was the face of Brendan Pritchard."

"Also fake?" Lou asked.

Gabe nodded. "A detective agency eventually determined that it came from a photograph in his college yearbook. The forger transposed it onto a body in the concert crowd."

"Incredible," Gordie said.

"It was more than just incredible," Gabe said. "It was vicious because it sealed Pritchard's lips."

"Why?" Gordie asked.

"The fakes looked authentic, and that was the rub. Pritchard was afraid that friends and colleagues would think they were real. It's like the babysitter accused of child-molesting. Even if the charges are dropped, you're going to have trouble getting more babysitting jobs. Same for Pritchard. In order to clear his reputation he'd have to risk destroying it."

"What did he do?" Lou asked.

Eventually, Gabe explained, Pritchard showed the file to one of his old colleagues at the Justice Department, who quietly looked into it. The mechanics of the prank were even more elaborate than Pritchard had suspected. The Department of Defense *had* given him security clearance. But someone had intercepted the clearance letter *before* it was mailed and replaced it with a fake denial. As for the FBI, they had no record of any Freedom of Information Act request from Pritchard, which meant that somehow the request had been diverted before it was docketed at the FBI. Furthermore, the FBI had nothing in the slightest bit incriminating in their actual file on him.

Obsessed, Pritchard hired a detective agency. It was inconceivable to him that anyone could pull off such an elaborate ruse without leaving a loose end. But after more than a year of investigation, the detective agency came up with nothing linking Marshall, or anyone else, to the scheme. Nevertheless, Pritchard was convinced that his old squash nemesis was the mastermind. He confronted him at an ABA meeting. Marshall laughed and told him he was crazy.

"So who did it?" Gordie asked.

Gabe smiled. "That's why I told you I didn't think Marshall's private papers would help you."

"Why?" Ray asked.

"When Marshall died," Gabe said, "his executor found a large sealed envelope in one of his safe deposit boxes. The envelope was addressed to Brendan Pritchard with instructions to mail it to him by registered mail. The executor followed the instructions. Inside that envelope Pritchard found a fake photograph of himself shaking hands with Adolph Hitler. Stapled to the photograph was a sheet of paper from Graham Marshall's memo pad. One of those 'From the Desk of' pads. Handwritten on the paper was one word."

"What?" Lou asked.

"Gotcha," Gabe said.

Gordie leaned back in his chair. "Wow."

Gabe nodded. "You see my point? Marshall *had* to make sure Brendan Pritchard found out it was him. His ego was too big to let a hoax like that go unclaimed. And that was just a private prank. This statue is a big deal. I saw the article on it in the *Wall Street Journal*. If Marshall went to that length to claim credit for what he did to Pritchard, he'd definitely make sure he got full credit for hiding the statue."

"But how?" Ray asked.

"Exactly what I asked myself after Lou called," Gabe said. "The best way for Marshall to prove he was the one who hid the statue is to tell the finder where to look for it."

"How would he do that now?" Ray asked.

Gabe looked down at the notes on his legal pad. "Copy this down." He read off a nine-digit number. "Go over to the Probate Court Clerk's office at the Daley Center and ask for that file. It's a thick one."

"Marshall's probate file?" Lou said.

Gabe nodded. "It's a public file. The key word is 'public.' If he's the one who hid the statue, your best bet is to start with that file."

Chapter Sixteen

It was Ray's idea, of course.

They'd just boarded the down elevator after their meeting with Gabe Pollack. As the doors slid shut, Ray turned to face them, eyebrows raised.

"What?" Lou asked.

"We can't see the court clerk, yet."

"Why not?"

"We got something to do first, boys."

"Huh?" Gordie asked. He was distracted, trying to cook up an excuse for getting out of his business lunch.

"We ain't the James Gang, yet." Ray was grinning. "Not 'til we liberate Bronco Billy."

On the taxi ride to Columbia Middle School on the northwest side of Chicago, Gordie and Ray worked out their scenario: Bronco Billy was under consideration for one of those MacArthur Foundation "genius" grants. They were the team of psychologists assigned to administer the personality tests required to determine his eligibility. It sounded ridiculous to Lou, but he was along for the ride—literally.

They were ushered into the principal's office. Behind a metal desk sat a corpulent man in his late fifties. The desktop was bare except for a BIC pen, a black rotary-dial telephone, and a tarnished brass nameplate announcing that the man behind the desk was Dr. Harold N. Silverfrick, Ph.D. With his bulging eyes, scraggly mustache, and sagging double chin, Silverfrick reminded Lou of an enormous catfish. His toupee was slightly askew. Judging from his sideburns, the rug was one shade darker than his real hair. His plaid sports jacket was buttoned, the ends of his shirt collars curled upward, and the thick knot of his tie was out of line.

Gordie, who had dressed for work that morning and thus was in a suit and tie, handled the introductions. He was Dr. Cohen. Dr. Gorman was the gentlemen in the khaki slacks and a green Polo shirt. Dr. Solomon was the man in faded Levi's and a white button-down shirt with the sleeves rolled up to the elbows.

Gordie gave an inspired performance, salting his *shpiel* with plenty of allusions to the Ying and Yang of American educational theory, namely, the "cognitive domain" and the "affective domain."

"Nice job, Doc," Ray told him as they walked up the stairs to the second floor.

They crowded by the door to Room 210 and peered through the glass. There were five long rows of desks facing the front, seven desks per row. A green-red-and-yellow donkey piñata hung from the middle of the ceiling fan. On the walls were brightly colored posters from Costa Rica, Chile, Peru, and Argentina. The blackboard was filled with Spanish words and phrases.

And there was Bronco Billy—just as skinny and pale as he'd been freshman year. He was leaning over a boy's desk in the back row, pointing out something in a workbook. He wore a short-sleeved blue dress shirt, a dark bow-tie, and pleated khaki slacks. He even had on the same style of metal-rimmed glasses— the ones that dug red trenches on both sides of his large nose.

Lou watched through the glass, smiling as Billy curled a finger around a strand of his lank brown hair. It was a gesture Lou had seen Billy do hundreds of times their freshman year—while studying calculus in the dorm room with his headphones on and bobbing his head over the textbook, while moving through the food line in the dining hall, while standing to the side during a Hampton College mixer.

Ray gestured at Bronco Billy, who had just noticed that there was a crowd at his classroom door.

"Come on," Ray hissed, waving his arm.

Billy squinted toward the door and then straightened in surprise. He grinned and held up his hands in a helpless gesture as he looked around the classroom.

Ray signaled for him to join them.

Billy paused, and then he turned toward the class. He made an announcement. All heads looked toward the door, where the three of them had assumed serious expressions. After all, they were doctors of psychology here on official business. Billy walked to the head of the class, flipped through a few pages of a textbook, gave them an assignment, and headed for the door.

Out in the hall, he grinned and shook their hands.

"What are you guys doing here?"

"Liberating you, gringo," Ray said. "Dr. Silverfish says you can leave when this period ends. He's sending up a substitute."

Billy looked puzzled. "How'd you do that?"

Lou explained the MacArthur Foundation shtick.

Billy chuckled. "You told him all that?"

Ray slapped him on the back. "Trust me, Bronco, you got something to do that's more important than teaching those jarheads how to conjugate Spanish verbs."

"What do you mean?"

"Sirena," Lou said.

Ray gave Billy a wink. "We're on a mission, Señor."

Gordie groaned. "No missions, Ray."

Billy raised his eyebrows. "You guys know where she is?"

"Not yet," Gordie said.

"But we're in the hunt," Ray said.

The school bell rang. From inside the classroom came the sounds of textbooks closing and students getting up.

"¿Vamos, Señor Bronco?" Ray asked.

Billy hesitated.

"Come on," Gordie said. He nodded toward Lou and Ray. "These guys have already hijacked my day. Your turn."

Billy shrugged. "Okay."

Bronco, Lou repeated with a smile as Billy ducked back into the classroom to gather his stuff.

Billy had started college as William McCormick. Not Bill or Will or Willie. William was the only name he'd been called since birth, and that remained the case until parents' weekend during the fall of their freshman year. His mother and father flew in from Shaker Heights for the event. On Saturday night, they invited their son's three roommates—all sans parents that weekend—to join them for supper at the Josiah Barrett Inn. During the meal, Mrs. McCormick passed around baby photographs of William while her only son frowned at his plate.

Later that night—much, much later—on the lawn behind Barrett Inn, long after Mommy and Father had retired for the evening and shortly after downing his eighth beer, William confessed his dark secret. Even though Father expected him to join the State Department after graduation and then return to Cleveland to enter the family merchant banking business, what he really, really, really wanted to do, what he'd dreamed about since childhood, was to move to Montana to become a rodeo cowboy.

He'd passed out just moments after that confession. As they would later discover, the closest he'd come to riding the range was on his ninth birthday, when his parents took him to the Cedar Point Amusement Park in Sandusky and bought him two rides on the Kiddy Kingdom Carousel. Nevertheless, as young William McCormick lay in a stupor on the lawn behind Barrett Inn, Ray Gorman announced that henceforth William would be known as Bronco Billy—a nickname so incongruous it stuck.

Billy emerged from the classroom with a sheepish grin, his sports jacket folded over one arm.

Ray put an arm around his shoulders as they headed down the hall. "We'll fill you in at lunch, Bronco."

To his occasionally exasperated roommates freshman year, Billy had been the quintessence of predictability. Majored in economics, minored in political science—just like Father. Ran on the cross country team—just like Father. Started studying to take the foreign service exam that was three years into the future—just like Father, who spent two years at Foggy Bottom before being assigned to the United States Embassy in Lima. After ten years, Father retired from the service and parlayed his overseas connections into a partnership at an investment banking firm in Cleveland. That was Bronco's career path, too.

Or so it seemed. After college and two years in D.C., he received his first overseas assignment: attaché to the political section of the United States Embassy in Managua, Nicaragua.

But then Bronco Billy veered off his career path.

Literally.

And permanently.

As the four of them were walking down the front stairs of the school, Billy stopped.

Lou turned to look back at him. "What?"

Billy was grinning. "It's just great to see all you guys together."

As they piled into Lou's van, Gordie shouted, "The James Gang is back!"

They'd named themselves after their dormitory, James Hall. Ray had been the gruff platoon leader, Gordie the manic-depressive joker, and Bronco Billy the good-natured nerd.

And just like freshman year, Lou thought, here they were dragging Bronco along. If asked, Bronco would always tag along—say, to the basement TV room on a Sunday afternoon to join the throng of freshmen watching the Celtics-Knicks game. But as the crowd grew more raucous, as more pretzels and beers were downed, as Bradley or Frazier hit one from the head of the key with less than a minute left and the New Yorkers roared and the Celtics fans cursed, you'd turn to say something to Billy... and he'd be gone. And when the game ended and you'd returned to the room with Gordie or Ray, laughing as you opened the door, there he'd be, hunched over his desk, head bobbing slowly to the beat in his headphones as he underlined a passage in his calculus textbook. And more often then not, Ray would grab his headphones, knock the books off his desk, and drag him out for another adventure.

They did it because it was their duty. As Ray explained to Lou one night on their way to the library to haul Billy out for a field trip to a reggae club in Springfield, "Think of what's waiting for that poor bastard—house in the 'burbs, mowing the lawn on Saturday, rooting for the Browns on Sunday, doing it missionary style once a week with the lights out. Hell, man, we gotta make sure Bronco puts in a little time on the dark side of the moon before that happens."

Little did they suspect what the fates had in store for their boring roommate.

As Lou pulled away from the curb, he glanced at Billy in the rearview mirror. Despite all that had happened to him since college, he looked the same as he had on that September afternoon twenty-four years ago when Lou returned from lunch to discover his new roommate unpacking a box of *Foreign Affairs*.

It seemed almost an optical illusion. How could you go through so much and change so little? How could such upheavals inside leave no trace outside?

Lou glanced over at Ray—a man who'd weathered a pharmacopoeia of controlled substances, a violent failed stint in grad school, a wretched marriage, two years in a Telluride commune, the rigors of the Southern California cocaine trade, and other assaults on body and spirit with no visible impact beyond a few gray hairs at the temples, reading glasses in the breast pocket, and twenty-five extra pounds around the middle.

Clearly, there was some fundamental lesson here. But what it was, Lou had no clue.

Chapter Seventeen

Lou gazed at the assistant probate court clerk and tried to keep his tone unruffled. "Okay, sir, and where would the file be?"

The assistant probate clerk scratched his ample belly as he stared at Lou. "I cannot say for sure."

"Why is that?"

The clerk had a grave expression, as if pondering the mysteries of the cosmos. "The presiding judge could have it if there's a hearing scheduled. Someone could have checked it out. Or—"

He shrugged.

"Or what?" Lou said.

The assistant probate clerk raised his eyebrows. "It could be missing."

"Missing?" Ray said. "How can an entire goddamned probate file be missing?"

The four of them were in the Office of the Clerk of the Probate Division of the Circuit Court of Cook County, which was located on the twelfth floor of the Daley Center in the Chicago Loop.

The assistant probate court clerk—a fat, bald, middle-aged white man in a white short-sleeve shirt and dark wrinkled slacks—stifled a yawn. "It happens, gentlemen. Yes, indeed, it happens. You are now standing inside the filing area for the biggest and busiest circuit court in the entire world. The entire world, gentlemen. Literally. You've got your court files back there." He gestured behind him toward the rows and rows of floor-to-ceiling metal filing stacks. "Tens of thousands of court files, gentlemen."

Lou looked to where he'd gestured. There were at least a dozen clerks moving up and down those aisles, most pushing metal carts filled with files. Occasionally, one would stop along the way to remove a file from the stacks or replace a file in the stacks. It reminded Lou of the vast underground government storage facility in the final scene of *Raiders of the Lost Ark*.

The assistant probate court clerk turned back to them. "What can I say, gentlemen?" He sighed and placed his hands on the waist-high counter that separated the clerks and their files from the public. "Sometimes a probate file goes missing."

The clerk drummed his fingers on the counter. "Sometimes the file gets itself misplaced. Sometimes, well, gentlemen, some-times the file gets itself stolen."

"Stolen?" Ray shook his head. "Who would steal a court file?"

"Who, you ask?" The assistant probate court clerk gave a weary chuckle. "Well, sir, a judge cannot hear a case, cannot issue a ruling on the merits, cannot even enter a continuance, without the file. Alas, lawyers are aware of that." He turned to Lou. "Am I correct, counselor?"

If this guy were a steer, Lou thought, he'd have the word PATRONAGE branded on his hip.

"Let us conjure the following scenario," the assistant probate clerk said, pausing to purse his lips. "A particular member of the bar is not quite ready for the trial call but he fears that the judge will refuse to grant him yet another request for continu-ance. What to do, eh? How to deal with this conundrum? As I say, sometimes the court file gets itself lost. Around here—"

He paused to chuckle.

"—around here, we call that a five-fingered continuance."

"I can't fucking believe this," Ray said.

Lou asked the clerk, "Do you suggest we start by checking the probate judge's clerk to see if she has the Marshall file?"

The assistant probate court clerk nodded solemnly, ignoring Ray's outburst. "That would be a prudent first step, counselor."

Thirty minutes later they were back in the Office of the Clerk of the Probate Division. This time the assistant probate court clerk they drew was a fat middle-aged black woman with reading glasses that hung from her neck on a gold chain that rested on an ample bosom.

"Where else could it be?" Lou asked her.

She raised her eyebrows and glanced to her right. "I suppose it could be in the refile bin, honey. We're just a little behind."

They leaned over the counter to see where the clerk had glanced. At the far end of the room behind the counter was a large canvas bin filled to the top with court files. Dozens and dozens of court files, piled helter-skelter.

"When will those be refiled?" Gordie asked.

She shook her head. "We been real busy down here since March, honey. We might get to them, oh, maybe next month."

"Next month?" Ray repeated, incredulous.

She shrugged. "This is Cook County, child."

Lou asked her to wait a second while he walked the other three over to one of the reading tables. Then he went back to her. After ten minutes of good-natured wheedling, she agreed to look through the refile bin for the probate court file in *In re Estate of Graham Anderson Marshall III*.

They waited at a table while she sorted through the files.

"Look at *that* dude." Gordie nodded toward a clerk who was approaching the counter carrying a court file.

He was a skinny white guy in a fat brown tie and a wrinkled beige short-sleeve shirt that was at least two sizes too large and ballooned over his black pants, which were belted so high on his waist that his hips looked like they were fused to his rib cage. They watched as he handed the file across the counter to an attorney.

"Keep your eye on him," Gordie said.

The skinny clerk moved deliberately, almost mechanically, down the counter toward a manual pencil sharpener bolted to the wall at the end. He was still holding the slip of paper with the court file number. Slowly, carefully, he crumpled the slip of paper, pressed it against the pencil sharpener and cranked the handle several times. Then he stuffed the wad into his bulging shirt pocket.

"I've been watching him," Gordie said. "He does that every time."

Ray said, "No doubt he's a blood relative of a precinct captain. It's a fucking halfway house in here."

The female clerk returned to the counter with a big smile.

"Look what I found," she said, holding two thick brown accordion file jackets.

Lou went up to the counter and handed her the check-out card. "Thanks," he said.

"You're welcome, honey." She handed him the two file jackets.

He started to turn and paused. "Do you know who last checked these out?"

"Hmmm, let me see." She reached across the counter and ran her finger down an index card stapled to the side of one of the file jackets. She tilted her head to read the information.

"That was just four days ago," she said, more to herself. "I'll go look it up."

Lou returned to the table and handed one of the file jackets to Billy and sat down with the other. Gordie moved next to Billy, and Ray slid his chair alongside Lou.

"There'll be lots of court documents," Lou explained. "Ignore them. Look for Marshall's papers—his will, any codicils, letters from him, instructions for his executor, references to other estate planning documents. Stuff before he died."

Twenty minutes later, Ray whistled softly and held up a legal-sized document. "This is some weird shit."

"What's that?" Lou asked.

Ray flipped back to the cover page. "Codicil A to the Last Will and Testament of Graham Anderson Marshall."

"What about it?" Lou asked.

"It sets up a trust fund—a forty-thousand-dollar trust fund—for the care and maintenance of—you ready for this?—a grave at a pet cemetery."

"Whoa," Gordie said. "What's the pet's name?"

"Canaan."

"Who?" Bronco Billy asked.

Ray gestured at the document and shrugged. "Canaan."

"A pet cemetery?" Gordie reached for the codicil. "The guy set up a trust fund for a pet's grave?"

Gordie studied the document.

"Canaan could be a cover," Lou said.

Fifteen minutes later Billy leaned back in his chair. "I think I found her."

The other three looked up from their documents. Billy was holding a legal-sized document about thirty pages long.

"Her?" Lou asked softly.

Billy smiled. "Has to be."

They all leaned forward.

Billy placed the document on the table. "His Last Will and Testament."

He waited as an attorney passed by their table toward the copy machine. Then he opened the document to a page in the middle.

"Article Fifteen." He looked down at the page. "Here. It's in his bequest to Barrett College."

"Read it," Ray said.

Billy looked around to make sure no one else was paying attention. He leaned forward, his voice low. "It says he gives, devises, bequeaths, et cetera the sum of three hundred thousand dollars—quote—'to Barrett College, whose most captivating and captivated first lady now resides where the sultan pointed on October first'—close quote."

They were silent for a moment.

"Damn," Ray finally said, "that's her."

"Read that again," Lou said.

Billy did, slowly.

Ray was beaming. "We found her, boys."

"We did?" Gordie asked.

"Of course."

"Where is she?" Gordie asked.

"Wherever that fucking sultan pointed," Ray said.

"Okay," Gordie said. "And where exactly would that be?"

Ray gave him an annoyed look. "We'll find out."

"Which sultan?" Billy asked.

"We'll find that out, too," Ray said.

"How?" Gordie said.

Ray leaned back in his chair with a frown. "We'll figure something out."

"It shouldn't be that hard." Lou lowered his voice. "She disappeared in June of 1959. What's the date on Marshall's will?"

Billy flipped to the last page. "The sixth of October, 1984."

Lou did the calculation. "That means there are…twenty-six October firsts between the time Sirena disappeared and the date of his will. Whoever this sultan is, he must have been famous enough—or the place he pointed to must have been famous enough—to get reported in the newspaper."

"Why do you say that?" Billy asked.

Lou said, "Remember what Gabe Pollack told us? Marshall would want to make sure that he got credit for hiding the statue. What's the best way to do that? By telling people where he hid it." Lou pointed at the will. "This is Marshall's evidence. That's why there has to be a newspaper article about that sultan."

Billy looked confused. "Why?"

"Because," Lou said, "if there's no public record of the event, it becomes an impossible clue. If you can't solve the clue, Marshall doesn't prove that he was the one who hid her."

Gordie nodded. "So we need to check the newspapers for each October first from 1959 to 1982."

"Actually," Lou said, "we want the October second issues. "If our sultan pointed on October first, it wouldn't appear in the newspaper until the following day."

Ray stood up. "Then let's get over to the library."

"Sir? Excuse me?"

Lou turned. It was the assistant clerk who had found the file for them. She was holding up a filing card. Lou walked over to the counter.

"Here's that check-out list for the Marshall file." She scanned both sides. "Mostly Chicago lawyers. And here—" she pointed to a name "—this gentlemen writes for the *Sun-Times*."

"When was that?" Lou asked.

"That was almost three years ago. No one's asked for the file since then, until four days ago. And then you today."

"Who asked for it four days ago?"

She squinted at the card. "Har…no, Henry…Wash, uh—"

"Washburn?"

"That's it. Henry Washburn."

Lou groaned.

Ray groaned. "Shit."

"It could be anyone," Gordie said.

Ray turned to Gordie, his face grim. "It's them," he said.

"Who?" Billy asked.

"Frank and Reggie," Lou said.

Billy's eyes widened. "Frank and Reggie? How do you know?"

Ray said, "They were at the nursing home in St. Louis. They saw his sister. They probably read the same damn letter. That means we're not the only ones who know Marshall hid her." He banged his fist against his thigh. "Fucking preppies."

"Come on, then," Gordie said. "Let's get over to the library and find the article."

Chapter Eighteen

Lou rewound the last reel of microfilm—the one containing all issues of the *New York Times* for the first ten days of October, 1959.

He shook his head. "I don't get it."

They were in the library of the Northwestern Law School. Lou and Gordie were seated at one reader, and Ray and Billy were at the other. More than a dozen reels of microfilm were piled between the two microfilm readers.

They'd been at it now for nearly three hours, reading every October second issue of the *Chicago Tribune* and *New York Times* from 1959 to 1984, along with all October issues of *Time* magazine for the same period.

Fifteen sultans had made the news over the course of those twenty-five Octobers. They'd delivered speeches, hosted world leaders, bought expensive diamonds, died in private plane crashes, sold oil, bought mansions in Beverly Hills, had their heads lopped off by revolting subjects, lopped off the heads of revolting subjects, and donated millions to charity. One of them—His Majesty Sultan Haji Hassanal Bolkiah Mu'izzaddin Waddaulah, the Sultan and Yang Di-Pertuan of Brunei Darussalam—even shook hands with Mayor Richard M. Daley and members of his staff in City Hall on October 1, 1973. *Time* quoted his Hizzoner's quintessential Chicago introductions: "Sultan, dese are da boys. Boys, say hi to da Sultan."

But in all those years—in all those articles and all those photographs—not one of those sultans pointed at anything. Or at least not in the presence of a reporter or photographer.

The thrill of anticipation they'd felt as Billy threaded that first reel of microfilm into the machine three hours ago had long since fizzled.

"We must be missing something here," Ray said.

Gordie said, "Maybe we're looking at the wrong newspapers. What if it was reported in the *L.A. Times*, or the *Boston Globe*?"

"What if it was only reported in a foreign paper?" Billy added.

"Damn," Gordie said, shaking his head. "I just thought of something."

Billy stifled a yawn. "What?"

"You remember that *New York Times* article a month ago, the one on the hunt for Sirena?"

They nodded.

Gordie looked around at them. "It mentioned all the different places where people are searching for her."

"So?" Ray said.

"It said there was a crew from the Class of Sixty-eight heading for Egypt."

Gordie paused. No one said anything.

"Get it?" he asked. "Egypt? Sultans? They must have had a good reason to head over there."

"Shit." Ray pushed away from the table and stood up. "I need a drink."

Chapter Nineteen

Lou called home from a pay phone in the bar back near the restrooms. He knew that Katie had her big math test that day and that Kenny had a ball game that night. Although conditions were hardly optimal for a long-distance family conversation—the noise in the bar was approaching airport-runway decibel levels—this would be his only chance tonight. It was already almost ten. He wouldn't be back to the hotel until after midnight. He missed his children and needed to hear their voices.

Both were home and still awake. He got to hear all their news, even though they had to shout for him to hear. Kenny went first, then Katie.

"I'll call tomorrow night, peanut," he told her when she was done filling him in on the day's events. "From a quieter place. I love you."

"Love you, too, Daddy. So?"

"So?"

"Are you getting warmer?"

He smiled. "I think so."

"You going to find her?"

"Hard to say."

"You having fun, Daddy?"

Lou smiled. "I guess so."

"Good. Go for it, Daddy. We love you."

He smiled as he hung up.

Turning toward the crowded bar, he repeated his daughter's words aloud. "Go for it, Daddy."

The James Gang was down to three for the rest of the night. Bronco Billy had called his wife from a pay phone at the law library. The strained conversation—tense whispers on Billy's end—lasted five minutes. Billy replaced the receiver, his shoulders hunched. They said good-bye to him outside the library before they caught a cab to the bar. They pretended not to notice his embarrassment.

From across the room, Lou watched as Ray and Gordie flirted with the waitress. Ray poured the last of the pitcher of beer into Gordie's mug and signaled for another one—a gesture right out of freshman year. All those nights at Pete's Fine Pizzas and Grinders, with Ray pouring the last of a pitcher into one of their mugs and signaling for another.

Well, Lou said to himself, *Ray was definitely going for it.*

Ray had wanted them all back together again for his quest—back together like they once were. A return to the past, if just for these few days together.

Lou wanted that, too, but it was complicated. You couldn't just surrender to nostalgia. Not when there were children and clients and a mortgage and future college tuitions summoning you back to the present. Today alone he'd checked his voice mail twice, returned a couple of client calls, and spent ten minutes on the phone with Brenda giving her a new research project on an idea for the Donohue appeal that had popped into his head at two in the morning.

Twenty years was a lot of years, he thought as he watched Gordie and Ray through the smoky haze of the bar. So much had happened since college. To each of them. Bronco Billy—good Lord, look how much had happened to him since college. To Gordie, too—those bleak years in Hollywood, tainted with the copper taste of failure. And Ray.

Death had changed things as well. Irreversibly.

Gordie's father was dead. Stanley Cohen—a diminutive, slightly stooped, balding accountant with a bushy mustache and a wonderful smile who loved to tell zippy little jokes in his rapid-fire, Borscht-Belt delivery. *Hey, Lou,* he said during Lou's visit with Gordie's family over one of the holidays, *they just opened a new Chinese German restaurant over on Dempster. Food's not bad*—pause two beats—*but an hour later you're hungry for power.*

Lou smiled. You could almost hear the snare drum riff in the background—*ra-ta-boom*—and then Stanley Cohen chuckled and repeated the punchline. *Food's not bad, but an hour later you're hungry for power.* More chuckles.

Both of Ray's parents were dead.

"I'm an orphan," Ray had told him last year with a sad smile.

Lou remembered Ray's parents so clearly from the time he had spent a weekend at Ray's house in Pittsburgh on his drive home at the end of freshman year. His father had seemed so young and vigorous, his mother weary but good-natured. Lou had joined the eight members of the Gorman family around the roughhewn dinner table that Ray's father had made in his basement shop. Ray's father died of a heart attack at the steel mill—dead before the ambulance arrived. Six months later, his mother died of liver cancer, quickly and painfully and quietly.

Billy, too, had been touched by death. His younger brother Robert had been killed in a car crash three years ago. Lou had met Robert at Barrett during the spring of his freshman year when he'd come up to visit his big brother. He was in eighth grade at the time—an extremely polite, formal boy with a slight stammer. And now he was dead.

And death had visited Lou as well. He frowned, staring down at the floor.

Not now, he told himself. *Not now.*

Gordie looked up as Lou rejoined them. "So? How're the kids?"

"Good. Katie thinks she aced her math test. Kenny hit the game-winning double."

Gordie pumped his fist. "Way to go, Kenny Ballgames."

The waitress set down their second pitcher of beer and another order of guacamole and tortilla chips.

Ray took a sip of beer and shook his head. "We're missing something here. There's got to be a way to figure this out."

Lou dipped a tortilla chip in the guacamole and ate it. "What do we know?" he said. "We know our sultan never made it into the *Chicago Tribune* or *New York Times.*"

Gordie groaned. "Don't even think what that could mean. We'd have to read through newspapers from around the country, or even the world, for chrissakes."

Lou crunched on a chip. "Worse yet, it might not even be in a newspaper. Or even in this century. We could be dealing with a mythical sultan. Like the one in Aladdin."

They sipped their beers in silence.

Gordie said, "Maybe it's got something to do with that crazy codicil with the animal cemetery. What was the pet's name?"

"Canaan," Lou said.

"The Promised Land," Ray said. He looked at Lou. "Gordie's right. Let's see if Gabe Pollack knows anything about it."

"We can drop by his office tomorrow."

They were silent for awhile, sipping their beers and crunching on tortilla chips.

Gordie printed the word SULTAN on his napkin and turned it to face them.

"What are you doing?" Ray asked.

"You think it's an anagram?" Gordie said.

For the next several minutes, they fiddled with the letters:

Stun.

Lust.

Salt.

Slut.

Slant.

Last.

They couldn't come up with any word using all six letters.

Other possible codes proved equally unenlightening, although Ray's idea of focusing on the first letters of the words in Marshall's will yielded a disturbing message: Sultan Pointed On October First.

"Spoof?" Ray said. "It better not be."

"We used to be good at this stuff," Gordie said.

"What stuff?" Lou asked.

"Figuring things out."

Ray gave him a dubious look. "We did?"

"Sure," Gordie said. "Don't you remember? It was Bronco Billy's finest hour."

"What are you talking about?"

"Come on, Ray," Gordie said.

"What?"

"I'll give you a hint."

"Okay."

"Yakov Blotnik."

"Who?"

"Yakov Blotnik."

Lou and Ray gave each other a baffled look.

And then Ray smiled. "Oh, yeah. Yakov Blotnik."

SCENE 34: THE EXAM {3rd Draft}:

DISSOLVE TO:

EXT. BARRETT COLLEGE QUADRANGLE - NIGHT

CAMERA ON CLASSROOM BUILDING

Dead of winter. Snow gently falling. The building is dark except for a single brightly lit classroom on the second floor. We are too far away to make out the identities of the four people inside, but we recognize them as they speak.

                    LOU
          (straining for the answer)
        Some sort of eye doctor, right?

               BRONCO BILLY
                 (patiently)
        But what is his name? You have to
        know his name.

INT. CLASSROOM - NIGHT

It's one of those seminar rooms with a long conference table surrounded by chairs.

Ray, Lou, Gordie, and Billy are in there cramming for an English exam. Books and notebooks are strewn around the table, along with empty cans of Coke, Styrofoam coffee cups, and a bag from Dunkin' Donuts. Billy sits at the head of the table, as much in charge as anyone could be after all these hours.

Lou leafs through a dog-eared copy of *The Great Gatsby*, looking for the answer. Gordie crumples sheets of loose-leaf paper and tries to toss them into the waste basket in the corner. Ray stands by the window and peers into the snowy night as he takes a drag on his Camel cigarette.

> BILLY
> (looking up at them)
> Well?

> LOU
> (still searching through the book)
> Egg-something. Egbert?

> BILLY
> No.

> GORDIE
> (as a crumpled paper
> drops in basket)
> Bradley shoots, he scores!

> LOU
> Okay, Bronco. We give up. Who?

> BILLY
> Dr. T. J. Eckleberg.

> GORDIE
> And who is he again?

> BILLY
> The face on the billboard in the valley of ashes in *The Great Gatsby*.

> RAY
> (disgusted)
> This is total chickenshit.

> BILLY
> Professor Berger said this kind of stuff would be on the exam.

                    RAY
This is college, for chrissake. What's he
doing giving us a goddamned seventh
grade quiz?

                    BILLY
To make sure we read the books he
assigned. He said we'd have to know
names, places, things like that.

                    RAY
Total chickenshit.

                    BILLY
It's fifty percent of our grade.

                    GORDIE
              (with a new "ball")
Dr. Eckleberg at the head of the key. Dr.
E shoots. HE SCORES!

                    LOU
How about some Philip Roth?

                    GORDIE
              (pausing in his game)
Goodbye, Columbus. What a great tush,
eh?

                    RAY
Whose?

                    GORDIE
Whose? My God, man. Whose? Ali
MacGraw's, that's whose. Remember that
scene at the country club when she gets
out of the pool and reaches back to snap
the bottom of her swimming suit down.
There's not a Jewish guy my age who
doesn't get a woody remembering that
scene.

LOU
He won't ask about *Goodbye,
Columbus*. Too easy. We need to focus
on the other stories.

BILLY
Good point, Lou.

RAY
(mimicking Billy)
Good point, Lou.

BILLY
(studying his class notes)
Okay, who was Yakov Blotnik?

GORDIE
(laughing)
Who?

BILLY
Yakov Blotnik.

RAY
(rolling his eyes heavenward)
Fuck if I know.

BILLY
Anyone?

GORDIE
Yakov Blotnik? Uh, Jay Gatsby's real
name?

LOU
F. Scott Fitzgerald's real name?

GORDIE
Ray Gorman's real name.

BILLY
This is serious. Yakov Blotnik.

> LOU
>
> We give up.

> BILLY
>
> Yakov Blotnik is the janitor in Philip Roth's short story, "The Conversion of the Jews."

A moment of silence, and then the other three burst into laughter.

EXT. QUADRANGLE - NIGHT

They are still laughing as the camera pulls further away until all we can be see is the illuminated windows of the otherwise dark building.

> GORDIE
>
> Cousy to Russell. Russell back to Cousy. Over to Hondo. Hondo to Blotnik. Yakov Blotnik shoots, HE SCORES!

> RAY
>
> The janitor in "The Conversion of the Jews"? Unbelievable. Total chickenshit.

CUT TO:

INT. LECTURE HALL - DAY

The next day. Exam time. All rows of seats in the tiered lecture hall are filled, a closed bluebook on every desk. Professor Berger stands at the lectern below as student proctors pass out the exams. Billy is seated down in the front row. The other three are interspersed among the rest of the class, with Ray all the way in back on the top row.

ANGLE ON PROFESSOR BERGER

as he glances back at the clock over the blackboard and CLEARS his throat.

> PROF. BERGER
> You will have exactly one hour to complete
> this exam. No talking whatsoever.

He pauses to glance back at the clock again.

ANGLE ON STUDENTS

Gradual zoom in on Ray Gorman, who is seated way up in the back row.

> PROF. BERGER
> (off screen)
> You may now…begin the exam.

The SOUND of 70 exam booklets opening.

CLOSE ON RAY

as he opens his booklet and starts reading.

INSERT OF FIRST PAGE OF THE EXAM

where the following question is visible:

> 1. Who is the janitor in Philip Roth's
> "The Conversion of the Jews"?

ANGLE ON RAY

His frown relaxes into a smile and he looks up.

RAY'S POINT OF VIEW

Three rows below Ray to the right, Lou turns and looks back with a grin and then glances down to his left, where Gordie is seated.

ANGLE ON GORDIE

as he looks back at Lou with raised eyebrows and an expression of wonder.

RAY'S POINT OF VIEW

From all the way down in the front row, Billy sneaks a look back at Ray.

ANGLE ON RAY

as he winks at Bill and gives him a thumbs-up.

ANGLE ON BRONCO BILLY

as he smiles.

Chapter Twenty

"Rachel Gold?" Ray said. "You trust her?"

"Gabe does," Lou said. "That's good enough for me."

"She's a lawyer?"

"She is. Used to be at Abbott & Windsor."

"What happened?"

"She left."

"Voluntarily?"

"Definitely. Gabe said she was one of their best associates. Smart, tough, hardworking. And apparently gorgeous."

"I like that last part. So why'd she leave?"

"According to Gabe, she wasn't crazy about life in a big law firm. She wanted to go solo. She's got her own practice now. Mostly litigation."

"That takes some balls. I like that in a woman."

They were in a small conference room down the hall from Gabe Pollack's office at Abbott & Windsor. Just the two of them this morning. Gordie was giving a presentation to one of his agency's big accounts, and Billy had a representative from the Spanish consulate visiting his classes.

"And she's from St. Louis, too?" Ray said.

Lou smiled. "Another graduate of U. City."

"Did you know her in high school?"

"Nah. She's at least ten years younger than us."

Having struck out on the newspaper angle yesterday, they'd shifted their focus to the Canaan bequest—namely, that odd codicil to Marshall's will that established a trust fund for the maintenance of a grave at a pet cemetery for something called Canaan. Although Marshall's will seemed to direct them toward wherever the mysterious sultan had pointed, the odd pet cemetery bequest was hard to ignore.

Gabe had been familiar with the codicil—or at least its existence. That was clear when they mentioned it to him.

"Ah, yes." He'd nodded and smiled. "The Canaan legacy."

The firm had discovered the codicil among Marshall's estate papers after his death. Its existence had been a surprise to all—from his widow, who knew nothing about it, to the trusts-and-estates partner at Abbott & Windsor, who'd drafted what he'd believed was the entirety of Marshall's estate plan. The firm had retained its former associate, Rachel Gold, to quietly investigate the matter. Although the results of her investigation had been strictly confidential at the firm, Gabe believed it was unrelated to Sirena.

Gabe had called Lou earlier that morning when he learned that Rachel was going to be at the law firm that day regarding another confidential matter for Abbott & Windsor. If they could come by around ten-thirty, she'd meet with them before heading back to her office.

There was a knock on the conference room door.

"Come in," Lou called.

The door opened and a young woman stepped in. A strikingly beautiful young woman. She gave them a friendly, confident smile.

"Hi, guys. I'm Rachel."

They stood, shook her hand, and introduced themselves.

Rachel Gold was tall and slender, with dark curly hair, high cheekbones, and intelligent green eyes. She was wearing a dark two-piece suit, the skirt hemmed at the knees, an ivory silk shirt underneath the jacket, and low heels. There was a calm, assured aura about her that conveyed the sense that she'd be happy to meet you in court or on a tennis court. Lou liked her immediately.

She took the seat at the head of the table and set her leather briefcase and purse on the floor beside her. Lou sat on one side of the table and Ray on the other.

"Well?" Rachel said.

"Thanks for meeting with us," Lou said.

She smiled at Lou. "We U. City grads have to stick together."

Lou grinned. "Agreed."

"So tell me why I'm here."

She listened as Ray gave her the background on Sirena.

When he finished, she frowned. "So you believe Mr. Marshall arranged for her disappearance?"

"Apparently," Lou said.

"Okay. And?"

Lou said, "We understand that after Marshall died, the firm retained you to work on a matter involving his estate."

She nodded. "That's true."

"Specifically, we understand it had something to do with that codicil for the grave in the pet cemetery."

"That's also true."

"We went over to probate court," Lou said, "and made a copy of it. Canaan, right?"

She nodded.

"What's the deal with the grave?" Ray asked.

Rachel shook her head. "I can't say anything more about the grave, Ray. Attorney-client privilege. But I can guarantee that your missing statue was *never* in that grave. Ever."

"You're that sure?" Ray said.

"I am."

After a moment, Ray said, "Was it one of his practical jokes?"

"Pardon?"

"That Canaan legacy thing."

Rachel leaned back as she considered the question.

"In a way," she finally said.

"When you were doing that investigation," Lou said, "did you come across anything having to do with Sirena?"

Rachel frowned as she thought it over. She shook her head. "No."

Ray asked, "Did Marshall know any sultans?"

"Sultans?" she repeated.

"Yeah."

She shrugged. "It's possible. Abbott & Windsor has an office in Riyadh. I think Marshall handled a commercial arbitration over there back when I was an associate. I assume they have sultans in Riyadh."

"Did he represent one?" Lou asked.

"I don't know." Another pause. "Why?"

Lou explained the sultan reference in the will.

"That is odd." Rachel leaned back in her chair. "You should ask Gabe to run off a list of Marshall's clients. That information should still be in the firm's database. That list may tell you whether he ever represented a sultan—or handled any matter that might have involved a sultan."

◇◇◇

"This is frustrating," Ray said.

They were heading back down the hallway toward Gabe's office.

"Raymond?"

They stopped and turned toward the voice. The speaker was a female attorney in her early forties. She held a yellow legal pad in one hand and a dark Prentice-Hall treatise on tax law in the other.

Lou glanced over at Ray, who had a rigid smile on his face.

"Elaine," Ray said. "What are you doing here?"

She was dressed in a conservative gray suit and dark flats.

"I work here, Raymond."

Ray said, "I thought you were at Winston and Strawn."

"I was. Things change. I came over her about eight years ago. What are *you* doing here?"

"Talking to one of your lawyers. Me and, uh, this is Lou. My friend Lou Solomon. Lou, this is Elaine, uh—"

Ray paused, glancing down at her left hand. She was wearing a gold wedding band.

"Sansbury," she said, reaching to shake Lou's hand. "Elaine Sansbury. Very nice to meet you. You were one of Raymond's roommates freshman year, right?"

"Right," Lou said, surprised.

"The normal one, right?"

"Normal?" Lou smiled. "Says who?"

"Raymond." She glanced over at Ray and winked. "Although he may not be the most reliable expert witness on the subject of normality."

Lou laughed. "No comment."

"There were two others, right?" She squinted in concentration. "There was Gordie. Gordie Cohen. He was the comedian. And then—hmm—cowboy name, right? Tex? Bronco? Bronco Billy. You called yourselves the James Gang."

Lou raised his eyebrows. "I'm impressed. How do you know all this?"

"Raymond and I were once married." She looked at Ray. "A long time ago, eh?"

"Seems that way."

Surprised, Lou glanced at Elaine and then Ray and back at Elaine. She had lively blue eyes, thick chestnut hair cut short, and a sprinkling of freckles over her high cheeks and broad nose. She had the round face and stout build of a Russian peasant.

She said to Ray, "I read that article about you in *Forbes*. I was impressed."

There was a moment of silence, and then Ray said, "You're looking fine, Elaine."

She laughed. "You're sweet, but you always sucked at bullshit. I put on forty-two pounds when I got pregnant. Everyone told me, 'Don't worry, Elaine. Once the baby's born, all that weight'll drop right off.' That was six years ago. Apparently, thirty-five of those pounds decided to take up permanent residence."

"So you have a child?" Ray asked.

"Hey," Lou said to them, "I've got to go check on that list with Gabe. When I'm done, where will I find you two?"

"My office," Elaine said. "I'm one floor down. When you're done just have the receptionist buzz me."

She turned to Ray with a warm smile. "Come on, Raymond."

SCENE 64: FRONT-END, PART II {Draft 3}:

CUT TO:

INT. BARRETT COLLEGE DINING HALL - NIGHT

Dinner. The usual mealtime sounds in the crowded dining hall: LAUGHTER, SHOUTS, CLANGING of plates and silverware.

ANGLE ON LOU AND RAY

They are wearing white cotton busboy jackets and pushing a large metal bussing cart through the dining hall.

A group of upperclassmen get up from a table and leave. Lou and Ray push their cart over to the table and go to work: scraping the plates into the garbage pail on the cart; stacking the trays, dirty dishes and glasses on the cart; putting the silverware into the divided rack.

                    RAY
          (as he scrapes a plate)
     I talked to the graycoat tonight. About
     front-end and back-end.

                    LOU
          (putting silver in rack)
     Yeah?

                    RAY
     Said he might let us try it on Buzz's
     night off.

                    LOU
You really want to?

                    RAY
Bussing is grunt work, man. Front- and
back-ends are the coolest job in the
dining hall. Let's unload.

Lou wipes the table with a wet towel and they push
the cart toward the front left side of the dining hall and
through swinging doors into the tiny area between the
dining hall and the dishwasher area. There's a large
square opening in the wall, which is where the busboys
pass the garbage and dirty plates and silverware and
glasses and trays into the dishwasher area to BUZZ,
the front-end man.

It's NOISY in there: CLANGING of dishes and silverware, GRINDING of the garbage disposal, STEAM
and SPRAY and ENGINE NOISES of the industrial
dishwasher.

                    RAY
              (poking his head
            through the opening)
Hey, Buzz, how's it hanging?

INT. DISHWASHER ROOM

BUZZ is bare-chested beneath his white cotton jacket,
sleeves pushed back above his elbows. His haircut
matches his name. Buzz looks like a cross between the
Marlboro Man and a Hell's Angel—and most definitely
at home on his range, which consists of a deep metal
sink area with a power sprayer the size of a handgun
and the front end of an industrial Hobart dishwasher.

Lou passes stuff through the opening while Ray
watches Buzz put on a master demonstration of
front-end man in action—stacking plates and trays
and glasses into the plastic racks with the speed and

dexterity of a Ninja warrior. As soon as a rack is filled, he slams it down onto the conveyor belt that moves the line of racks through the various chambers of the stainless steel dishwasher.

At the back end, the racks emerge, one by one, pushing through the hanging canvas flaps in a cloud of steam. Waiting there is CHARLIE, the back-end man. Like Buzz, Charlie is bare-chested under his white jacket. With his long blond hair kept out of the way by a tie-dyed headband, he looks like a ski bum. Charlie wears rubber gloves. He yanks each rack out of the machine, slams it down on his work area, and rapidly removes and stacks the contents, his hands almost a blur. When the rack is empty, he whips it onto the return conveyor belt and spins toward the back end in time to grab the next rack as it emerges.

Angle on Ray as he peers at the action, a smile of wonder on his face.

Chapter Twenty-one

"Well?" Ray asked.

They were waiting for a down elevator in the lobby of Abbott & Windsor.

"No match," Lou said. "The firm wouldn't give me a printout, but Gabe put Marshall's client list up on his computer screen and let me browse through it. No sultans. In fact, no clients at all from the Middle East."

"Shit."

"It was a long shot." Lou smiled at Ray and raised his eyebrows. "So?"

Ray frowned. "So what?"

"Was it nice to see her?"

"I guess." He shrugged. "It's like running into a friend you haven't seen since grade school. It didn't take us long to realize that we don't have much in common anymore—not that we ever did."

"She was more than a grade school friend."

"Barely. We were kids back then. Young and stupid and mismatched. Her dad's a lawyer. A big mucky-muck in Cleveland. Brother's a lawyer, too, and so are two uncles. We met during her four minutes of rebellion. I was about the furthest thing you could find from a lawyer," He hesitated, pensive. "Man, I was an even bigger asshole back then."

"How so?"

"Doing drugs, hanging out in bars, stumbling home at three in the morning. And good old reliable Elaine was getting up early everyday and going to classes and cooking our meals and studying hard in the library and working on the law review and putting on fancy clothes for interviews with the downtown firms and getting herself primed to join the Yuppie labor force."

He shook his head. "Poor gal totally freaked when she found out I was selling drugs out of our apartment."

The doors slid open and they stepped onto the empty elevator. Lou pressed the button for Lobby. "She seems nice."

Ray nodded as the doors closed. "She is. I'm a dick, but Elaine's a good person. I'm glad her life worked out well."

"What's her new husband do?"

Ray gave him a smile. "Lawyer." He paused, his eyes going distant. "Her kid's cute."

"Boy or girl?"

"Girl."

Lou observed his friend for a moment. "Any regrets?"

Ray gave him a curious look. "About what?"

"Her. You and her."

Ray shook his head. "As Satchel Paige said, 'Don't look back.' I don't."

"That's bullshit, Ray."

"Actually, it's the best advice out there. If you like where you are today, it's ridiculous to have regrets about yesterday."

"What's that mean?"

"You are where you are today because of where you were before today. Like that Beatles song—it's a long and winding road." He paused. "Last year I got roped into speaking to a business class at UC San Diego. Some sort of marketing seminar. During the question-and-answer part, one of the students said that he wanted to become a shopping center developer, too. Just like me. 'What was your career path?' he asked me." Ray chuckled. "My career path. Jesus."

Lou smiled.

"But that's my point," Ray said, suddenly serious. "You can't possibly duplicate someone else's career path—or their life, for that matter. Why am I here today? Because I spent a couple of

years in a commune in Telluride? Because I bought that box of
bottle rockets freshman year and about scared the living shit
out of poor Bronco when I fired them out his window? Because
I married Elaine? Because I wrecked that marriage? Or any of
a thousand other things I did? Or didn't do?" He shrugged. "I
have no fucking idea. All I know is that if you trace my, quote,
career path—or yours, or anyone who's ever done anything in
life—it's gonna look like one of those Rube Goldberg contrap-
tions where the ball hits the boot that spooks the dog that pulls
the leash that's connected to the bowling pin that knocks over
the candle that starts the cannon ball rolling down an incline
toward the bucket of red paint and so on and so on and so on.
And at the end of all that convoluted lunacy, there you are, still
standing, and with a big shit-eating grin. Life happens."

Lou nodded, thinking of his own. "Maybe."

The elevator slowed as it reached the lobby level.

"Just maybe?" Ray said. "No, definitely. This is reality, man,
not some board game. You don't get a do-over, which is probably
just as well, 'cause if you really could go back, if there really were
do-overs in this life, the odds are you'd fuck it up even worse
the second time around."

They stepped off the elevator.

Ray gestured toward the newsstand. "Hey, you want a candy
bar?"

"Sure."

Lou was amused by the way Ray shifted from the sublime to
the mundane and back again. This, too, was the Ray Gorman
he remembered from freshman year.

Ray studied the choices at the candy counter. "What was
your favorite when you were a kid?"

"These," Lou said as he reached for a Snickers. "How 'bout you?"

"These." Ray reached down for a Baby Ruth.

Out on LaSalle Street, Lou said, "I read somewhere that Baby
Ruth isn't named after the ballplayer."

"Really?" Ray peeled the wrapper off the candy bar and took
a bite. "Is it named after anyone?"

"Some president's daughter. Grover Cleveland, I think—or maybe William Taft. One of them had a baby named Ruth while he was in the White House."

"Well, that's fine with me," Ray said. "Never been a baseball fan. Any sport that predates "American Gladiators" is highly suspect."

Lou stopped.

Ray turned to stare him. "What?"

"Whoa," Lou said.

They were on a sidewalk on the east side of LaSalle Street. People hurried past them on either side.

"Whoa what?" Ray asked.

"Babe Ruth."

Ray glanced down at his half-eaten candy bar and back at Lou. "So?"

"Ray, what did they used to call Babe Ruth?"

"Lard Ass?"

"I'm serious."

"The Yankee Clipper?"

"You're kidding me. The Yankee Clipper was Joe DiMaggio."

"Well, *excuse* me, Mr. Vin Scully. Babe Ruth." He frowned. "The Manassa Mauler? I don't know. What's the answer?"

"You're going to love it."

"So tell me already. What was his goddamned nickname?"

"The Sultan of Swat."

"Good for you, young man. You get a gold star." But then Ray stopped, eyes widening. "You really think—?"

Lou felt his heart racing. "Got to be."

Ray looked down at the half-eaten Baby Ruth and frowned. "Did he ever point at anything?"

Lou smiled. "I can't believe you don't know this, Ray. Follow me."

"Where we going?"

"Just follow me."

Chapter Twenty-two

They were in a Barnes & Noble underneath the El tracks on Wabash Street. Lou headed back to the sports section, skimmed the titles quickly, and found a hardbound book on the history of the Chicago Cubs. He checked the index at the back and then flipped to page eighty-three.

"Here we go," he said.

"What?"

"Nineteen-thirty-two World Series. Yankees and Cubs. Game three. In Chicago. At Wrigley Field."

Lou scanned the text. "Game tied four-to-four in the fifth. Ruth comes to the plate. Charlie Root is pitching for the Cubs. First pitch, called strike. Next two are balls. Then another called strike. Two and two. The Chicago crowd is going wild."

Lou looked up with a smile.

"Okay," Ray said. "What happened?"

Lou looked around to make sure no one was near or listening. He handed the open book to Ray and pointed at the text.

"Read that," he said. "To yourself."

The text quoted the wire story filed by a reporter covering the Series for the *New York World-Telegram*. Lou peered over his shoulder and read along silently:

> Ruth stepped out of the batter's box. The stadium shook and rattled with the boos and jeers of the Chicago faithful. While forty thousand spectators hurled verbal

assaults at him, the Sultan of Swat merely grinned, held his bat high, and pointed it toward the scoreboard in dead center field. This dramatic gesture only further infuriated the partisan throng.

Ruth stepped back into the batter's box and dug in, wagging his bat over his shoulder. Root threw a change-up curve, low and away. Ruth swung, and punched a screaming liner over the head of Johnny Moore in center field. Moore could only turn and watch as the leather spheroid caromed high off the scoreboard.

Ray looked up. "The scoreboard? The one at Wrigley Field?" Lou nodded.

Ray frowned. "You think?"

Lou said, "He's the only sultan we have. And the only one that pointed anywhere."

Ray looked down at the page and then back at Lou. "You're a fucking genius, Solomon."

Lou took the book from Ray and turned to the next page. "It gets better. Look at the box score. Check the date."

Ray studied the page and looked up.

"Holy shit."

Lou nodded. "October first, 1932."

When they were back out on the street, Ray said, "Let's figure this out. If that's where she is, if Marshall really stashed her there back in 1959, that's, what, thirty-five years ago?"

"A long time," Lou said.

"No shit."

"You think she could still be there?"

Ray gave him a wink. "We're gonna find out. Wait here a sec."

He walked over to the corner newsstand and came back with a copy of the *Sun-Times*.

"Where're we supposed to meet Gordie?" he asked Lou.

"In front of that Nike store on Michigan Avenue."

He flipped to the sports section that began on the last page of the tabloid.

"When?" he asked.

Lou checked his watch. "In about a half-hour."

An El train rumbled by overhead.

Ray was scanning the sports page. "And we're supposed to be at the Bronco Billy's for dinner at six, right?"

"Right."

Ray closed the paper and tossed it into the trash can. "Perfect."

"Perfect?"

Ray nodded. "Cubs are in town today. Game starts at one. Let's get Gordie and head up to the ballpark. Time for a little recon."

SCENE 64: FRONT-END, PART III {Draft 3}:

CUT TO:

INT. BARRETT COLLEGE DINING HALL - THE NEXT NIGHT

5:15 p.m. Dinner service starts in 15 minutes. The dining hall is empty except for the two dozen students working dinner shift as servers and busboys and runners. All wear white coats. They're eating in groups of two or three scattered throughout the dining hall.

ANGLE ON LOU AND RAY

seated at a table finishing their meal. The graycoat comes over. He is the supervisor of the dinner shift—an officious upperclassman wearing a white shirt and tie under his gray cotton jacket.

                    GRAYCOAT
          I'll give you boys a tryout on back-end
          tonight.

                    RAY
                  (grinning)
          Cool.

                    GRAYCOAT
          Buzz says he'll train you. If you're any
          good, he'll teach you front-end, too.
          He's pre-med, you know, and he's got
          organic chemistry next semester. He's
          quitting front-end before Christmas.

                    RAY
          Which one of us?

> GRAYCOAT
What?

> RAY
Which one of us is going to work back-
end tonight?

> GRAYCOAT
Which one? Three of you would be
lucky to keep up with Buzz.

The graycoat departs.

> RAY
This'll be great!

INT. DISHWASHER ROOM - LATER

CLOSE ON BUZZ as he leans back against the counter, arms crossed, facing the back-end area, slowly
shaking his head.

ANGLE ON BACK-END

Lou and Ray have long since lost the battle. Total
chaos. One rack of plates after another emerges, steam
billowing up. Filled racks of clean dishes and glasses
are piled everywhere. A plate slips out of Lou's hand
and falls with a CRASH. Ray drops an entire silverware
rack, the contents CLANGING to the ground as the
knives and forks and spoons scatter all around.

And still the racks keep coming. Relentless. One after
another.

[Note to director: This scene should be reminiscent of
the "Sorcerer's Apprentice" episode from the movie
Fantasia. Same music should play as Ray and Lou
struggle to stem the rising tide.]

INT. BARRETT COLLEGE DINING HALL - LATER THAT NIGHT

The dining hall is empty. Chairs are stacked on the table tops. Most of the lights are off. There are only two people in the room: Lou and Ray. They're slumped forward on a pair of chairs—disheveled, soaked, exhausted. They stare numbly at each other, dazed.

RAY
Toward the end there I was starting to think we were getting the hang of it.

LOU
Toward the end there I was starting to think about hanging you.

Chapter Twenty-three

Lou scanned Wrigley Field, shading his eyes with his hand. The sun was shining, the sky was blue, the outfield grass was bright green, and real ivy covered the red brick walls.

"Is this heaven?" he said. They were in the center field bleachers.

Gordie cracked a peanut shell in his hand and popped the nuts into his mouth. "Definitely."

Ray was up getting beer and doing some scoreboard reconnoitering.

"When I was a kid," Gordie said, "I used to come here two, three times a week in the summer. They were all day games back then. We'd ride down on the Skokie Swift—me and a couple buds. Always sat in the bleachers. Usually over there." He pointed toward the left-field bleachers. "That's where most of the homers landed, and that's where we could cheer Billy Williams."

"Billy Williams." Lou smiled. "What a ballplayer."

"Greatest line-drive hitter of all time. Used to bounce singles off the ivy."

Gordie leaned back on the bleacher bench. "Good times back then. We'd get a Coke and a hot dog and a bag of peanuts, watch the game, hop back on the El, and be home in time to play some ball before dinner."

He smiled at the memory. "No better place in the world to be a kid than Wrigley Field in 1964."

"Actually," Lou said, "Busch Stadium wasn't too shabby that year. We beat the Yankees in the World Series. My dad took me to the seventh game. Bob Gibson was the winning pitcher. Talk about a memory."

Ray returned with a cardboard tray holding three large cups of Old Style. "Got the brews."

He took the aisle seat. Gordie was to his left, and Lou to Gordie's left. Ray handed them each a beer.

Lou took a sip of his beer and leaned toward Ray. "So?"

Ray glanced around and edged closer. "There's a ladder. Leads up to a trap door. Door's open now. Presumably 'cause they got guys inside operating it. Hanging from the door latch is what looks like an ordinary combination lock."

Lou and Gordie both turned to glance back.

The rows of bleachers in center field ended just beneath the dark green scoreboard, which towered over the ballpark. The upper half of the scoreboard showed the status of other games around both leagues. On the left side, under the word NATIONAL, there were rows of metal slots for the inning-by-inning scores of the National League games; the right side—AMERICAN—had slots for the American League games. The only game underway in either league that weekday afternoon was the one they were at.

In the scoreboard's middle panel were the sections where the balls, strikes, and outs were flashed, along with the number of the player at bat. Atop the scoreboard was a clock, and above it a T-shaped flagpole with team flags fluttering in the breeze.

To true baseball fans, Lou mused, the Wrigley Field scoreboard was a comforting sight—as reassuring to fans as the Statue of Liberty was to immigrants. In a sport awash with retro-nostalgia—Ye Olde Ballparks—the Wrigley Field scoreboard was the real thing, a genuine relic from an era when all scoreboards were operated by men moving around inside them. Indeed, it was THE scoreboard from every boy's childhood—whether the games you attended back then were at Forbes Field, Connie Mack, Tiger Stadium or, for Lou, the old Busch Stadium (aka Sportsmen's Park) along Grand Avenue across from the Carter Carburetor factory.

He could still remember his first Cardinals game, his first sight of the playing field. He was nine years old. As he stepped through the passageway holding his father's hand, there it was, spread out before him—the magic carpet of bright green, the sparking white bases, the smooth brown infield, the pitching mound with the white rubber and the rosin bag, the bright yellow foul lines that seemed to shoot out from home plate and hit the outfield walls with such momentum that they leapt to the top of the foul poles.

In the second inning of that very first game, his hero Ken Boyer, number 14, smashed a two-run homer into the left field bleachers. As Boyer trotted into the dugout after circling the bases, Lou looked out toward the scoreboard in time to see the blank metal plate in the second inning slot removed and replaced with a yellow "2," which in turn was replaced with a white "2" when the inning ended.

And now, as he gazed up at the Wrigley Field scoreboard, one of the keepers slid a green metal plate with a white zero into the visitors' slot for the fourth inning.

"How many people work inside that thing?" Gordie asked.

Ray said, "Guy working the beer concession said two guys for day games, three for nights."

Lou shaded his eyes as he studied the scoreboard. "How big is it?"

Gordie squinted. "Three stories?"

Ray took a sip of beer as he appraised the structure with the savvy eyes of a real estate developer. "I'd say thirty feet from top to bottom. Double that from side to side."

"Hard to believe she's in there," Lou said.

"Is?" Gordie shook his head. "We don't even know about *was*. And even assuming she ever was, what are the odds she still is?"

"Pretty good," Lou said.

"Come on, man," Gordie said. "Thirty-five years is a lot of years."

"I don't think that matters," Lou said. "Assuming we're right about the sultan, that means that of all the possible hiding places in the world—in the *whole* world—he selected this one. You can be sure he didn't pick it casually. Not for hiding something that important. He had to be convinced that it was a safe hiding place. Right?"

Gordie shrugged. "I guess."

"Don't forget," Lou said, "this scoreboard is private property. Back in 1959, the Wrigley family owned Wrigley Field. That's an important fact. Think of who Graham Marshall was: a well-connected Chicago lawyer in a well-connected Chicago law firm. Guy like Marshall would have known important people within that organization. I'd bet he knew a Wrigley. I bet he cleared the whole thing in advance and got a commitment from them before he stashed her in there."

"Maybe," Gordie said. "But the Wrigleys don't own the Cubs anymore. They sold them to the *Tribune*."

"I know," Lou said. "I thought about that. It's still okay. The dates are key. Marshall's will is dated in October of 1984. That was *after* the *Tribune* bought the Cubs. What's that tell you? He must have gotten assurances from someone at the *Tribune*. Otherwise, he would have moved the statue out of the scoreboard before the *Tribune* bought the Cubs and he would have changed his will."

They were all silent, gazing up at the scoreboard.

"Makes sense," Ray finally said.

"Let's hope so," Gordie said.

The roar of the crowd turned them back to the playing field just in time to see a Cubs player round first base and dig for second. Everyone in the bleachers stood. Lou located the ball in the gap between center and right field. The Pirates' Andy Van Slyke grabbed it barehanded off the ivy and in one motion spun toward third base and threw. The ball reached the third baseman on one bounce and he slapped the tag on the sliding Cub. The umpire didn't hesitate.

"Out!"

The stadium erupted in boos and catcalls. The runner jumped up and started jawing with the umpire, who turned his back and walked away.

As the bleacher crowd settled down, two hot blondes in tight jeans and halter tops sashayed up the aisle. Several guys whistled. The girls smiled and kept moving. The beer man came by, followed by the peanut man. Someone sailed a red Frisbee overhead.

Lou turned to Gordie. "I love this game."

◇◇◇

During a pitching change two innings later, Gordie said, "Did you know I started shaving in sixth grade?"

Said it just like that. Out of the blue.

Ray and Lou exchanged puzzled looks over his head.

"Shaving what?" Ray said.

"My face."

Gordie had his arms crossed over his chest. He was staring at his half-empty beer cup on the ground in front of him. "I started shaving in sixth grade."

The Pirates' pitcher walked off the mound, head down, to a polite round of applause.

"That's young," Lou finally said, for want of anything better.

Gordie turned to him. "You're damn right."

Gordie reached for his beer, finished it in one gulp, and crumpled the cup. "Sixth grade. Started shaving and stopped growing."

"No shit," Ray said. "What are you, five seven?"

"Five six."

"You were five six back then?"

"Yeah."

Ray nodded. "You were once a big motherfucker."

"Sure was. I played center on the basketball team. Batted clean-up on the baseball team. I was the Jim Thorpe of sixth grade—picked first in every sport. When I used to come down here during junior high, I just assumed—and all my buddies just assumed—that I'd be playing here myself one day."

"I hear you on that," Ray said, smiling. "I used to dream of driving in the Daytona 500."

"No, Ray," Gordie said, "you don't understand. I was a superstar back then. A real superstar. You have no idea what that's like. You get the girls. You even get an entourage. I had a seventh-grade entourage. But then one day you wake up and realize you aren't the biggest and strongest kid anymore. Even worse, you realize you aren't growing out of your clothes or your shoes anymore. By eighth grade, I was barely average. By tenth, I was cut from the basketball team. My senior year, one of the kids who used to idolize me—Ronny Goldenberg—was out there on the court playing varsity basketball while I was up in the stands sitting on my butt."

He stared down at his hands. Lou and Ray exchanged glances.

Gordie shook his head. "How do you think that felt? To know in high school that your days of glory are already six years past."

"Jesus, Gordie," Ray said, "lighten the fuck up. Sounds like your mind got stuck in sixth grade, too."

"Ray, you have no conception of what I'm talking about."

"Bullshit, Gordie. I have a total conception of what you're bitching about. It's the same whiny bullshit I heard from you freshman year, man. Since when does being big and strong qualify you for anything more than pulling a fucking farm plow?"

"I'm not talking about plows," Gordie said.

"Ah, you're talking about them?" Ray made a sweeping gesture toward the field. "That herd of cattle grazing down there in the pasture?"

"Yes, Ray," Gordie said, his voice fierce. "Down there."

"Come on, man, you think those bozos are somehow tuned into the music of the spheres? Give me a break. Talk about dumb luck. You're looking at guys one major league fastball from pumping unleaded at Bud's Amoco or stocking paint thinner at Sears." Ray shook his head. "So you're not big enough to play down there. So what? Who says playing down there has anything to do with anything?"

"You're missing the point."

"No, Gordie," Ray said, "you're missing the whole god-damned boat. Size and speed don't mean shit in the real world. What counts is brains and savvy, baby. Moreover, you got no grounds to bitch. You had exactly what these ballplayers have now. You were once king of the hill, right? Now they are. So what if your turn came in sixth grade? Most people never get a turn. Most people aren't king of diddly. I was never picked first for any sport. I never batted fourth. I never played center. Shit, man, I can barely dribble a fucking basketball."

Ray pointed to one of the outfielders. "Look at that bozo in left field. King of the hill? Not for long, dude, He'll be washed up by forty. You think it's tough reinventing yourself at fourteen? Wait 'til that yutz gets *his* wake-up call. Christ Almighty, Gordie, you're sitting here moaning about—"

Ray stopped in mid-sentence.

"Well, well, well," he said, craning back his head. "Look what the goddamned cat dragged in."

Chapter Twenty-four

"Hello, chums."

It was Reggie Pelham. Standing next to him in the aisle was Frank Burke.

They're here, Lou said to himself as he looked up at them. *At last.*

"Louis." Reggie leaned over to shake Lou's hand. "I said to Frank, good God, man, isn't that Raymond and the other fellows over there?"

Frank nodded at them. "Boys."

A beer man came by. Reggie stopped him. "Think I may wet the whistle. Anyone else?"

"Sure," Lou said, reaching for his wallet.

"Frank?" Reggie said.

Frank shook his head.

Ray said nothing. He was sitting with his arms crossed over his chest, studying Frank.

"I'll take one," Gordie said.

"Put away your money, fellas," Reggie said. "This round's on me."

Reginald Harrison Pelham was short and plump. He was dressed today for a round of golf: bright yellow Polo shirt (collar up), iridescent green slacks (pleated and cuffed), and cordovan loafers (with tassels). He'd grown up on Park Avenue, prepped at Choate, and returned to Manhattan after college to join Pelham Bros Ltd., the family merchant banking firm. He'd been a late-night poker player in college, Lou recalled, and a high roller today—comped at major casinos around the world, according to the Class of '74 ramblings of their goofy class secretary, Bryce Wharton.

After the beer man departed, Reggie kneeled in the aisle by Ray. "What brings you chaps to Chicago?"

"Gordie and Bronco Billy live here," Ray answered. "I'm wending my way back to Barrett for the reunion. I stopped in St. Louis to spend a few days with Lou and his kids. Then it was on to the Chi-Town to catch the sights."

Reggie nodded enthusiastically. "Excellent."

Ray paused, the hint of a smile on his lips. "And what about you, Reg? What's a nice rich boy from New York doing out here?"

Reggie grinned and leaned toward Ray. "Frank and I are in the hunt for Sirena."

"Really?" Gordie said, acting surprised. "You think she's in Chicago?"

Lou winced. Gordie was overdoing the naiveté bit.

Reggie shrugged. "Just might be. Afraid I can't reveal more than that, you know." He gave them a wink. "The bleachers have ears, eh?"

Lou smiled. Even though Reggie was a consummate snob, there was a hale-fellow quality about him that Lou had always found endearing.

He remembered the time freshman year that Reggie had called out to him as he passed his open dormitory door. "Louis, old boy. Can I inveigle you to join me in a stogie and some hootch?"

They'd passed a pleasant half-hour puffing on Cuban cigars, sipping single malt whiskey, and searching with sporadic success for conversational common ground.

"Excellent fun," Reggie had announced as Lou got up to leave. An amused chortle, a comradely pat on the back, and Lou was ushered out the door, his head still buzzing from the whiskey.

It was only much later that Lou wondered whether Reggie's bonhomie was just a practice session to sharpen his skills. After all, a merchant banker these days had to deal with all types, even Hebes from the sticks. Then again, Lou conceded, it was always possible that Reggie's performance wasn't a performance.

Lou took a sip of beer and asked Reggie, "Have you run into anyone else looking for her?"

"Not in Chicago, Louis. But there are most assuredly several searching parties out there. Indeed, do you fellows remember a chap named Dan Broussard?"

"Tall guy?" Gordie asked. "A year behind us?"

Reggie nodded. "That's the one." He turned to Frank. "A fellow Blue, eh?"

Frank nodded.

Reggie turned to Gordie. "They both went to Hill School."

Francis Ambrose Burke III had an equally snooty pedigree: born into Grosse Point society, prepped at the Hill School, summered at the family compound on Mackinac Island, returned home after Barrett to help manage the family investments, which included timber holdings in Oregon and rubber plantations in South America.

"As I was saying," Reggie continued, "Dan called last night from Maine. Up near the Canadian border. He's there with a group of classmates. They thought they'd tracked Sirena down to an abandoned loggers' camp in northern Maine. Turned out a bust, but he's got a detective agency that thinks she might be in Gary, Indiana. Great stuff, eh? But we still think the real action might be right here in Chicago, don't we, Frank?"

Frank nodded.

Lou shifted his gaze to Frank Burke. Nothing soft focus about him, and never any effort to ingratiate himself with the pubes, which was his prep school's shorthand for public school grads. Back freshman year, he'd seemed to possess all the advantages that wealth and breeding could supply: tall, chiseled good looks, thick brown hair that he wore long and brushed straight back, like a Viking warrior. He'd installed a small refrigerator in his dorm room, and kept it stocked with gourmet cheeses and sausage and bottles of French wine. He and Gordie used to watch in envious disbelief as Frank returned from mixers, from the library, from fraternity parties, from seemingly anywhere, and always escorting a delectable coed into his dorm room.

"So it's just you and Frank?" Ray asked.

"Just the two of us." Reggie leaned forward and smiled at Gordie. "Sure you're not just a bit in the hunt yourself, Gordon?"

"Nope," Ray said before Gordie could respond. "But if we hear anything promising, Reg, I can sure promise one thing: you and Frank will be the very last to know."

Reggie chuckled and looked up at Frank. "There's some pluck, eh?"

Frank didn't reply.

Lou studied Frank's face. Something was slightly off, as if the man standing in the bleacher aisle was someone else wearing a Frank Burke latex mask. And then Lou remembered. Several years ago, according to the Class of '74 grapevine, Frank had undergone massive plastic surgery after being launched, face first, through the windshield of his Jaguar, which had rammed into a tree late one night on his way home from a topless club in Windsor, Canada. His "restored" features were just a bit too rigid. It gave him an eerie otherworldly aura, as if, in the privacy of his room, Frank might reach beneath his chin and pull back the skin, revealing the head of a space alien.

Reggie stood. "Well, see you chums around."

When they were out of earshot, Ray grunted. "Good."

"What?" Lou asked.

"They're worried."

"Why do you say that?" Gordie asked.

"For starters," Ray said, "what the hell are those two preppies doing in the bleachers? They're following us."

"You think so?" Gordie said.

"I know so." Ray scratched his neck pensively. "We have to assume they've seen Marshall's will. But if they'd figured it out, they wouldn't have given us the time of day, which means we're still a step or two in front of them. For now, at least. But we're going to have to move fast."

"And," Gordie added, "we're going to have to start watching our butts."

Ray leaned back, took a sip of his beer, and shook his head. "What a miserable piece of shit."

"Reggie?" Gordie asked.

"Reggie?" Ray shook his head. "Reggie's harmless. You see Frank watching us while Reggie talked. Like a fucking predator. You can be sure it was his idea to come over and pump us for information. He told Reggie exactly what to say, how to play it. Frank's the dangerous one. Motherfucker's got ice in his veins."

"I never liked him," Gordie said.

Ray took another sip of beer. "You ever hear what he did to those girls senior year?"

"What girls?" Lou asked.

"Two local high school girls. He and one of his pals from Williams picked them up. Took 'em to a motel in New Hampshire, along with plenty of reefer and beer and Quaaludes. Had themselves a twenty-four-hour fuckathon. Next afternoon Frank's pal is antsy to get back to campus. Problem is, the girls are still stretched out on the bed—'luded up and totally zonked. Frank tells his buddy to get in the car. Ten minutes later, he comes out of the motel, hops in the car, and drives off. Tells his buddy that the girls decided to sleep it off and go home later."

Ray finished his beer. The others waited for him to continue.

"Cops have a different story," Ray said. "According to them, Frank went back in the motel room, tried to wake them up, got angry, pulled out his dick, and took a whiz on one of them.

"Oh, Christ," Gordie said.

Ray said, "Turns out Frank pissed on the wrong goddamned girl. Her dad was a Belchertown cop. He raised holy hell. Frank's father had to hire F. Lee Bailey to get him out of the jam. Ended up dropping a wad of dough on the girl's family to settle. Believe me, Frank is a nasty son of a bitch."

Ray turned to stare up at the scoreboard, squinting and shading his eyes. After a moment, he glanced over at Lou.

"Tonight," Ray said.

Lou nodded. "Tonight."

SCENE 64: FRONT-END, PART IV {Draft 3}:

INT. FRATERNITY BASEMENT BAR - NIGHT

Ray, Lou, and Buzz are on barstools, each with a beer.

> BUZZ
> Dudes, you're on your own tomorrow night.

> LOU
> How so?

> BUZZ
> This was my last night.

> RAY
> Who's front-end tomorrow?

> BUZZ
> Draw straws, you poor bastards.

CUT TO:

INT. BARRETT COLLEGE DINING HALL - THE NEXT NIGHT

There's a line of bussing carts near the front of the dining hall waiting to unload. Busboys hang around, growing impatient. One of them peers through the pass-through window and shakes his head in disgust.

INT. DISHWASHER AREA—VIEW THROUGH THE PASS-THROUGH WINDOW

Total chaos. Ray is on front-end. Dirty dishes and glasses and pails of garbage are piled everywhere.

Broken plates and stray pieces of silverware are scattered on the ground.

ANGLE ON LOU

at the back-end, waiting. He pushes aside the canvas flaps to peer inside to see if anything is coming. Nothing.

ANGLE ON RAY

as he attempts to stack a set of dirty dishes in a rack. Two dishes slip out of his hands and CRASH to the ground.

> RAY
>
> Shit!

ANGLE ON LOU

Steam is coming out of the back-end. Lou raises his eyebrows in surprise. A loaded rack is actually coming out of the dishwasher. As soon as the edge of the rack pushes against the flaps, Lou grabs it and pulls it out. Hot water sloshes all over the place.

> LOU
> What the—? Jesus, Ray—

CLOSE ON THE RACK

Ray has sent a pail of garbage through the dishwasher.

RAY turns to look. He's overwhelmed, on the verge of panic.

LOU smiles. RAY gives him a quizzical look. LOU starts to laugh.

> RAY
> (starting to grin)
> I sent garbage?

                    LOU
You know what they say? Garbage in—

                    RAY
    —garbage out.

                    LOU
        (in a bad Mexican accent)
    Garbage? We don't need no stinking
    garbage.

The two of them collapse in laughter.

INT. DINING HALL

The line of busboys is still out there waiting. Several
of them frown at the HOOTS and HOWLS of laughter
from the dishwasher area.

Chapter Twenty-five

Evanston, Illinois.

Six hours later.

They were squeezed around the kitchen table in Bronco Billy's brick bungalow.

Billy turned toward Lou. "Really? Tonight?"

Lou nodded.

Billy looked at Gordie, and then at Ray.

"Yep," Ray said.

Billy's eyes blinked rapidly behind his wire-rim glasses. "Why so fast?"

"No other option," Ray said. "Reggie and Frank are sniffing around like dogs in heat. Others might be, too. I'm feeling—feeling—"

He turned to Gordie. "What's that Yiddish word of yours?"

"*Shpilkes.*"

"That's me. *Shpilkes* out the wazoo."

"But how are you going to get in there?" Billy asked.

"*We*, Kemosabe." Ray grinned.

"Okay." Billy forced a smile. "We. How?"

Ray shrugged. "We may not have the key to the front door, but we got the next best thing."

"What's that?" Billy asked.

"Heavy-duty bolt-cutters."

Billy looked at Lou.

Lou nodded. "Ray and I went by Home Depot after the game."

"We stocked up," Ray said. "Bolt-cutters, rope, tarp, duct tape, other shit. They're all in the back of Lou's van."

"Whoa." Gordie made a time-out signal with his hands. "Bolt-cutters? Are you seriously thinking about using them?"

"If we have to," Ray said.

Gordie turned to Lou. "Counselor, am I correct to assume that breaking-and-entering is still against the law in the State of Illinois?"

"My heavens." Ray put his hand over his heart in feigned shock. "Really?"

Gordie shook his head in exasperation. "I'm serious, Ray. We're not in college anymore. We get caught, and we're in deep shit, man." He turned to Billy. "You think your principal would like that?"

Ray said, "Chill out, Gordie. If we have to actually use the damn bolt-cutters, you two Girl Scouts can sit on your thumbs in the van and wait."

"Ssshhh," Dorothy said as she entered the kitchen buttoning the top button of her peasant blouse. "You'll wake up Santino. Anyone for more coffee?"

They told her no.

Lou said. "Dinner was great, Dorothy."

She pulled up a chair and smiled. "My pleasure."

Lou reflected again on the unlikelihood of her marriage to Billy—which was just part of the unlikelihood of Billy's bizarre career in Nicaragua. The U.S. Embassy in Managua had been his first overseas posting. During those initial months he lived the life of an embassy functionary—sending cables to Washington during the day, donning a tuxedo for an evening cocktail party up at Tiscapa with Somoza's Guardia Nacional henchmen.

But one day he failed to report for duty. And by that night he was huddled in back of a 1949 Ford truck with six other recruits bouncing along dirt roads to the outskirts of Matagalpa, where they began a three-day trek through the mountain jungles to the guerrilla training camp of Carlos Aguero Echeverria of the *Frente Sandinista de Liberación Nacional*, known in the States as the Sandinista National Liberation Front. Carlos himself—in green fatigues and carrying an M-15—greeted the bewildered recruits. One year later, on July 20, 1979, Bronco Billy was among that crowd of 250,000 that jammed into the Playa de la Revolución in downtown Managua in celebration of the over-throw of Anastasio Somoza Debayle.

Lou was the first to learn. He'd stayed in touch with Billy after college and knew about his Nicaragua posting with the State Department. Indeed, he'd called him in D.C. a few weeks before his departure to wish him good luck. But when he received the long letter from Billy describing his Sandinista conversion, Lou initially thought it was a spoof. But by page seven of the eighteen-page handwritten epistle, he realized his college room-mate was telling him the truth.

Bronco Billy a Sandinista guerilla? Lou had been stunned.

He wrote back, though, and they stayed in touch. Billy joined the Literacy Crusade, a massive Sandinista operation in which seventy thousand volunteers (known as *brigadistas*) headed into the countryside to teach reading and writing in remote rural villages. Billy had led a group of thirty-two Managuan teenage *brigadistas* on a six-month tour of duty in a remote area of the Neuva Segovia province where they eventually brought literacy to hundreds of peasants.

As Lou could tell from the letters, it was a time of fierce pas-sions and emotions, exhilaration and anguish. Billy had been in the village the day Jaime Cordova, a coffee farmer who once couldn't even recognize his own name in writing, proudly pre-sented the *brigadistas* with a wood plaque on which he had carved the words of the revolutionary hero Augusto César Sandino, who'd been killed by Somoza's father in 1934: *Death is no more than a moment of annoyance, and it's not worth taking seriously.* But he was also there in May of 1980 when ex-National Guards-men slipped across the border from Honduras and murdered his comrade and fellow teacher, Georgina Andrade.

Alas, things change. Especially revolutions. Six years ago, Billy returned to the States. That was when the catalyst of his mysterious life detour was revealed: Dorothy Becker. She'd been a University of Chicago graduate student in urban anthropology who'd dropped out of her doctoral program while on her field placement in Nicaragua. By the time she and Billy met at a fruit vendor's stall in Managua, she was a paramedic in a ramshackle clinic in a Miskito barrio near the rancid waters of Lake Managua. Billy saw her across the aisle at the banana bin—a tall woman, twenty pounds overweight, dark curly hair, thick glasses, Earth-mother breasts. She looked up, and it was love at first sight. Literally. For both. Within a month, Billy's unswerving internal gyroscope had jumped its base.

It was Dorothy who introduced Billy to Pedro Joaquín Chamorro, the courtly editor of *La Pensa* and a leading opposition figure. It was Dorothy who showed her naïve embassy boyfriend the canned food in the supermarket bearing the Red Cross stamp—the same food that had been donated by international relief organizations in the aftermath of the 1972 earthquake and then intercepted by Somoza's accomplices to sell in supermarkets Somoza owned. And it was Dorothy who took Billy to visit the three stark white buildings in the center of Managua, officially named *Centro Plasmaferesis* but unofficially were known as *La Casa de Vampiros*—or the House of Vampires. It was there that the poor of Managua, at the rate of 1,500 a day, came to sell their blood plasma for five dollars a pint, which was then marked up three hundred percent and sold on the U.S. market for millions of dollars in profits a year. Who owned *La Casa de Vampiros*? The ultimate vampire, Anastasio Somoza Debayle, bleeding his people to death. Chamorro's newspaper first exposed Somoza's involvement in the House of Vampires, and Chamorro's assassination in early 1978 was the catalyst that caused Billy to make his first, tentative contacts with the Sandinistas.

Dorothy was, Lou believed, a good soul, albeit in her own tiedyed, vegan, unshaved-underarm, hippie-commune-matriarch sort of way. Passionate about causes for which Lou could either muster no passion—such as the importance of breast feeding beyond the child's second birthday—or for which he mustered guilt over not sharing her passion—such as the need to improve mental health care for prisoners. A serious person, and, as far as Lou could tell, without an ounce of frivolity in her. The world needed more people like Dorothy. Just so long as he didn't have to marry one.

Dorothy poured herself a cup of herbal tea. "Are you still talking about that statue?"

Billy said, "Ray wants to go for it tonight."

She glanced her watch and gave her husband a puzzled look. "They'll let you in to look for it at this hour?"

"Well, not exactly," Billy said. "We'd have to, uh, sneak in."

She studied Billy.

The rest of them waited.

"I do not understand," she finally said. "Why would you do that?"

Billy pursed his lips but said nothing.

Ray leaned forward and put his arm around Billy.

"That statue is an important part of our school's heritage, Dorothy," Ray said. "It vanished thirty-five years. No one's seen it since. If we can find it and bring it back, the school gets twenty-three million dollars, and we get famous and divide up three million dollars. Not exactly chump change."

Dorothy took off her steel-rimmed glasses and wiped them on a cloth napkin. She held them up to the light, squinting at the lenses, and then put them back on.

She gave Ray a severe look. "Breaking in? Doesn't that seem—well—irresponsible?"

Ray smiled. "What if it was Michelangelo's David? What if it had been missing for decades? Would it seem irresponsible if we were going in there to recover Michelangelo's David?"

"Of course not," she said.

"And why not?" Ray asked.

Dorothy gave him a tolerant smile. "Because Michelangelo's David is a great work of art."

"And you've concluded that Sirena is not?"

"Raymond, Michelangelo's David is one of the most significant works of art in the world."

"Says who?" Ray was grinning. "A bunch of snooty art critics? Who says they're right? What if Michelangelo's David is just Renaissance kitsch? Just the sixteenth-century equivalent of one of those Norman Rockwell figurines they hawk in the back of *Parade* magazine?"

Dorothy sighed. "I am not going to let you bait me, Raymond. You know that your statue is not a significant piece of art."

"Actually," Ray said, "I don't know that. All I know for sure is that it's a pretty significant piece of art to graduates of Barrett College. It's part of the college's history."

"But in the grand scheme of things, Raymond, that statue is not significant."

"All a matter of perspective, Dorothy," Ray said. "To some guy in Tunisia, the Magna Carta is an insignificant scrap of paper. But if the *original* document, signed by old King John himself, had been stolen and hidden inside that scoreboard, well, you'd think it was pretty noble for Billy to go up there and rescue it."

Dorothy sighed again. "Raymond, Sirena is not the Magna Carta, and it is not Michelangelo's David, and it is not the Mona Lisa. And it certainly is not worth the risk of getting arrested over."

The other watched the back and forth, captivated.

"Not worth the risk?" Ray rubbed his chin. "Who has the right to decide that? Let me ask you this. Was Charles Lindbergh's flight across the Atlantic Ocean worth the risk? Did he save anybody, or cure any disease, or make the world safer for democracy by flying across the ocean? Same with Neil Armstrong. And Sir Edmund Hillary. And Hank Aaron. And all the crazy bozos that run the Boston Marathon each year. What's the point of training six months to run twenty-six miles in three hours when you can drive the same goddamned distance in thirty minutes? But you know what? My opinion doesn't count. I got no speaking privileges. You wanna run the fucking Marathon or climb Mount Everest or explore the Titanic or seek the goddamned Fountain of Youth or play golf on the fucking moon, I say go for it. It's your quest, not mine."

He glanced at Lou and winked. "Same with a bunch of dudes from the Middle Ages who decided to devote their lives to the search for the wine cup that Jesus used at the Last Supper. Talk about irresponsible." He shook his head, grinning. "Shit."

"Raymond," Dorothy said, smiling despite herself, "that last one is just a story."

"Hey, maybe someone will write our story some day." Ray was grinning. "Sirena may not be the Holy Grail, Dorothy, but she's the closest the four of us will ever get."

He leaned back in his chair and looked around the kitchen table, his eyes suddenly widening.

"Check out the shape of this table, Dorothy. Milady, we're your knights of the round table."

Lou was grinning. Ray had done it. He'd charmed Dorothy and, in the process, he'd charmed the rest of them, too. A few moments ago they were four guys in their early forties scrunched around a little table in a cramped room in a brick bungalow on the outskirts of Chicago. Now they were a band of brothers in a magic circle.

Ray stood, gestured toward the others around the table, and gave her a sweeping bow. "How do we look, Lady Guinevere?"

She bowed toward him. "Most noble, Sir Lancelot."

Ray turned to Billy. "Hear that, Sir Bronco? Get your skinny ass upstairs and pack an overnight bag." Ray checked his watch. "We're departing Camelot at zero one-hundred hours."

Chapter Twenty-six

At 1:40 a.m., Lou pulled the van to a stop directly beneath the El tracks at West Addison Street. The CTA station was to their right—brightly lit and empty except for the transit authority employee in the ticket booth.

Ray was riding shotgun. Gordie and Bronco Billy were in back.

Lou eased the van up to the corner of Addison and Sheffield. The four of them stared up at the curving gray façade looming in front of them. Above the dark row of ticket windows the unlit sign welcomed them to *Wrigley Field, Home of the Chicago Cubs*.

Ray rubbed his chin as he looked through the windshield. "The scoreboard is above the center field bleachers, which means—"

He turned toward the backseat.

"That way." Gordie was pointing north up Sheffield. "The bleachers' entrance is at the end of the block."

Lou turned right onto Sheffield and drove slowly along the street. To their left, running the length of the block, was the east wall of Wrigley Field. Lou slowed to a stop at the corner of Sheffield and Waveland Avenue. To their right was a bar called Murphy's Bleachers. They could hear music and laughter from inside. To their left were the entrance gates to the Wrigley Field bleachers.

Lou turned left onto Waveland and parked the van halfway down the block alongside the back wall of the ballpark. He turned off the engine, reached into the glove compartment, took out two flashlights, and handed one to Ray.

Ray looked back at Billy and Gordie. "Ready?"

They nodded.

The four of them got out. Lou had the rope, Ray had the bolt-cutters, Billy had the duct tape, and Gordie had the rolled-up tarpaulin.

Lou gazed upward. The sky was clear, the stars were bright. Towering above the ballpark was the scoreboard—three stories tall, with a T-shaped flagpole on top. From his angle on the sidewalk, Lou had a side view of the scoreboard. The front of it—the "wall" facing the playing field—was flat. The back, however, bulged in a convex curve. At its broadest point—front to back—the scoreboard was about twenty feet deep.

"Good evening, Mr. Phelps," Gordie said in his *Mission: Impossible* voice. "The man you are looking at is Lupo 'The Werewolf' Barboni, a deranged Wrigley Field security guard. For the last three hours he's been drinking black coffee and popping bennies. His orders are to shoot first and ask questions later."

"You think they have security guards?" Billy asked.

"Probably," Ray said. "But we're talking rent-a-cops, not former Navy Seals. C'mon, let's scope it out."

At the entrance to the bleachers were a pair of imposing metal gates—ten feet tall, five feet wide, and held shut by a heavy metal chain wrapped around the bars and padlocked from inside.

Gordie lifted the chain and glanced down at Ray's bolt-cutters. "You think that'll cut it?"

Ray positioned the cutters against one of the chain links. "Let's find out."

Snap.

Lou grasped the loose ends of the chain and turned to Billy. "Help me get this off."

Billy took one end and they pulled the chain loose, careful to minimize the noise.

Gordie peered through the gate into the darkness. "Don't hear a thing."

"Let's get in there," Ray said.

"Wait," Lou whispered. He gestured toward the bar across the street.

The four of them stood motionless in the shadows as two guys in jeans and leather jackets came out of the bar. They passed by on the other side of the street, arguing over whether Ron Santo or Ernie Banks was the most valuable member of the 1969 Cubs.

Lou waited, hand raised, until they turned the corner. Then he nodded.

Ray pulled the gate open. "Let's do it."

Gordie followed him in, shaking his head. "Remind me to get my head examined."

A few minutes later, the chain back in place in such a way as to make the cut undetectable unless examined up close, the four of them headed onto the broad concrete ramp that spiraled up two floors and opened onto a corridor formed by a chain-link fence on either side. Above their heads was the night sky. They moved down the corridor to where it opened onto the center field bleachers about midway up the rows of benches.

The four of them stood in silence, staring at the field spread out below. The tarpaulin that covered the infield reflected a blurry image of the myriad stars overhead. Rising behind home plate and the dugouts were tiered decks of empty seats.

Lou scanned the outfield. He could make out the numerals 368 painted on the wall in right-center field. He turned. Looming behind them was the huge scoreboard. According to the clock near the top, it was now three minutes after two in the morning.

"Down," Ray whispered.

They all kneeled.

"Where?" Gordie said.

"In the stands." Ray pointed. "There."

Down along the third-base side a beam of light swept across the empty seats.

Lou could just make out the profile of a heavy-set man walking along the aisle that separated the box seats from the reserved seats. He was moving down the third-base side toward home plate, sweeping his flashlight back and forth over the seats. He turned into an entranceway behind home plate and disappeared inside the stadium.

Ray stood up. "Okay."

They followed Ray up the concrete steps toward the top row of the bleachers. He stopped directly beneath the scoreboard and turned toward them. A metal ladder hung down from the bottom of the scoreboard. With the flashlight beam, Gordie followed the ladder up to the trapdoor.

"There's a lock," Billy said.

"Not for long." Ray turned to Gordie. "Let me have that flashlight."

Gordie handed it to him. Ray clicked it off, put it in his pocket, and clambered up the ladder one-handed, holding the bolt-cutters in the other. Lou turned on his flashlight and trained it on the lock on the trapdoor as Ray positioned the cutters against the lock.

Snap.

Ray removed the lock and pushed against the trapdoor, which opened upward into the scoreboard. He took the flashlight out of his pocket, clicked it on, and climbed through the opening and out of sight.

A moment later, he poked his head out and smiled down at them. "C'mon up, boys. Water's fine."

Billy went up the ladder first, and then Gordie, who mumbled, "We must be nuts."

Lou followed them up through the opening into the scoreboard. Once inside, he clicked on his flashlight and swung the beam around the interior. The trapdoor opened into the center of what at first resembled an empty metal shed three stories high. You could look straight up through thirty feet of open space to the ceiling.

As Lou's eyes adjusted to the darkness, he could make out the elaborate configuration of the far wall. That was the wall facing the playing field—or, more precisely, the backside of the wall facing the playing field. The upper half consisted of a dozen or so horizontal rows of rectangles, broken in the middle by the backside of the large panels that flashed the balls, strikes, and outs. Those horizontal rows of rectangles were the places for posting the inning-by-inning results of the Cubs game and games around both leagues.

A metal stairway against the far left side of the front wall led up to a catwalk flush against the front wall. The catwalk was about midway up the scoreboard and ran the full length of the wall. It had guardrails and was maybe three feet wide. Lou could see that it was designed to give a person working the scoreboard access to three or four rows of the inning-by-inning slots. From that catwalk a second metal stairway led up to a second catwalk, also flush against the front wall closer to the top of the scoreboard. It gave access to the rows of slots not reachable from the lower catwalk.

As the others started climbing up the ladders toward the catwalks, Lou surveyed the ground floor. He'd worked one summer during college for the Missouri Highway Maintenance department, and the ground floor reminded him of the work shed where the crew returned for the lunch hour. A dusty water cooler stood near a battered card table on which playing cards were scattered. On the floor near the water cooler were three empty five-gallon Culligan's water bottles. On the other side of the card table were a few Hefty bags filled with trash, a torn-open package of Jewel's charcoal briquettes, a can of lighter fluid, a rusty hibachi, a dustpan, a broken fruit crate and an old broom.

He shook his head, amused. He could hear his daughter Katie's words to him over the phone in the bar the prior night: *Go for it, Daddy.*

Smiling, he turned toward the back wall, which was the side of the scoreboard facing away from the field. Anchored to the floor along the entire length of the back wall were a row of large rectangular metal containers. Eight in all. Each stood about four feet high, six feet long, and three feet wide. The back side of each container stood a few inches higher than the front side, which meant the hinged lids slanted downward. Lou ran the flashlight beam over the container nearest him. The stenciled black letters on the lid read PROPERTY OF THE CHICAGO NATIONAL BASEBALL TEAM, INC. There was a padlock fastened to the clasp.

Overhead came a loud bang, and then a muffled, "Shit."

Lou flashed the beam in the direction of the noise. Gordie was up on the first catwalk, his back to Lou, bending down.

"What the fuck was that?" Ray said. He was on the second catwalk, leaning over the guardrail to look down at Gordie.

Gordie turned and lifted a sheet of metal about the length and width of a small window. It was painted green and with a large numeral zero stenciled in white.

"This damn thing fell off," Gordie said.

He turned back toward the wall to try to put it back in.

"Keep it quiet, for chrissakes," Ray said.

Lou climbed up the stairs to help Gordie. The metal rectangle had literally fallen out of the front wall. Lou bent to peer through the opening. He was looking down at the center field bleachers and the playing field beyond. He scanned the stands from the third-base side toward the first-base side. He spotted the security guard moving along the back row of seats on the first-base side.

Gordie said, "I think you have to turn these clasps to lock it back in."

Lou helped Gordie align the sheet of metal. He held it against the slot while Gordie turned the metal clasps and locked it in place.

As Gordie moved on, Lou looked at the array of equipment on the first-level catwalk. Along the back edge was a slanted metal countertop that ran the length of the scoreboard. There were neat stacks of green metal rectangles along the countertop. The rectangles in each stack had a different numeral stenciled in yellow or white—a stack of yellow twos, and then a stack of white twos, and then yellow threes, and then white threes, and so on. In the middle of the catwalk were two battered chairs, presumably for the men operating the scoreboard. The chairs faced the front. On the small table between the two chairs was a black rotary telephone.

"Up here," Ray called down. "Check it out."

Lou and Gordie took the stairs up to the second-level catwalk. Billy was already up there, standing at the foot of a metal ladder in the middle of the catwalk. The ladder was bolted to the front wall of the scoreboard and ran up through an opening in the ceiling, where Ray's legs had just disappeared. They followed him up the ladder.

Lou was last. He climbed through the opening and stepped onto the tar-papered roof of the scoreboard. The flagpole rose above them. A slight breeze made the slack flagpole ropes click against the metal.

Lou turned toward the field, but the view was blocked by a metal façade that rose above the roof of the scoreboard. He turned toward the east. Off in the distance, beyond the high-rise condos, was Lake Michigan. He could see the red lights of a tanker on the horizon. Down below, a southbound El train rumbled into the Addison station. Lou watched from above as the train's doors clattered open. A young man stepped off the train, and then the doors clattered shut. With a metallic grunt, the train pulled out of the station, heading south down the tracks toward Belmont. As it picked up speed in the darkness, an occasional white spark illuminated the tracks.

"Maybe it's in one of these," Billy said.

He pointed at the two metal crates anchored on the roof and partly shielded from the elements by an overhang. Both crates were padlocked.

"Let's find out," Ray said.

He positioned the bolt-cutters against the padlock on one of the crates and snapped through the steel. Lou slipped off the lock and lifted up the hinged top, which made a rusty creaking noise. Gordie pointed the flashlight beam inside as Ray and Bill rifled through the contents. There was nothing in there but team pennants and a mildewed sheet of canvas.

Ray snapped the lock off the other crate. More pennants, along with about forty feet of nylon rope and a heavy tool kit filled with rusted tools.

"Damn." Ray let the lid drop closed with a metallic bang.

"Now what?" Gordie asked.

Lou said, "There are several more of these containers down on the first floor."

Moments later they were standing in front of the container on the far right side of the back wall. Ray cut through the lock and Lou pulled up the lid. Inside was a collection of dirty raincoats, a rusty teletype machine, and the furred, matted skeleton of an enormous rat.

The second container held more discarded odds and ends, including several leather Chicago Bears helmets—relics from the early years of the NFL—and a cardboard box filled with baseball gloves circa 1930. Lou was tempted to grab one for Kenny.

They paused in front of the third container. Like the other two, this one had the PROPERTY OF THE CHICAGO NATIONAL BASEBALL TEAM, INC. legend stenciled on the lid. But unlike the other two, beneath that legend, in red letters, were the words DO NOT DISTURB. Like the others, this container was padlocked. Unlike the others, this padlock was old and encrusted with rust.

Ray got the bolt-cutters into position and snapped through the lock. Lou twisted off the old lock and pulled back the latch. He tried to lift the lid.

"Give me a hand," he said. "It's rusted shut."

Gordie and Ray joined him.

"Ready?" Ray crouched alongside them. "One, two, three."

They strained in silence for a few seconds and then, with a metallic screech, the top popped free. It groaned as they lifted it. Billy shined the flashlight inside. The four of them stared at a large object that was wrapped in gray burlap and tied with several loops of rope. It took up almost the entire container, one end wider than the other.

"Holy shit," Gordie said. "You think it's her?"

Ray leaned into the container and wrapped his arms around the narrow end. He grimaced as he tried to lift it out. It didn't budge.

"Thing is heavy," he said.

Finally, with two of them crouching on the lids of the adjacent containers and using loops of rope for added leverage as the other two worked from the front, they were able to winch the thing out of the container and set it down heavily on its side. Carefully, they tilted it up until it stood on its base. Ray used his pocketknife to slice through the two loops of rope nearest the top. He and Lou pulled the burlap wrapping away from the top portion and stepped back.

Billy clicked on the flashlight.

Gordie finally broke the silence. "Wow."

They were staring at the top half of Sirena's head. It protruded from the burlap as far down as her nose. Illuminated by the flashlight, it was as if she were emerging, cold and stiff, from a tattered chrysalis. The beam of light reflected in her blank eyes.

Lou leaned back against the empty storage bin, arms crossed over his chest and shaking his head in wonder. He looked at Ray and smiled. "Wow is right."

Ray nodded. "We need to get her the hell out of here. Fast and quiet."

◇◇◇

Almost thirty-five years ago, presumably in the wee hours of a night much like this one, Sirena made her stealthy ascent into the Wrigley Field scoreboard. And now, at 4:47 a.m. on the morning of June 11, 1994—after spending 12,771 days inside a locked metal container in that scoreboard—Sirena left through that same trapdoor, still in her burlap shroud.

Billy was the spotter at the foot of the ladder.

"Careful," he called up softly.

Sirena swayed at the end of the nylon rope as she slowly descended. Gordie straddled the trapdoor opening and guided the ropes that Ray and Lou, standing behind him, were letting out hand over hand.

Billy reached up to steady the burlap-wrapped statute.

"Five more feet," he said, his voice barely above a whisper. "Four…three…two…slow…slow."

She touched down with a gentle clunk. They tossed the rest of the ropes through the trapdoor and clambered down. Lou pulled the trapdoor shut.

"Get down," Ray whispered, pointing toward a security guard in the grandstands near the bullpen in left field.

Fifteen long minutes passed as the security guard made his rounds and finally departed up the aisle behind home plate.

Ray tilted the statue back toward him. "Move it."

No one spoke again until Lou had turned the van onto the southbound entrance to Lake Shore Drive at Irving Park. Sirena was stowed in back, still wrapped in burlap and now covered with a blanket.

"Holy shit," Gordie said. "We did it."

Lou turned to Ray. "Nice work, Captain."

Ray grinned. "It only gets better."

SCENE 47: THE HUTCHISON PRIZE - THE IDEA
{Draft 3}:

CUT TO:

INT. DORM ROOM - NIGHT

Ray and Lou are in the outer room smoking a joint and
listening to the Grateful Dead's "Uncle John's Band" on
the stereo. Bronco is at his desk, headset on, underlin-
ing passages in his textbook with a yellow highlighter.

The door BURSTS OPEN. In steps a despondent
Gordie Cohen.

> RAY
> (holding out the joint)
> Hey, Gordo. Want a hit?

Gordie trudges past them into the bedroom, slamming
the door behind him.

> LOU
> Shot down again.

> RAY
> (standing)
> Gotta take a leak.

Ray leaves.

> BILLY
> (taking off his headset)
> What's wrong with Gordie?

> LOU
> Met a girl at the bookstore today. Asked

her to meet him at the student union tonight. Looks like she didn't show.

> (holding out the joint)
> You want some?

                    BILLY
               (replacing his headset)
          No, thanks.

Ray returns.

                    RAY
          You ready for this? Reggie Pelham is
          standing in the shower stall. Guess
          what he's doing?

                    LOU
          Jacking off?

                    RAY
          Worse. Practicing his speech for that
          Hutchison competition. Something
          about the architectural works of Thomas
          Jefferson.

                    LOU
          Carrying on the grand tradition.

                    RAY
          What tradition?

                    LOU
          They've been giving out the Hutchison
          Oratory Prize since the 1920s. Jerry told
          me more than half the winners prepped
          at Choate. That's why some folks call it
          the Choate Competition.

Gordie comes out of the bedroom, head shrouded in a towel, toothbrush in his hand. He leaves for the bathroom.

> LOU

Gordie should enter that competition.

> RAY

And do what? One of his comedy
routines?

> LOU

Exactly.

> RAY

Huh?

> LOU

He can do a comedy routine that looks
like a speech. He's the funniest guy on
campus. He won't win, but people will
love it, especially chicks. Cheer him up.

> RAY

You think he'd do it?

> LOU

We'll make him do it.

Gordie returns from the bathroom, head still shrouded
in the towel.

> RAY

Gordo, we got a great idea for you.

Gordie trudges past and disappears into the bedroom,
slamming the door behind him

> LOU

I'll bring him around.

Lou goes over to the bedroom door and opens it. He
peers in.

> LOU

Gordie?

GORDIE
(off screen)
Leave me alone.

Lou looks back at Ray and winks. Then he steps inside
the bedroom and gently closes the door behind him.

Chapter Twenty-seven

The highway curved southeast out of Chicago into Indiana, the dark waters of Lake Michigan intermittently visible off to the left. Their first goal was Ohio: get across the border, find a motel, catch some Z's. Then they'd figure out their next move.

They saw the sun rise over Gary, Indiana—or rather, Lou did. The rest were asleep—Ray slumped against the passenger door, snoring; Gordie and Billy in back.

As he drove through Indiana, alone with his thoughts, Lou marveled over what they had done. The four of them, the goofy James Gang. Search parties spread literally across the globe, here they were, cruising along I-80 with the legendary Sirena in the back of his minivan.

And, incredibly enough, as Gordie announced before he fell asleep, waiting for them at Barrett College was three million dollars—$750,000 for each of them.

"A recipe for happiness!" Gordie had declared.

To which Ray responded, "Don't be a douche bag, Cohen. Anyone who thinks a lot of money will make them happy has never had a lot of money."

To which Gordie answered, "I'm happy to test that hypothesis."

Lou, however, had been thinking about another possible use for that money. But he didn't dwell on it, reminding himself not to tempt the gods.

Cruising along the interstate as the sky began to lighten, Lou drove past a high school football field on his left. It was an older field with concrete stands that reminded him of his own high school football field. His thoughts drifted back to the summer of 1969, to that afternoon in late August during the last week of two-a-day practices. He'd been waiting for the huddle to form. As his teammates trotted back, he glanced toward the sidelines, where the cheerleaders—all wearing short shorts and gold-and-black U. City T-shirts—had just arrived and were now practicing.

"Push 'em back, Push 'em back, WAY BACK! Push 'em back, Push 'em back, WAY BACK!"

She was the third from the right, a pom-pom in each hand. She had dark curly hair, a deep tan, and long athletic legs.

"Who's that?" he'd asked Steve Becker, his fullback and best friend.

"Which one?"

"Curly hair, tan."

Steve had straightened, squinted toward the sidelines, and leaned back into the huddle.

He removed his plastic mouth guard. "Andi Kaplan. A junior. Moved here from Baltimore last Spring."

Lou called a play-action pass to the right and rolled out almost to the sidelines for a better look. He trotted back to the huddle alongside Steve.

"She's pretty."

"Yeah, but I hear she's stuck-up."

She wasn't, but it took Lou more than a month to find out—two weeks to get up the nerve to ask her out, and several more weeks of asking before she finally had a free Saturday. They went to the Brentwood Theater to see *Midnight Cowboy* and then to the Steak 'n Shake on Olive Boulevard for cheeseburgers and Cokes. She was funny and smart and had lovely green eyes. She kissed him good night at her front door—a good kiss with a hint of musk. He'd wandered back to his car in love.

Gordie and Billy began stirring around eight o'clock. Lou pulled off the interstate just beyond Elkhart for breakfast at a Denny's. They made sure to get a table by the window with an unobstructed view of Lou's minivan, which he'd backed into a parking space alongside the restaurant.

Perhaps it was lack of sleep—he'd been up for more than twenty-four hours—but the whole Denny's ambiance felt surreal to Lou. There on the table before him was the bright plastic menu with its profusion of Slams—Grand Slam, Farmer's Slam, Lumberjack Slam, French Slam. And out there on that most ordinary of asphalt parking lots in the back of that most ordinary of minivans sat that most extraordinary of statues, still wrapped in the burlap that had swathed her for more than three decades. Staring through the plate-glass window at his van, his vision blurred by a wave of fatigue, he felt as if he'd been beamed into an alternative universe.

"We can reach Barrett by tomorrow night," Gordie said. "How do we protect her once we get there?"

Ray looked up from the road map spread on the table in front of him. "We can try to make an arrangement with one of the local banks. See if they'll let us put her in their vault. If not, maybe rent a storage locker. We'll figure something out."

He looked down at the map again. After a moment, he pointed at a dot along Highway 80.

"Let's shoot for Milan," he said. "We can be there by lunch."

It was a quarter to one when they pulled into a McDonald's near Milan. Ray had driven the last seventy miles with Gordie riding shotgun and Billy and Lou in back trying to sleep. They took a vote as they waited in line to place their orders, and agreed to press on after lunch. Their new goal: the Pennsylvania border.

Ray unfolded the roadmap at the table and studied it as he ate his sandwich.

Gordie held up his McRib sandwich. "You ever wonder if the people who come up with these names get their jollies from making adults sound like buffoons?"

Ray looked up from the map and frowned. "What the fuck are you talking about now?"

"What are you eating?" Gordie asked.

Ray glanced down at his sandwich and back at Gordie. "What's it look like? A Big Mac."

Gordie grinned. "See?"

"See what?"

"The name, dude. You're an adult."

"So?"

"Listen to it, Ray. Big Mac. It's ridiculous. Same with the others." He gestured toward the menu posted on the wall behind the counter. "Egg McMuffin. Chicken McNuggets. And not just McDonald's. Don't forget Burger King."

"The Whopper," Bronco Billy said. "And the Whaler."

"And America's favorite drink," Gordie said. "The Big Gulp. That's democracy in action, boys. The great equalizer. You get in that drive-thru lane at Jack in the Box, wait for a voice inside the clown head to ask what you'd like, holler out an order for a 'Jumbo Jack,' and by the time you pull up to the window you're just another grinning butthead."

"Gordie," Ray said, "how 'bout shutting your trap before I shove a Happy Meal up your McAsshole."

◇◇◇

About an hour into Pennsylvania, somewhere between Sharon and Clarion, they pulled off I-80 and got a room at the Thrifty Dutchman Motel. It was almost four in the afternoon.

They covered Sirena with the tarp, lugged her into the room, and set her on the carpet near the corner. There were two twin beds in the room. They took the mattresses off the boxsprings, set them on the carpet, and flipped for who got what. Gordie won a coin toss, flopped face down on his mattress, and uttered a lengthy groan of exhaustion.

"Wake me tomorrow," he said.

"Hold on," Lou said. "Before we crash here, let's take a look at her."

Ray heaved himself up from his boxspring. "Yeah. Why not?"

"I can't move," Gordie said, still face down.

Billy, Lou, and Ray unwrapped the burlap. It was a slow and messy process, with chunks of rotting material crumbling in their hands or tearing away. But eventually they removed it all.

Ray stepped back, crossed his arms over his chest, and gave her an appraising look. He bowed slightly. "Greetings, Your Highness."

"This is neat," Billy said.

Lou felt a mixture of elation and disappointment. The elation was obvious. To be face-to-face with Sirena—well, it was extraordinary. By the time of Lou's freshman year, she'd been gone for more than a decade, and as the years passed the world came to seem so vast a burying ground that her disappearance took on the permanence of death. But here she was. And here he was—one of the first four people to stand in her presence in thirty-five years.

But it was also disappointing, the letdown perhaps the result of seeing too many movies. When he'd tried to envision Sirena's return—when he'd finally acknowledged that Ray's crazy quest might actually succeed—his imagination choreographed a Busby Berkeley arrival with rolling tympani and blaring trumpets and swirling lights as a camera zoomed up the tiered catwalk to a gleaming white goddess.

But instead of a rousing soundtrack there were the muffled sounds of a marital spat through the thin wall separating their tacky motel room from the next one. Instead of brilliant multi-colored spotlights, there was murky light from a table lamp. And instead of a towering Art Deco icon—well, she was sure smaller than he'd imagined. The sculptor had posed her in a seated pose, but even standing Sirena would barely reach four feet. A bit on the short side for a goddess. Also a bit on the dingy side—more gray than white, with rusty streaks and stains and dents. Yes, this was their goddess—but she was in her morning-after condition, sans makeup.

He reached out to touch her bare shoulder. It was cold and hard.

"One rule," Ray said. "We got to make sure it's unforgettable."

"What's unforgettable?" Billy asked.

"Her return to the college. We've got to make her entrance an event they will always remember." Ray paused as he looked at each of them. "Agreed?"

"Agreed," Gordie said.

Ray slapped Lou on the back. "I told you this'd be awesome, didn't I?"

Lou nodded.

Ray turned to Billy. "Give me five, Bronco."

Actually, Lou thought to himself as he studied her, *the rusty streaks aren't so bad. Gives her character.* He smiled. All things considered, she didn't look so bad for a hundred-year-old gal who'd spent the last thirty-five years wrapped in burlap inside a metal box.

Chapter Twenty-eight

"Chow time!"

Lou rolled over in bed, squinting in the light. The tangy scent of hot pizza filled the motel room as Gordie entered carrying three takeout boxes of pizza. Right behind him came Ray with a case of Rolling Rock. Lou glanced over at Bronco Billy, who was on his boxspring trying to find his glasses. Lou checked his watch. 6:45 p.m. He sat up and looked around the room. Over in the corner, Sirena seemed lost in her own reverie, oblivious to them.

The pizza was delicious, the beer ice cold.

"There's a roadhouse about a hundred yards away," Ray said. "Right next to that water tower. Looks cool. They got beers on tap and an awesome jukebox. Bartender told me it gets pretty wild after dark. What say we go over there after dinner? We can do it in shifts—two at a time with the other two standing guard back here."

Lou and Billy drew short straws, which meant they had guard duty for the first two hours. It was still light out when Ray and Gordie headed off to the roadhouse. Lou had brought along a Frisbee. He and Billy sailed it back and forth on the motel parking lot until they'd worked up a sweat.

It was a pleasant night. There was a pair of folding chairs on the concrete walkway just outside their room. They each grabbed a beer and came back out to cool down and watch the sunset.

Lou opened his beer, smiled at Billy and shook his head.

"What?" Billy said.

"I still have trouble picturing you as a guerilla fighter for the Sandinistas."

"I wasn't a guerilla for that long."

Indeed, he'd lasted only three weeks in the camp before Carlos sent him back to Managua, trying to soften the blow by explaining that some men had special talents to contribute to the revolution. In Billy's case, that meant poring over newspapers and diplomatic journals from around the world to prepare reports for the Sandinista high command on the likely reactions of various world leaders to Somoza's impending overthrow.

As short as his stint had been, though, it had been long enough for one moment of sheer horror. The moment occurred one afternoon during the second week. Bored after four days of storms and depressed by the steady drum roll of rain on the green plastic covers suspended overhead, he wandered over to the mess area for company. He'd lifted the flap to the kitchen tent just as the cook was lowering what appeared to be the headless, skinned body of a child into a large cooking pot. It turned out to be a monkey that one of the patrols had shot for dinner, but the image would haunt his nightmares for years.

"Do you miss those days?" Lou asked.

Billy leaned back in his chair and studied the green bottle of Rolling Rock. It gleamed in the fading light.

He took a sip of beer. "No, but sometimes I miss the feeling."

Lou studied his friend. "How so?"

Billy gazed at the setting sun. "Do you remember that concert you and Ray took me to freshman year?"

"Which one?"

"Jethro Tull. Down in Springfield."

Lou vaguely recalled it. "Okay."

"There was a guy down front—I don't know how it started—but all of a sudden he was up in the air getting passed around. He was kind of sprawled on his back, totally relaxed, big smile on his face, eyes closed, floating along on a current of people's hands. I watched him with such envy, trying to imagine what it would feel like to be so connected to the moment, to be so in sync with others around you."

He took a sip of beer and shaded his eyes. The sun was now an orange ball hovering just above the horizon.

Billy said, "I'd never had that kind of experience, Lou. Never. Not at pep rallies in high school, not at church services, not even at camp. I was always outside the circle watching the others."

"Until Nicaragua," Lou said.

Billy nodded. "That was the first time I wasn't a spectator."

"Until last night."

Billy looked puzzled at first, but then he smiled. "Right. Until last night."

They watched the orange sun slide beneath the horizon.

"Last night was neat," Billy said.

"Tell me something," Lou said.

Billy looked over at him.

"After all you went through down in Nicaragua, how did you end up a public school teacher in Chicago?"

Billy stared for a while at the empty horizon as the sky started to darken.

"I suppose," he said, "I'd always thought about becoming a teacher, especially after the Literacy Crusade down there."

"But what made you finally do it?"

Billy looked down at his beer bottle. "Hollywood."

"Huh?"

Billy gave him a sheepish grin. "A movie. *A Man for All Seasons*."

"The one with Paul Scofield?"

Billy nodded.

Lou said, "That movie came out a long time ago." He tried to remember exactly how long. "When we were in junior high."

"I never saw it back then."

Lou leaned back in his chair and studied Billy. "Tell me what happened."

Off in the distance was the hum of the traffic on I-80. Billy frowned as he thought back to that day seven years ago.

After Somoza's downfall, he'd landed in the Sandinista equivalent of the State Department. It was thrilling at first. After all, Nicaragua was on the world stage, Ronald Reagan was rattling his saber, Castro was blowing kisses. Diplomacy was the place to be in those days—the white hot center of the revolution.

But after a few years, the bureaucracy resurfaced. He was surrounded once again by backstabbers and opportunists—a Latin American version of Foggy Bottom. And even though he kept moving up the ladder, the constant scheming and in-fighting was discouraging. He tried to keep to himself, to avoid being sucked into the intrigues, but one morning an aide-de-camp to one of the faction leaders came into Billy's office and closed the door behind him. In a low voice he explained that his boss needed Billy's assistance in toppling the head of the department. If Billy went along, they would certainly remember him after the power shift. If not, well…

Billy paused, took a sip of beer, and shook his head. "I was so…bummed."

"What did you do?" Lou asked.

"I didn't know what to do. I left the office at lunch and wandered through the streets of Managua, trying to figure out what I should do."

In his wanderings, he'd found himself in front of the Cathedral on the Playa de la Revolución. Depressed, he'd thought back to the glory days of the Revolution. At that same plaza, just a few years earlier, he'd joined the ecstatic crowd celebrating the overthrow of Somoza. The Cathedral was still in ruins from the 1972 earthquake—roof gone, walls crumbled, dusty grass growing in the empty pews and on the floor of the nave. Suspended over the outer wall was a huge portrait of Augusto César Sandino in a cowboy hat and ammunition bandoleer—the revolutionary hero from the '20s, namesake of the Sandinistas, future namesake of Billy's only child.

Billy had wandered on, eventually coming to a movie theater. It was showing *A Man for All Seasons*. He bought a ticket and went inside. It was mid-afternoon, the darkened theater was practically empty. He took a seat on the aisle, his thoughts in turmoil.

Billy paused to finish his beer. He leaned over and placed the empty bottle on the concrete next to the chair. Lou waited.

Billy looked over and shrugged. "I was a mess. They were offering me a big career advancement. I wasn't that crazy about my boss in the first place, but I couldn't stomach the thought of doing what they wanted me to do to him."

And then the movie started. Instead of the usual cheesy dubbing, it was the English language version with Spanish subtitles. Early in the film, Sir Thomas More is summoned to Cardinal Wolsey's headquarters, a day's trip down the river. Wolsey informs him that King Henry VIII wants More to publicly endorse his plan to divorce his wife. To support the King would require More to compromise his religious and moral beliefs, which he refuses to do. He travels home through the night and arrives at his dock the next morning exhausted. There he is met by Richard Rich, the young man who will eventually betray him.

Rich is an intense scholar, tormented by self-doubt and alarmed by his own ambitions and his weaknesses. Rambling, he tells More that he's decided to go into politics.

Billy had sat alone in the dark theater, spellbound, as the scene unfolded.

More tries to warn young Rich to stay away from politics. He tells him of the bribes and the other temptations that the wealthy and the powerful would use to corrupt him.

"A man should go where he won't be tempted," More tells him. "Why not be a teacher, Richard? You'd be a fine teacher. Perhaps a great one."

But if I were just a teacher, Richard replies, even a great one, who would ever know it?

"You," More says, "your pupils, your friends, God—not a bad public that." And then he gives a wistful sigh. "Oh, and a *quiet* life."

Billy paused.

Lou waited.

"Two weeks later," Bill said, "we left Nicaragua."

Lou looked toward the horizon. The colors had faded. The sky was light gray.

He said, "That's beautiful."

"More like embarrassing."

Lou turned to him. "Embarrassing?"

Billy shrugged. "To trace the turning point in your life to a scene in a movie."

Lou looked puzzled. "Why?"

Billy sighed. "Makes you realize what a basically middlebrow person you really are."

Lou laughed. "I have news for you, Billy. Middlebrow is where life is lived. Down here on ground floor—with Elvis, Evita, and E.T." Lou winked. "Not a bad public that."

Lou finished his beer and stood. "You want another one?"

Billy looked at his empty bottle and nodded. "Sure."

"I have to call home," Lou said. "It won't take but five minutes."

◇◇◇

When Lou came back out carrying two beers, the sky was dark gray.

"How's everything at home?" Billy asked.

"Good." He took his seat and handed Billy one of the bottles. "I'm bringing Katie and Kenny to the reunion. I called the travel agent this morning to make sure she dropped the plane tickets off at home. I just called the housekeeper to confirm the tickets got there. Everything is set. They arrive on June fifteenth. Two days before our big day."

They sipped their beers and watched the lightning bugs start to appear.

After several minutes of silence, Billy cleared his throat. "I don't know how to say this."

Lou looked over. "What?"

"I didn't find out about…about Andi until the day after the funeral."

Off in the distance, at the edge of the parking lot, a street lamp came on. Lou shifted in his chair.

"It was too late for the funeral," Billy said, "and then afterward I didn't know what to say, or what to do. I didn't know whether to send flowers or a contribution to a charity or what and meanwhile time kept passing and I kept thinking about what I should do but as each day went by it got harder to know what was the right thing to do and I guess I just sort of, I don't know, ended up doing nothing at all because it seemed like too much time had passed but I want you know it wasn't because I didn't care because I did. I really did, Lou. She was a special person. I felt just awful—for her and for you and for your kids and…and—"

There were tears in Billy's eyes. Lou reached over and patted him on the knee. "It's okay, man."

The moths circled the streetlight at the edge of the parking lot.

"I don't understand how they can make that kind of mistake," Billy said. "How can something like that happen?"

Lou watched the moths reel and whirl around the light as he struggled to keep his mind blank. He tilted his head back. The stars were coming out.

It was dark now.

Chapter Twenty-nine

Gordie glanced over again.

"Damn" he said. "I think she is smiling at me."

Ray turned toward the bar. The chick was definitely a looker—and one helluva lot more sophisticated than you'd expect to find in a roadhouse in rural Pennsylvania. A tall blonde in a leopard print silk blouse, a leather miniskirt, and fuck-me pumps. Face out of a *Vogue* cover, legs out of a Vegas chorus line.

He grinned at Gordie. "So go ask her to dance, stud."

Gordie glanced over at her again. "Yeah, I might just do that."

He stared at her for a moment and then turned to Ray. "You think so?"

"For fuck's sake, Gordie, you could talk anything to death."

Gordie looked back at her. After a moment, he nodded. "Maybe I will."

"Just fucking do it, you douche bag."

"Oh, damn, she's leaving.

Ray turned. "She's not leaving, bozo. She's going to play some tunes."

They watched as she leaned over the jukebox. The tight skirt showed off long, tanned legs and a firm ass. She put two quarters in the slot and made her selection. A moment later, the opening guitar riff to the Rolling Stones' "Brown Sugar" sounded over the speakers.

She turned toward them and started swinging her hips to the music.

She smiled at Gordie. "Wanna dance?"

◇◇◇

Lou and Billy were watching a Yankees-Orioles game on ESPN when there was a knock on the door. Lou checked his watch and glanced at Billy with a frown. He went over to the door.

"Who is it?" he called.

"Gordie. Open up, Lou."

Lou opened the door.

Gordie was standing there with a stunning blonde. She was almost a head taller than him.

"Lou," he said, grinning, "this is Sheila."

Lou reached out to shake hands.

"Hi, Sheila."

She shook his hand. "Hello, Lou."

She had a sexy, confident voice.

Lou glanced at Gordie, who gestured toward the door with his head, eyes wide. "Ray's waiting for you guys back at the roadhouse."

He put his arm around Sheila's waist. "Sheila and I can stand guard for a few hours."

Lou turned toward Billy, who quickly got to his feet and turned off the television.

"Sheila," Gordie said, "say hi to Bronco Billy."

Sheila laughed. "Bronco? That's cute."

Billy blushed. "Nice to meet you, ma'am."

Sheila was staring past him at Sirena. "Wow, what is that thing?"

"That?" Gordie said with a dismissive wave. "Just one of those lawn ornaments."

He turned to Lou and gestured toward the door. "Ray's waiting for you guys. He's lonely."

Billy paused at the door and turned toward Sheila. "There is some beer in the bathtub."

"Thanks, Bronco," Gordie said. He gently pushed Billy through the doorway. "We'll take care of things here."

Gordie gave them a wink and closed the door.

Lou and Billy stared at one another as they listened to the deadbolt lock snap shut on the other side.

Lou shrugged and smiled. "Let's see what's on tap."

Chapter Thirty

Sheila giggled. "You're a real stitch, Gordie."

Gordie finished his second beer and stood up. "Time for a refill."

He paused at the bathroom door and turned toward her. "Another beer?"

She shook her head, holding up her bottle. "Still have plenty."

Gordie used the toilet, brushed his teeth, did a quick sniff check on both armpits, sprayed on another layer of Right Guard, cupped his hand in front of his mouth and breathed out, rearranged his thinning hair, checked his front and side profiles in the mirror, took a deep breath, exhaled slowly, and reached for the door.

When he stepped out of the bathroom, the lights were way down in the bedroom—the only illumination coming from a lamp in the corner that had a towel draped over it. Sheila was standing by the boxspring unbuttoning her blouse. Gordie watched from the bathroom doorway as she slipped it off, revealing a frilly black push-up bra.

"Have you ever done Bungee jumping?" she asked.

"Uh, no. I'd like to but I haven't gotten around to it."

He watched as she unzipped her skirt, let it drop to the floor, and stepped out of it.

She winked at him. "It's very stimulating."

Gordie stood transfixed. It was as if a Victoria's Secret model had just walked out of the catalogue and into his motel room.

She was wearing black satin string bikinis cut high on the hips, a black push-up bra, and black spike heels.

She turned toward the dresser and reached for her purse. He stared. She was tall and slim and toned. Her panties were a snug black triangle framing a firm, round butt. She pulled something out of her purse, set it back on the dresser, and turned toward him. She gave him a mischievous smile.

Dangling from her left hand were four Bungee cords. She grasped the loose ends of the cords in her other hand and pulled them taught in front of her. It made her breasts swell against the cups of her black bra.

"Do you know what's even better than Bungee jumping?" she asked.

"No," he said, his voice hoarse.

She moved toward him, her smile shifting into a leer. "Bungee fucking."

◇◇◇

"You have to admire the purity of it," Lou said.

"Why?" Ray leaned back and gestured toward the stars. "Unless you believe there's someone up there keeping score, Lou, the guy pissed away half his life on nothing."

The topic was Ronnie, the roadhouse bartender that Ray had been talking to when Lou and Billy showed up a half-hour ago. The three of them were now upstairs on the rooftop patio, where they had a panoramic view of the highway and motel and, farther off, the cornfields and silos. They were leaning back on their chaise lounge chairs and gazing at the canopy of stars overhead.

"Still," Billy said, "I do admire his dedication. He had a dream. He devoted ten years of his life to pursuing it."

"And failed," Ray said. "Totally."

He popped the tab on a can of Iron City beer and took a sip. "Never got higher than Triple A ball. What's he got to show for it?"

"He knows he tried," Billy said. "He knows he gave it his best."

"No, Bronco," Ray said. "All he knows is he's a loser."

"That's not fair," Lou said as he followed the arc of shooting star. "He gave it his all."

"And failed."

Lou said, "Just because you fail doesn't make you a loser. Failing to try is what does."

Ray chuckled. "Since when did you start writing epigrams for Hallmark Cards?"

"I don't know why you are so cynical," Billy said.

"He's not," Lou said. "It's all a pose."

"Pose my ass. Someone's got to maintain the edge."

"Maintain what?" Billy asked.

"The edge. Look what's happening to our generation, dude. Loose-fit jeans. Low-fat ice cream. Lean fucking Cuisine, Led Zeppelin unplugged." He paused. "Led Zeppelin unplugged? I mean, what is the point? I say plug 'em back in, crank 'em back up, and kick out the jams, motherfucker. We're only here for a short time anyway, and I sure as hell don't plan to spend it cruising down the slow lane and listening to some balding rock star play 'Heartbreaker' half-speed on an acoustic guitar."

"I kind of like the slow version of 'Layla,'" Billy said.

Ray's voice filled with mock compassion. "Don't go soft on me, big guy."

"Ah," Lou said, "it's all coming clear to me now."

"What is?" Ray asked.

"You."

"What about me?"

"That you're full of shit."

"What are you talking about?"

"This cynical crap." Lou shook his head good-naturedly. "A complete masquerade. You're a bigger sentimental fool than the rest of us."

Ray snorted. "Yeah, right."

Lou was smiling at him.

"What?" Ray said.

"This." Lou made a sweeping gesture. "You, me, Bronco, Gordie, Sirena—this whole crazy quest. It sure wasn't my idea, Don Quixote."

"Call me Sancho," Billy said.

"I think we're all Sanchos on this bus," Lou said. "Except our driver."

Ray was grinning. "Only thing makes me sentimental, boys, is money, and there's going be a whole truckload waiting for us at Remington Field on June seventeenth." He turned to Lou. "Speaking of which, what are you going to do with your share?"

"I've been thinking."

"And?"

"I'm doing fine. The firm pays me well."

"Go on."

Lou paused. "I have this client—a mom—a widow actually—quadriplegic—two little kids. A terrible accident. It's a long story. I'm handling her appeal, but the odds are pretty steep."

"You're going to give her your share?"

Lou shrugged. "Maybe."

Billy suddenly sat up. He pointed toward the northern part of the sky. "Look."

Another shooting star. The watched the night sky in silence.

After the star vanished near the horizon, Billy said, "That girl Gordie met is pretty."

"Pretty?" Ray said. "She's a total babe. Probably screwing his brains out right now."

"He's due." Lou took another sip of beer. "Let's hope she makes it a memorable event."

Chapter Thirty-one

It was certainly off to a memorable start.

Gordie was naked and spread-eagled on the box springs, his wrists and ankles lashed to the bed frame by the Bungee cords. Sheila was straddling his waist, her knees on either side of his chest. Gordie gaped up at her, nearly blinded by lust, as she reached behind and unsnapped her bra. Every part of him felt aroused. He'd never been so turned on in his life.

Sheila tossed her bra onto the carpet and bent over him. Her swollen nipples brushed against his chest as she bit him gently on the neck. She raised herself until her perky breasts swayed inches above his face, her nipples like cherrystones.

She stared down at him, her eyes half closed.

"Bite me," she whispered.

Gordie lurched upward, but the Bungee cords stopped him just shy of the target.

"Come on," she teased. She raised herself a little higher. "Try harder."

He strained against the cords, his body shaking, his mouth snapping closed on nothing but air. He fell back, gasping.

"I can't reach," he said.

Her smile faded into something far more businesslike. "Good."

She got off the bed and picked her bra up from the floor. Gordie watched, anxious for whatever was coming next. He felt as if he were mainlining pure lust.

Sheila walked around him, bending to study the bungee cord connections. She slipped on her bra and snapped it in the back as she moved toward the dresser.

"Come on," Gordie said. "I'm dying."

She reached for her purse and looked inside. He watched eagerly. Maybe she was going to pull out one of those sex toys. A French tickler? A cat-o'-nine-tails? He was up for anything. *Anything.*

She snapped her purse closed and reached for her blouse. He watched as she slipped it on.

"What's going on?" he asked.

She turned to him as she buttoned the blouse. "Sorry, Gordie. I think this is kind of shitty."

A wave of dread passed over him. "What do you mean?"

She shrugged. "A girl's got to make a living."

"I don't understand."

She pulled on her leather skirt and zipped it up as she walked over to the door.

"Oh, my God," Gordie moaned. "Don't do this to me."

She paused with her hand on the doorknob, her back to him.

"Please," he begged. "At least untie me."

Her shoulders seemed to tense for a moment, but then she shook her head and opened the door. She stepped out without looking back, leaving the door wide open.

"Everything's ready," he heard her say.

"Wait in the car," a male voice answered.

Gordie felt a jolt of panic. Who was that? The voice was familiar. And then Frank Burke stepped through the door. Behind him came Reggie.

Frank was carrying a flashlight and a small canvas attaché. Reggie had a walkie-talkie. Frank flashed the light in Gordie's face and then swung it around the room until the beam fell upon Sirena.

Smiling, he turned back to Reggie. "Nice, eh?"

Reggie nodded as he rubbed his hands together. "Outstanding. Most definitely."

"You fucks!" Gordie said. "That statue is ours."

Frank came over to the bed. "Not anymore, little guy."

"Fuck you!" Gordie leaned his head back and shouted. "Ray!"

Frank reached into his attaché, pulled out a rolled-up sock, and shoved into Gordie's mouth. Holding it in place, he turned to Reggie. "Get me some tape."

Frank looked down at Gordie. "This isn't horseshoes, Shylock. Close doesn't count."

As Gordie squirmed and tried to move his head from under Frank's hold, Reggie pulled a roll of duct tape out of Frank's bag. He tore off a long strip and handed it to Frank, who taped it over the sock in Gordie's mouth and wrapped it around his head.

Frank nodded. "That's better."

He straightened and looked over at Reggie, who was closely inspecting Sirena. "Let's get this show rolling."

Reggie turned, shaking his head in admiration. "Great stuff, Frank. Great stuff." He held the walkie-talkie to his mouth. "Okay, gentlemen. I believe we are ready for liftoff."

There was a crackling noise and then a voice: "Roger. We're heading in."

Frank walked to the door and poked his head outside. "Everything's set," he called into the darkness.

He turned back to Reggie and nodded. "Showtime."

And then he stepped out.

A moment later two workmen came into the room. One was rolling a two-wheeled dolly, and the other was carrying several coils of heavy-duty rope. They glanced at Gordie as the moved past the bed toward Sirena.

Reggie paused at the door and turned toward Gordie. "I guess I win the prize this time, eh? Nevertheless, awfully sorry about this part, chum."

Chapter Thirty-two

Ray leaned forward. "What the hell is that?"

"Sounds like a helicopter," Billy said.

Lou pointed. "Over there."

A helicopter passed over the highway heading toward the motel.

"What's going on?" Lou asked.

Now the copter was hovering above the motel parking lot.

Ray scrambled to his feet. "I don't like this."

A powerful spotlight beneath the helicopter flashed on. The shaft of light illuminated a figure in the parking lot motioning up at the helicopter.

"Shit!" Ray turned toward the stairs. "Shit!"

◇◇◇

Reggie was in the driver's seat, hands on the steering wheel, engine idling. Sheila was in the backseat, twenty crisp one-hundred-dollar bills folded in the wallet in her purse. A good night's pay.

Both were watching Frank, who stood on the motel parking lot supervising final preparations. The helicopter hovered thirty feet above Frank, creating a gale-force downdraft that scattered gravel and litter across the parking lot like tumbleweed in an old Western.

WUPA-WUPA-WUPA-WUPA-WUPA-WUPA-WUPA.

The noise was deafening.

The two workers had rolled Sirena out to the middle of the parking lot. They were finishing the job of trussing her with the ropes. She looked every bit the kidnap victim—bound by ropes, illuminated by the bright shaft of light.

Above her, a large metal hook slowly descended, unreeling from a spool of steel cable attached to the bottom of the helicopter. The hook wobbled and swung back and forth as it lowered. *WUPA-WUPA-WUPA-WUPA-WUPA-WUPA-WUPA.*

One of the workers reached up and grabbed the hook. He guided it down and slipped it through a loop in the ropes around the statue. He checked the grip, turned toward Frank, and gave him the okay sign.

Frank stepped back until the pilot above could see him. He gave him a thumbs-up. The workers steadied the statue as the cable tightened.

There was a creaking noise above the pounding throbs of the blades. The helicopter engine revved higher, and Sirena rose off the ground, rocking in the air a few inches above the asphalt.

Frank jogged toward the car, opened the passenger door, and hopped in.

"Hit it," he said as he slammed the door closed.

◇◇◇

They were sprinting toward the parking lot, Lou in the lead. He could tell they weren't going to make it. They'd been at least a football field's length away when Frank gave the pilot the thumbs-up sign. They were maybe twenty yards back when the statue lifted from the ground and the car pulled out of the parking lot with a squeal of the tires.

Lou slowed to a jog as he watched Sirena glide across the asphalt parking lot at a diagonal away from them, gliding along a few feet off the ground, a fleeing ghost, shimmering in the shaft of light from above.

"Damn," he said, slowing to a walk. Hands on his hips, gasping for breath.

Ray charged past him.

"No!" Ray shouted, running after Sirena. "No!"

It took Lou a moment to grasp Ray's intent.

"Ray!" He started after him. "Don't!"

"You fucks!" Ray screamed toward the helicopter, his arms and legs pumping furiously.

As he closed in on the statue, the spotlight clicked off and the helicopter seemed to shift into a higher gear. Lou was ten yards behind him and gaining when Ray dove for Sirena.

As Lou watched in disbelief, Ray got his arms around the base of the statue as it started to rise. He was grasping at the ropes, trying to pull the statue down, his legs churning crazily, as if someone had hit the fast-forward button. And then he was off the ground, his legs bicycling in the air.

"Let go, Ray!" Lou shouted. "Let go!"

The helicopter climbed higher, Sirena and Ray dangling from the end of the cable. The added weight had momentarily slowed the statue's forward momentum. But now the two of them were swinging forward in an arc at the end of the long cable as they headed toward a grove of trees.

Ray was ten feet off the ground.

Now fifteen.

Now twenty.

He was kicking his legs, struggling for a firmer grip on the ropes, trying to hook his right leg up on the base of the statue. The two of them now swaying side to side at the end of the cable.

Billy came trotting up from behind, out of breath. "Where is he?"

Lou pointed.

"Oh, my God."

They stood at the edge of the parking lot, watching, helpless.

The trees were coming on fast.

Too fast.

Ray was thirty feet off the ground, now forty. He was clinging to the base of the statute, his feet thrashing in the air, when they smashed into the treetops.

The cable snagged for a moment, as if the trees were trying to hold on to their prize, which had disappeared into the leaves. The helicopter engines whined louder, and then Sirena leapt clear of the trees, swinging forward in a wide arc on the end of the cable, soaring upward into the night sky.

Alone.

Lou was running toward the trees.

"Ray!" he shouted. "Ray!"

Chapter Thirty-three

At 11:14 a.m. the next day, Ray opened his eyes.

"Morning, Spiderman," Lou said.

Ray tried to speak but all that came out was a raspy sound.

"Don't talk." Lou touched his own throat. "Doctor's orders. You're pretty banged up."

Ray winced as he tried to turn his head. He gave Lou a questioning look.

"You had *two* chopper rides last night." Lou gave him a sympathetic smile. "We're in a hospital about sixty miles outside of Pittsburgh. The paramedics flew you down here after they carried you out of the woods." He lifted the large cup of water off the tray and bent the straw toward Ray. "Want some?"

Ray nodded slightly, careful not to move his head much. Lou positioned the straw and watched as Ray took three sips. Then he put the cup back on the tray.

He said, "You reminded me a little of Major King Kong last night."

Ray frowned and mouthed the word *Who?*

Lou said, "Gordie's favorite character from his favorite movie of all-time, *Dr. Strangelove*. Kong is the commander of the lead bomber heading into Russia. Played by Slim Pickens."

Ray tried to nod, though the motion made him wince.

"Remember at the end? He grabs his ten-gallon hat, straddles the bomb and rides it down to Earth hollering like a cowboy and waving his hat."

Ray smiled.

"Unfortunately, your ride got away. You fell almost fifty feet. The paramedics said the only thing that saved you were the tree branches. They gave you a pounding on the way down, but they slowed your descent." Lou shook his head. "You scared the hell out of me, Ray."

Ray glanced down. His right leg was in a cast up to his knee and suspended off the bed by a cable. Lou followed his gaze and nodded.

"Compound fractures," he said. "Tibia and fibula. They put pins in there when they set it. You have a broken left wrist. Just a hairline fracture, but serious enough for a cast. Forty-seven stitches on your right arm. Fifteen in the back of your head. Cuts and bruises all over your body. And two black eyes."

Ray looked down at the cast on his left arm.

"I called Brandi," Lou said. "She'll be here late afternoon. Billy's driving the van down to Pittsburgh to pick her up at the airport."

Ray scowled.

"She loves you, Ray. And believe me, buddy—" Lou winked "—I'm not changing your bedpan when you get out of here."

Ray seemed to ponder the information as his gaze wandered around the room. Then his eyes snapped back to Lou.

Lou shook his head. "She's gone. Reggie and Frank had the whole thing planned out. Gordie's hot date was a setup. Probably a hooker. They must have been following us the whole time." Lou sighed. "Poor Gordie."

Ray looked puzzled.

"I found him in our motel room afterward. Bound and gagged on the bed. Totally naked. Totally humiliated. He's sitting out there now. In the waiting room. Refuses to talk to anyone."

A nurse came bustling into the room. "And how's our patient doing?"

Lou stood up. "He's awake."

She came over to the bed and flashed Ray a matronly smile.

"Good morning, Mr. Gorman. Let's check our temperature and blood pressure. The doctor should be here in a few minutes."

Ray's eyes moved toward Lou, who smiled and gave him a wink.

Chapter Thirty-four

Brandi lowered her voice. "The doctor thinks he'll be able to leave in three days."

It was close to six p.m. Lou and Brandi stood in the hall outside Ray's hospital room. Billy was at the pay phone down the hall talking to his wife. Gordie was alone in the lounge, staring at the television, which was tuned to a Pirates-Mets baseball game. The color was out of whack, the outfield grass orange.

"Three days," Lou repeated, doing the mental addition. "June fifteenth."

Brandi pulled a small calendar out of her purse and paged through it. "The reunion starts the sixteenth. You know he's gonna want to be there. The Sirena part is going to drive him crazy, but that's okay. He needs to be there." She smiled. "I'll get him good and drunk that morning and strap him into a wheelchair."

Lou nodded. "Good idea."

"I'll book us flights out of Pittsburgh." She jotted a note in the calendar and looked up at Lou. "You're still going, right?"

"Definitely. My kids are flying in on the fifteenth. Late afternoon. I've got the exact time in the van. If you can book a flight that arrives around then, I can pick you up when I get my kids."

"That'd be great." She glanced beyond him down the hall toward the pay phones and the lounge. "What are you guys going to do for the next three days?"

Lou turned. Billy was off the phone and walking back to the lounge.

Lou turned back to Brandi and shrugged. "Guess I'm about to find out."

◇◇◇

Billy shook his head. "I don't know, Lou. It seems impossible."

"It seemed impossible the first time, too. But we found her, right?"

"Yeah, but now they know who we are."

"And we know who they are, Billy. This time we know exactly who took her. Even better, we know exactly where they're headed, and exactly where they'll be on June seventeenth. If we did it once, we can do it again."

"Twice?" Billy said. "In less than a week?" He glanced over at Gordie, who was staring at the television and pretending to be oblivious to the conversation.

Billy looked back at Lou. "That's a lot to ask."

I know it's a lot to ask, Lou thought, frustrated. *Probably too much to ask—especially in our current situation: dazed and confused marooned somewhere on the edge of western Pennsylvania.*

Lou sighed. "We found her, Billy. We were the ones."

"Once. But not anymore."

"And what? Just walk away. Just slink off to the reunion."

"I know it's a lousy option, Lou, but it's the only realistic one."

Lou turned toward the window overlooking the parking lot, trying to organize his thoughts.

It wasn't just the unfairness of what Reggie and Frank had done to them, although he certainly wanted his vengeance there—total vengeance, which included embarrassing them in the process.

And it was more than just a desire to reclaim Sirena and whatever glory and money were associated with that. Those were reasons, sure, but he knew they weren't the real reason. At least for him. At the core of this crazy quest was Ray. This was about Ray. Especially now. Especially with that final image of him in Lou's mind—clinging to Sirena, legs thrashing in the air as the helicopter lifted them ever higher into the night sky, framing him for one moment against the stars, Ray's predicament was at once hopeless and insane.

And marvelous.

Ray's actions had been crazy, but gloriously crazy. A moment of mad inspiration so amazing that you just couldn't let it fade away in rural Pennsylvania. Ray's madness deserved something more—even if that something more ended in more failure.

Lou stared out the window, searching for the right words. He turned to face Billy.

"Remember last night on the rooftop patio?"

Billy nodded.

"Remember what you said?"

Billy frowned. "I'm not sure."

"You were the one, Billy. You were the one who was so impressed by that bartender. You were the one who said you admired a person who would spend ten years trying to reach his goal even if he never reached it. Ten years, Billy. Think about that. All we have to do here is spend four more days. She's ours, Billy. We found her. We can't just walk away."

"But where would we even start?"

"I have no idea." Lou came over and sat down across from him. "We'll think of something. Even if we go down in smoke, Billy, let's do it trying to get her back. We owe Ray at least that much."

Billy frowned. "Boy, I don't know, Lou."

Lou took a deep breath and exhaled slowly, feeling the burden of Ray's absence—and the frustration.

He stood up. "What do you want from me, Billy? A win-one-for-the-Gipper speech?"

Billy shrugged. "Jeez, Lou, it's just…"

Billy's voice faded and he turned to Gordie, who was glowering at the television, his arms crossed over his chest. "What do you think, Gordie?"

Gordie turned toward them, his eyes fierce. "I want to totally crush those preppie motherfuckers. Nuclear humiliation. Period. I don't care about anything else."

He turned back to the television.

"The best way to crush them," Lou said, "is to take back the statue."

Gordie scowled at the screen.

"This whole thing was Ray's idea." Billy shook his head. "But now Ray's out."

"Exactly." Lou stood. "That's the point, Billy. Ray's out. We're not."

Lou stared down at them. Neither said a thing. He checked his watch.

"Here's the deal, guys. It's quarter to seven, and I'm bushed. I'm going to bed. I'm getting up tomorrow early and driving to Massachusetts. And when I get there, I'm going to try to find her. You want to come along, be in the motel lobby tomorrow morning at six. If not—" he paused, looking first at Billy, who was studying the carpet, and then at Gordie, who was frowning at the television "—if not, well, I'll look for you guys at the reunion."

And then he left.

Chapter Thirty-five

Ray opened his eyes at six twenty the next morning.

Lou leaned in close and put his finger to his lips. He gestured toward the other hospital bed, where Brandi was asleep on her side facing them, her hands tucked under the pillow.

"I came to say good-bye," Lou whispered.

Ray nodded, expressionless.

"It's not over—yet. You'll be out of here in two days. Brandi gave me the flight info. I'll meet you two at the airport."

"Good morning, Louis."

Lou looked up. Brandi was smiling at him.

Lou winked at her. "Just checking in with Major Kong." He looked down at Ray. "Barrett's an eleven-hour drive from here. That'll leave us plenty of time. Frank and Reggie are going to have to stash her somewhere near the college. I'll find her."

Ray grimaced and shook his head.

"I know, I know." Lou smiled. "They have helicopters and they have armed guards and they have lots of money. But guess what I have?"

He gestured behind him with his thumb. In the doorway stood Gordie and Billy.

Gordie stepped into the room. "Did you just call him Major Kong?"

Lou nodded. "I told him the sight of him riding Sirena into those trees reminded me of Slim Pickens on the bomb."

"Major T.J. 'King' Kong." Gordie was grinning as he stepped into the room. "A great American. Remember the pep talk he gave his bomber crew?"

"No," Lou said, "but I bet someone here does."

"Well, boys," Gordie said, slipping into a Texas drawl— *"Way-ell, boys*, I jes' may. Yes, sir."

"Let's hear it, Major," Lou said. "We could use a little inspiration this morning."

"Now looky here, boys," Gordie said in his best Slim Pickens voice, "I ain't much of a hand at makin' speeches, but I got a purty fair idea that somethin' doggone important is goin' on back there. And I got a fair idea of the kinda personal emotions that some of you fellas may be thinkin'. Heck, I reckon you wouldn't even be human beans if you didn't have some purty strong personal feelin's about combat. I want you all to remember one thing, them folks back home is a-countin' on you and, by golly, we ain't about to let 'em down."

Gordie paused and hooked his thumbs under his belt.

"I tell you somethin' else, boys. If this thing turns out to be half as important as I figure it just might be, I'd say that you're all in line for some important promotions and personal citations when this thing's over with. That goes for ever' last one of you regardless of your race, color or your creed. Now let's get this thing on the hump, boys—'cause we got some flyin' to do."

Brandi applauded. Gordie bowed, and then he gave Ray the thumbs-up as he backed out of the room.

Lou turned to Ray and leaned over. "Heal fast, buddy. I expect you out there on Remington Field with us."

As he turned to go, Ray grabbed him by the wrist. Lou looked down. Ray held out his hand. Lou clasped it.

Ray stared up at him. Lou could feel the passion in those eyes. In a raspy voice, Ray whispered, "Good luck."

Part 4:
The Chase

We are stardust,
We are golden,
And we've got to get ourselves back to the garden.
                    —Joni Mitchell

Chapter Thirty-six

Billy hung up and turned to Gordie, who was on the bed, head propped against two pillows, watching MTV.

Gordie looked over at him. "Well?"

Billy shook his head.

Gordie groaned. "Terrific. That's fucking terrific." He turned to Lou. "Well?"

Lou was seated on the floor with his back against the wall, telephone directory open on his lap. He looked up and shook his head. "That was the last one."

"How many have we called?" Gordie asked.

Billy counted the phone numbers he'd jotted down on the notepad. "Nineteen."

They were in the Barrett Best Western Inn just off Route 39 on the outskirts of Barrett, Massachusetts. For the past two hours they'd been calling area motels and hotels, trying to find where Frank and Reggie—and possibly Sirena—were staying.

Lou checked his watch. Almost noon. Today was June fourteenth. The kids arrived tomorrow. The reunion officially started the morning after that.

He flipped back to the beginning of the phone book and skimmed the first few pages. He looked up and shook his head. "This one only covers towns within about a twenty-mile radius of Barrett. There must be another directory for all of western Massachusetts."

He stood and moved toward the door. "I'll see if they have one at the front desk."

"Assuming they registered under their real names," Gordie said, "which is doubtful." He leaned back on the pillows and shook his head. "There's got to be a better way to do this."

"Actually," Billy said, "there just might be."

Lou stopped at the door and looked back. "Oh?"

"Last summer someone stole my wallet at the public beach in Evanston," Billy said. "I had my MasterCard in there. The police never caught the thief but they were able to trace him to Hammond, Indiana."

"How?" Gordie asked.

"He bought some gas in Hammond. He charged it on my card. Apparently, there's this national credit data system. Every time a clerk runs your card through one of those readers it registers in the data bank."

"That's great if you're a cop looking for a criminal," Gordie said. "No credit card company is going to tell one of us what Frank and Reggie are charging."

"But they might tell Ray," Lou said.

Gordie frowned. "Why Ray?"

"He owns shopping centers. His organization must have contacts with every credit outfit in America. I bet they run credit checks on people all the time."

Lou reached for the phone. "All I need is a name and an address. I bet we can get their home addresses out of our class reunion directory."

He punched in the number for Ray's hospital room. Brandi answered. Lou explained the idea to her.

As Lou listened to Brandi describe it to Ray, Billy handed Lou the class reunion directory.

Brandi came back on the phone. "Ray can do it, Louis." She sounded excited. "He says it may take a few hours to get what you need, but he'll put his people right on it."

Chapter Thirty-seven

"One more question," Billy said.

Gordie rolled his eyes. "Jesus, Bronco."

"Just one."

"One. And that's it."

"Do I get to make more than the Major League minimum?"

Gordie turned to Lou. "Can you believe this yutz?"

Gordie turned back to Billy. "No, Bronco. The money part has to be irrelevant. That's the whole point."

"Okay," Billy said, "let me make sure I understand. The Devil says I can keep my wife and my son, but I have to give up everything else, including my college education *and* my savings, right?"

"Right," Gordie said. "And in exchange, the Devil will put you on the Major League Baseball team of your choice and give you the necessary skills to start at the position of your choice for five years."

"And when the five years are up?"

Gordie snapped his fingers. "So's your baseball career. Poof. You have to start all over—school, job, the works."

Billy frowned and rubbed his chin.

"So?" Gordie asked. "Would you do it?"

Billy twirled a strand of hair around his finger as he pondered the question. Finally, he shook his head. "I guess not."

Gordie turned to Lou. "What about you?"

"In a heartbeat."

Billy looked at Lou with surprise. "Really?"

Lou nodded.

"Who and where?" Gordie asked.

"Cardinals. Third base."

Billy said, "But you'd have to give up your legal career."

Lou shrugged. "So?" He glanced over at Gordie. "You?"

"Come on, man. Of course."

"Cubs?" Lou asked.

"Absolutely. Left field."

Gordie turned to Billy. "Bronco, you're in a very select group."

"How so?"

"I've been posing that Deal With The Devil for years. Most guys say yes. Doctors, lawyers, writers, whatever—almost all of them say yes. And you know what? The women *never* understand. Never. Doesn't matter who they are or where they live, they can't fucking believe a guy would say yes to that deal." Gordie leaned back and shrugged. "How do you explain that?"

Lou smiled. "If I were the Devil, I wouldn't be talking baseball with Billy."

"Oh?" Gordie said.

Lou looked at Billy and raised his eyebrows. "I'd be talking rodeo."

Billy blushed.

Gordie laughed. "Oh, yeah."

Lou said, "I'd offer the same five-year deal, but instead of center field, Billy would get a chance to be a barrel racer or maybe a bull rider."

"There you go," Gordie said. "You on board, Bronco?"

Billy smiled. "That would be tough to turn down."

"I can see it now," Gordie said, leaning back and sweeping his arm in the air as if reading the words on a billboard. "The Sandinista Steer Wrestler. Bronco the Bareback Bronc Rider. Oh, yeah. And guess what else, Billy? You'd have so much cowgirl pussy you'd need to mainline Viagra."

They laughed.

They were having a late dinner at Pete's Leaning Tower of Pizza and Grinder, a Greek-style pizzeria two blocks from the Barrett College campus. The James Gang had consumed mass quantities of Pete's pepperoni pizzas and meatball grinders during their freshman year. Two to three times a week, usually after the library closed, and at least once each weekend—and almost always at the table by the far window, which is where they were seated tonight. Although prices had tripled since their college days, their favorites were still on the menu, and the Greek-style pizzas still arrived with a light coating of grease that Billy still tried to blot up with a napkin.

"Hey," Lou said, "isn't that Pete?"

Gordie and Billy turned toward the front door, where a short stocky man in his sixties with a pencil-thin mustache had just entered. He had his hands in the front pockets of his baggy black slacks and was jangling his change, just like the old days.

Gordie stood and waved. "Yo, Pete!"

Pete turned toward them, squinting, jangling his change. His face broke into a broad smile.

"Heya 'dere, boys."

As Pete approached their table, Lou realized how many years had passed. Pete's hair, once thick and coal black, was gray and thin. His face was creased, his skin splotched with age spots.

They shook hands all around.

"So how youse boys doin', eh?"

"We're back for our reunion," Gordie said. "Your pizza still tastes great, Pete."

Pete grinned and nodded, jangling his change. "Da bes', eh? Dat's what I'm talkin' 'bout."

They started asking him questions about the restaurant, but Pete cut it short. "Gotta see my night manager, boys. Got two other restaurants now—Pete's Greek Islands over in Hadley and Pete's Gyros and Heroes down in Belchertown. Busy, busy, eh? All da time. Dat's what I'm talkin' 'bout. Enjoy my pizza, eh? Good to see youse boys."

They watched as he huddled with the manager for a few minutes, nodding as he listened to the younger man explain something, hands still in his front pockets. Then he turned and moved quickly through the restaurant toward the front door, nodding and smiling at a few of the tables of patrons.

"Guess what?" Gordie said to Lou. "We spent four years eating pizzas and grinders in this joint. We talked to Pete every time we were in here. Every time, right?"

"Just about," Lou said.

Gordie shook his head. "Guy has no fucking idea who we are."

"I think he sort of recognized us," Billy said.

"No way." Gordie took a huge bite out of his pizza slice, chewed, and washed it down with a gulp of beer. "Not a fucking clue, Billy. Dat's what I'm talkin' 'bout, eh?"

Lou patted Gordie on the back. "If it makes you feel any better, I think his pizza sucks. It sucked then, and it sucks now."

"Pardon me."

They turned. Seated alone at the next table was a woman about their age. She wore granny glasses and had curly brown hair flecked with gray. A copy of James Joyce's *Dubliners* was on the table next to her meal, which appeared to be an eggplant grinder.

She was staring at Gordie, an impish smile on her face. "Aren't you the Galapagos turtle?"

Gordie looked surprised. After a moment, he nodded. "You could say that. Yeah, that's me. Or was me. Once upon a time."

"I was in the audience that night."

Gordie raised his eyebrows. "No kidding?"

"I've never so laughed as hard in my life."

Gordie was grinning. "Yeah?"

She nodded. "It was one of the most—" she paused, searching for the right word "—luminous performances I've ever seen."

"Luminous?" Gordie blushed. "Thanks. Luminous, eh? No one's ever called me that. Lummox, maybe. Lunatic, sometimes. But never luminous." He wiped his hands on his napkin and reach over to shake her hand. "I'm Gordie. Gordie Cohen."

She shook his hand. "Sally Jacobs."

She wore a navy turtleneck and black jeans. She had a friendly, intelligent face, high cheekbones, bright hazel eyes.

"I was a freshman at Hampton," she said. "Our dorm mother drove several of us over to hear the speeches. She told us that the Hutchison competition would be an 'intellectually elevating experience.'" Sally enunciated the phrase with a snooty accent.

She leaned back and shook her head. "I was prepared for a totally dull evening. And most of the speeches were just that. Do you remember that pompous little preppie with his sermon on Thomas Jefferson?"

Gordie nodded. "Ah, yes. That was the great Reggie Pelham."

"So pretentious. The others weren't much better. I thought it would never end. But then you came on." She paused to study Lou. "You were the other one, right? The scientist?"

Lou nodded. "The straight man. Gordie wrote the script." He reached across the table to shake her hand. "Lou Solomon. This is Bill McCormick. We were roommates freshman year."

"You guys were wonderful." She turned to Gordie. "When you came up on stage in that green hospital gown with your head wrapped up in that crazy flashing thing—well, I was laughing so hard I almost peed in my pants. What *was* that thing?"

"An ACE bandage," Gordie said. "With about two dozen nails sticking out." He gestured toward Billy. "This man gets credit for the props. He put that contraption together."

Sally smiled. "Your Galapagos turtle was my favorite, but I loved that dog in heat routine, too. What were those dogs again?"

"An elderly male toy poodle putting the moves on a Doberman in heat," Gordie said.

"Oh, my God. I can still see it."

Lou said, "My favorite was Abraham Lincoln choking on a piece of steak fat."

Billy said, "Mine was the Volkswagen bug going up the mountain road."

"You definitely deserved to win," she said. "I think there would have been a riot if the judges had given first prize to anyone else."

"I don't think Reggie ever got over that loss," Lou said.

Gordie snorted. "I think he's feeling better now."

"So you guys are back for your reunion?" Sally asked.

"Yep," Lou said. "You, too?"

"Not exactly. I plan to go, but I actually live here now. I'm in the English Department at Barrett."

"No kidding." Gordie glanced at her ring finger.

Lou caught the glance. He looked, too.

"This is my fifth year," she said. "I love it."

"Where were you before?" Lou asked.

"I started off at the University of Oklahoma. That's where I met my husband. Ex-husband. He's in American history. We both accepted positions at Wisconsin. He's still in Madison." She paused. "I like it better here. I love the surroundings, too. I've become an outdoor sports nut. I hike and backpack in the warm months, and cross-country ski and snowshoe in the winter."

Lou gave her an appraising glance. Sally Jacobs was a far cry from the thong-bikini babes and anorexic models that fueled Gordie's lust during his Hollywood years. Sally could have stepped out of an Eddie Bauer catalog, a canoe paddle over her shoulder. There was a hearty sturdiness about her, amplified by the splash of freckles on her face. She had the look of a woman who could steer a kayak through the rapids, build a fire in the rain, and pitch a tent in the dark. And then, Lou thought, join you in that tent for some enthusiastic sex.

He felt a pang as he thought of Andi.

"New England is the perfect place for me," she was saying.

"That's really great," Gordie said.

Lou caught the effusive tone in Gordie's voice. He made a conspicuous show of checking his watch and turned to Gordie. "Billy and I better get back to the room." He stood. "We'll see whether Ray called."

Billy got to his feet.

Lou looked down at Gordie. "You still have some pizza left. Why not stay here and keep Sally company? I can come back and pick you up in a half-hour."

"Oh, don't bother," Sally said. "I can drop him off."

"You sure?" Lou asked.

Sally nodded, her eyes shining. "I'm positive."

"Thanks." Lou turned to go but paused to look back at Gordie. He couldn't resist. "Give me a call if you get tied up."

Chapter Thirty-eight

Gordie sat up in bed and announced, "I'm in love."

Lou came out of the bathroom drying his hair with a towel. "When did you get back?"

"Three."

Billy looked up from the *New York Times*, which he was reading in the easy chair in the corner of their motel room.

"In the morning?" Billy asked. "Where did you go?"

"We walked all around the campus. Just walked and talked and walked and talked. She's awesome. A real intellectual, but down-to-Earth, too. She's totally great. I'm in love."

Billy smiled and returned to his paper. "That's nice."

"I told you something good would come out of that competition," Lou said.

"True," Gordie said. "But you didn't tell me I'd have to wait twenty years for it."

Lou nodded, thinking back to Gordie's night of glory at the Hutchison competition. Sally Jacobs was right. He had been luminous. They'd kept the performance a total secret until the night of the event. Only Lou had been listed on the event's program—about two-thirds of the way down the column of competitors, right after Reggie and an earnest, lantern-jawed senior from Shaker Heights named John Calvert:

- Reginald Harris Pelham (Class of '74): "Thomas Jefferson: America's Renaissance Man."

- John B. Calvert, Jr. (Class of '71): "The Assassination of John F. Kennedy: Time to Reopen the Investigation?"

- Louis A. Solomon (Class of '74): "Electronic Stimulation of the Brain: A Preview of Things to Come."

There'd been a curious buzz when Lou stepped to the podium wearing not the standard suit and tie but a scientist's white smock. The buzz turned to puzzled laughter when, after some brief introductory remarks, he explained to the audience that to better illustrate the possibilities of this exciting new frontier of science, he'd commissioned a team of neurosurgeons to implant electrodes into the various regions of the brain of a volunteer, who would now join him on the stage for a live demonstration.

He'd signaled toward the back of the room, where a solemn Bronco Billy, also in a white smock, stood next to Gordie. They started down the aisle toward the front amidst puzzled whispers from the audience.

Billy held in his left hand his portable tape deck, which he'd disguised to resemble a control panel. His right hand grasped the upper arm of Gordie, who was dressed in blue hospital scrubs. Gordie's face was blank, his eyes dull. A cable ran from the top of the tape deck to the back of Gordie's neck, where it disappeared under the ACE bandages wrapped around his head. A dozen or so nails poked out from the bandages, and each one had a tiny blinking light attached to it.

Billy escorted Gordie to the front and helped him onto the stage. Then he handed Lou the tape deck, helped Gordie take a seat next to the podium facing the audience, and backed offstage as Gordie gazed vacantly at the audience.

They began the demonstration with stimulation of a part of the medulla oblongata, dating back, Lou explained, to our reptilian ancestors. He tossed a leaf of lettuce on the floor in front of Gordie, turned a knob on the control panel, and then dramatically pressed a button. Gordie flinched and then dropped forward onto his hands and knees, instantly transforming himself into a Galapagos turtle. He slowly munched on the lettuce as the audience erupted into laughter.

Gordie kept them howling and applauding throughout a fifteen-minute tour de force of bizarre and dazzling impersonations. At the end of the performance, the audience gave them a ten-minute standing ovation. At the end of the competition, the judges gave them first prize.

"Turns out you were wrong, too," Lou said to Gordie.

Gordie frowned at him from the bed. "About what?"

"Don't you remember what you said at the end of that night?"

"No."

"You disappeared from the victory party. I found you sitting on the steps of Thompson Chapel. Sitting alone in the dark and all depressed."

Gordie smiled sheepishly. "Oh, yeah."

"Remember what you said?"

"No."

"I told you that you were a celebrity and that everyone at the college was talking about you. I asked why you were sitting alone and moping. You said that you'd realized that being famous for one night at a little college in New England meant absolutely nothing in the grand scheme of things. 'How can you say that?' I asked you. Your answer was, and I quote, 'Twenty years from now, no one on this goddamned planet is going to remember who won the goddamned Hutchison Prize our year or what they did to win it.'"

Lou paused and smiled. "Looks like you were wrong, pal. At least one special woman on this goddamned planet remembered."

Gordie grinned. "Glad I was wrong." Then his expression grew serious. "Sally thinks I should go back to writing screenplays."

Lou looked up from buttoning his shirt. "Maybe you should."

"And leave advertising? I don't know. The bread's good."

"Not if you're not happy."

Gordie leaned back in bed, his fingers laced behind his head. "I'm definitely in love."

The phone rang.

Billy answered it. "Oh, hi. Sure. Nothing much. Yeah, he's right here." He held the phone toward Lou. "It's Ray."

Lou took the phone. "Well?" he asked.

◇◇◇

"Hawthorn, Hawthorn, Hawthorn," Gordie mumbled.

The three of them were huddled above the map of Massachusetts opened on the motel room dresser.

"Here it is." Billy pointed to a spot about thirty miles northwest of Barrett.

"*That's* where they're staying?" Gordie asked.

"According to Ray," Lou said, "Reggie's American Express had a charge there two days ago."

"Are they still there?" Billy asked.

Gordie reached for the phone. "Only one way to find out."

He dialed directory assistance and got the number for the Hawthorn Inn in Hawthorn, Massachusetts. He frowned as he waited for the connection to go through.

"Reggie Pelham, please," he said into the phone.

He looked up with a grin and covered the mouthpiece with his hand.

"She's ringing his room," he whispered.

The hotel operator came back on the line and said something to him.

"Uh, no thanks," he said into the phone. "I'll just try back later."

Gordie hung up the phone and pumped his fist. "We got those miserable pricks! Got 'em right in the old crosshairs!" He was beaming. "Let's go nail them."

"Not yet," Lou said.

"Why not?"

"We need some more information."

"Like what?"

"For starters, their room number—or numbers."

"Good point," Gordie said, reaching for the phone.

"Whoa," Lou said to him. "Not so fast. They're not going to give you someone's room number over the phone. And if you call back now, they'll get suspicious. Even worse, they may mention something to Frank or Reggie. We don't want those guys any more on guard than they already are. Let's just slow down. We need to plan the next move carefully."

Twenty minutes later, Lou dialed the number.

"Good afternoon," a cheerful female voice said. "Hawthorn Inn."

"Yes, ma'am," Lou said. "This is Mike Richards at Airborne Express, Detroit office. We're checking on a package delivered to one of your guests earlier this week."

"Is there a problem, Mr. Richards?"

"No reason to think so, ma'am. I'm in Quality Control. This is just a random confirmation check. Strictly routine. Keep the troops on their toes, if you get my drift."

He paused and glanced over at Billy and Gordie. Billy raised his eyebrows nervously. Gordie gave him the OK sign.

"With respect to this delivery," Lou continued, "our Springfield office shows a small package drop-off at your establishment on the evening of June thirteenth. That package was addressed to a Mr. Francis Burke. Did you have a Francis Burke registered at your establishment on June thirteenth?"

"Let me see." A pause. "Yes, we did."

"You're sure, ma'am?"

"Oh, yes. According to the book, I registered him myself. On June twelve."

"And were you the one who would have received our package on the evening of the thirteenth."

"No, that would have been Harold. He works evenings."

"I see. Does your establishment have a standard procedure for handling packages?"

"We certainly do. If it's small enough, we place it in the room slot at the front desk. If it's too large to fit in the slot, we place a note in the slot and hold the package in the vault."

"Okay," Lou said. "And which slot would that have been for Mr. Burke, ma'am?"

"Um, that would be 209."

"209, eh? And why that number?"

"Because that is his room number."

"I see. So the person on night duty at the front desk would have placed it in Mr. Burke's mail slot. Now is there anyone else who could pick up his mail?"

"Certainly not. Unless, of course, someone else is registered in that room with him."

"I see. And would that have been the case for Mr. Burke on that night?"

"I don't believe—oh, yes. There is another gentlemen in there. A Mr. Pelham. There are two beds in there. Doubles."

"Thank you, ma'am. I'm going to mark this delivery down as confirmed. Just for my records, your name is?"

"Virginia Brandon. Mrs. Virginia Brandon."

"Thank you, Mrs. Brandon. You've been very helpful. On behalf of Airborne Express, we hope you have nice day."

"You, too, sir. Thank you."

Lou hung up and turned toward the other two.

"Not bad," Gordie said.

Lou said, "We'll go there tonight after six."

"Why not now?"

"That woman registered them. She's more likely to know what they look like than the guy on night duty. We'll wait until she gets off, which is just fine. We need some time to think this one out."

Gordie frowned. "I'm still not clear on the details here."

Lou shrugged. "Me neither."

Chapter Thirty-nine

Gordie was out of the question. Unless Harold had been in a trance for the past several days, he would know in an instant that he had never before seen this short, burly, balding, bearded guy who was claiming to be one of the inn's guests.

Billy disqualified himself, knowing he'd be way too jittery to pull it off.

Which left Lou. Though his hair and his eyes were darker than Frank's, the two were roughly the same height and build. By no means a perfect match, but way closer than the others.

Which is why, at twenty minutes past six on the evening of June 14, 1994, it was Lou Solomon who climbed out of the minivan at the edge of the commons in the center of Hawthorn, Massachusetts. He heard the minivan pull away as he walked across the commons, across the freshly mown grass, past the wood bandstand and the granite Civil War monument, toward the Hawthorn Inn, which faced the commons on the other side.

The plan was for Gordie and Billy to park in back, come in through the rear entrance, and meet him upstairs at Room 209. They'd confirmed that the room was empty. Five minutes ago, Gordie had called the inn from a pay phone and asked for Reggie. There was no answer in his room.

Small comfort, Lou said to himself as he placed his hand on the entrance door, took a deep breath, and stepped into the lobby.

He faltered a moment, overcome not by nerves but the rush of memory. Straight ahead was an enormous stone fireplace with three long logs stacked inside. Couches and upholstered chairs were arranged in a cozy semicircle in front of the fireplace. An enclosed library was off to the right, and the front desk was to the left. On an antique table near the front desk was a big pewter bowl filled with shiny red apples.

The lobby of the Hawthorn Inn was almost identical to the lobby of the Woodstock Inn in Woodstock, Vermont.

There was no fire in the fireplace. Too late in the spring for that.

It had been winter in Vermont. A snowy afternoon. He'd been out for a hike through town while Andi stayed back at the inn. She'd been spotting again and feeling nauseous. The snowflakes—big fluffy Vermont ones, the kind you could actually catch on your tongue—had been floating down out of the gray sky for hours. He'd paused at the front door of the inn to stamp his feet on the mat. There'd been a fire in the big fireplace. Andi was curled on the couch in front of the fire, an apple in her hand as she read an old hardback edition of *Winesburg, Ohio* that she'd found in the inn's library.

As she told him later that day, she'd just finished "Adventure"— the story of a prim spinster who is suddenly overwhelmed by yearning during a violent thunderstorm one night. She disrobes and runs naked into the rain, seeking something—passion? salvation?—but returns wet and ashamed and alone. The story closes with her staring at the bedroom wall and struggling "to face bravely the fact that many people must live and die alone, even in Winesburg."

Andi had just read the final line when Lou returned. He'd remembered that she'd looked up with tears in her eyes, her lips quivering slightly. She'd been wearing faded Levi's and a wheat-colored crewneck sweater over a green turtleneck. As he'd gazed at her—at those almond-shaped green eyes and full lips and strong nose and dark curly hair—he'd realized again that his wife was the most beautiful woman he had ever seen and that marrying her had been the one truly significant accomplishment in his life.

Both facts were still true, Lou thought as he forced himself back to the present and the task at hand. He looked toward the front desk. There was an elderly man shuffling through papers. Harold?

As Lou approached, the man looked up from his papers.

"Yes?" he said, peering over his reading glasses in a friendly way.

Lou gave him a sheepish grin. "If I keep losing my key, Harold, you're going to add a special locksmith charge to the room."

Harold slipped off his reading glasses and placed them in his front shirt pocket. "Lost your key, eh?"

Lou nodded, chagrined. "Second time. First was yesterday afternoon. I accidentally left it in my room when I went to lunch. I must have done it again." He leaned forward with a conspiratorial smile. "Please don't tell Mrs. Brandon you had to give me another one. She'll think I'm bonkers."

After a moment's hesitation, Harold grinned and joined the conspiracy. "Mum's the word, Mr.—?"

"Burke," Lou said, forging ahead. "Room 209."

"Our secret, sir."

Harold chuckled and turned toward the room slots. He found the slot labeled 209, reached in, removed a spare key. He turned but then paused with a frown. He studied Lou, pressing the key against his cheek. "Burke, you say?"

Lou tensed. "Yes?"

"Virginia left me a note regarding you. Something about a package?"

Lou smiled. "You mean that Airborne Express delivery?"

"Yes, that is exactly it."

"I happened to be out front when the delivery guy pulled up in his truck. I had him give me the package. Is there a problem?"

Harold seemed relieved. "Oh, not all. Not one bit. Virginia received a call from the courier service today. Apparently, they wanted to confirm that you had received the delivery, sir."

"You can tell her I did."

"I will do that. But—" he winked as he handed Lou the room key "—I will say nothing about this minor mishap, sir."

As Lou took the key with his right hand, he reached into his pocket with his left hand and removed the five-dollar bill he'd placed there. He pressed the bill into Harold's hand and said, "Thank you."

"Oh, my. Thank *you*, Mr. Burke. Thank you very much."

Lou took the stairway up to the second floor. Gordie and Billy were waiting outside Room 209. Gordie had the two-wheel dolly and Billy had the rope.

"Any noises in there?" Lou asked in a whisper.

They shook their heads.

Lou knocked on the door and glanced up and down the hall. Empty. After a full minute had elapsed, he inserted the key and opened the door.

◇◇◇

Thirty minutes later, they were back in the van.

Gordie banged his fist on the dashboard. "Damn!"

Lou frowned. "They're not taking any chances."

They'd found nothing in the room but clothes, toiletries, and reunion materials.

"They probably did what Ray said we were going to do," Billy said. "Put her in a bank vault or a storage locker."

Gordie shook his head with frustration. "How the hell are we supposed to find her? Storage companies won't tell us a thing. Neither will the banks. And I'm sure as hell not in the mood to play Bonnie and Clyde."

"Tomorrow's the fifteenth," Billy said.

"And two days later is D-Day," Gordie said. "Dammit. We're out of time."

Lou started the engine and pulled the van out of the parking lot behind the Hawthorn Inn. They drove in silence back to Barrett.

Chapter Forty

An hour later, Lou poured the last of the second pitcher of beer into Gordie's mug. They were in a booth at the Rusty Scupper. Back in college the Rusty Scupper was *the* place to take a special date or to have your parents take you when they came to visit. But school was out, and the crowd tonight had that smarmy young professional look. Up at the bar were two twentysomething guys in Brooks Brothers suits chatting up a pair of women. The guys puffed on cigars and sipped what appeared to be martinis.

Lou surveyed the rest of the restaurant. With the exception of a foursome of blue-haired ladies two tables away, and what looked like a husband and wife in a booth along the side wall, Lou, Gordie, and Billy were the oldest patrons that night.

Lou's gaze held on the couple in the booth. The man looked about his age. The woman—well, she was around the age Andi would have been. They were leaning toward each other across the table and holding hands as they talked.

"Where would we even start?" Gordie said.

The question snapped Lou out of his reverie.

"Inside their heads," he said.

"What the hell does that mean?" Gordie said.

"Think about them," Lou said. "Here are two guys with a big investment in that statue. Lots of time and lots of emotion and lots of money. Especially money, right? Think of what they had to pay for that helicopter hijacking alone."

"But what does all that mean?" Billy asked.

"Here's what it *might* mean," Lou said. "They're just a day and a half away from their moment of glory. You know they're going to want to make sure that moment is truly glorious, right? They want the scene of her return to be unforgettable. Agreed?"

Gordie and Billy nodded.

Lou said, "So that means they're probably planning to do something a little more dramatic than driving onto Remington Field with Sirena sitting in the bed of a Ford pickup."

"You're right," Gordie said. "Especially now that they know that *People* magazine will be there. They'll have something flamboyant planned. Something with a flair. That's Reggie's style."

"Maybe another helicopter," Billy said.

"Or an armored car," Gordie said.

Billy scratched his chin. "A stretch limo could be dramatic."

"Not bad," Gordie said. "Do it up fancy. Have a chauffeur in gray livery get out, come around to the back door, open it slowly, and—*voilà*—there she is."

"That'd be good," Billy said.

Gordie tilted his head back and frowned at the ceiling. After a moment, he said, "Or they could drop her out of a plane.

"Drop her?" Billy said. "She'd break."

"Not just shove her out, Bronco." Gordie shook his head with exasperation. "With a parachute. On a pallet. Like one of those military drops." He leaned back, trying to picture the scene. "Can't you just see her? Descending out of the clouds?"

Lou shook his head. "No way. Sirena weighs nearly two hundred pounds. If she blows off course and lands in the stands, she could wipe out a whole row of alumni."

The three of them pondered the matter in silence.

"Damn," Gordie said. "There's just not enough time. We'd have to call every stretch limo service, helicopter rental outfit, and armored car company in Massachusetts, and maybe in Connecticut and Vermont and New Hampshire as well. And even if we got incredibly lucky and stumbled onto the right company, why would they tell us anything? Hell, if I were Frank and

Reggie, the first thing I'd want to make sure is that whoever I hired would keep it strictly confidential."

Billy turned to Lou and shook his head. "Gordie's right."

"Probably," Lou said. "But you'd have to admit that our chances would improve if we knew who they hired."

Gordie snorted. "Yeah, and my chances of playing professional baseball would improve if I were six feet tall."

"I'm serious."

"What are you getting at?" Billy asked.

Lou turned to Billy. "We'd be a lot closer to Sirena if we knew that they'd hired, say, Joe's Limo Service."

"Okay, Einstein," Gordie said. "And how are we supposed to narrow it to Joe's Limo Service?"

"We call Ray," Lou said.

"All of a sudden he's the Oracle of Delphi?" Gordie said.

Lou smiled. "No, he's the Oracle of Credit Cards."

Gordie frowned. "You think?"

"Possibly. Especially if there's a deposit involved. Let's assume they're planning to transport Sirena to the college in a stretch limo. Or on a helicopter. If you want to reserve one of those, you probably have to put down a deposit, right? If they used a credit card for the deposit, Ray's people should be able to find it."

Lou looked from Billy to Gordie. "Right?"

Gordie's scowl faded as he turned toward Billy.

Billy nodded. "Lou might be right."

Gordie looked back at Lou. After a moment he smiled. "You just might be."

Chapter Forty-one

As the justification for America's involvement in Vietnam, the Domino Theory has been discredited. As the explanation for air traffic delays across America, the Domino Theory is reaffirmed every time rain, sleet, or snow hits the runways ten miles northwest of the City of Chicago. As frustrated air travelers have long since learned, as goes O'Hare, so goes the nation.

The O'Hare problem that afternoon was hovering above the runways in the form of fog. But haze over O'Hare still meant that all planes heading toward Bradley International Airport—including, for some mysterious reason, those with flight paths nowhere near Chicago—were running late. Lou had no inkling of that problem as he drove south on I-91 under clear blue skies. It was only after he got into the airport terminal that he learned that TWA Flight 342 from St. Louis and US Air Flight 1447 from Pittsburgh were both showing ETAs roughly one hour later than the originally scheduled arrival times.

With an hour to kill, he wandered through the airport. Business had brought him through Bradley several times since college, but as a business traveler he'd always hurried past the gates and through the terminal the same way he always hurried past the gates and through the terminal of every other airport—quickly glancing at the advertising posters along the walls as he passed by, scanning for signs for Ground Transportation and Car Rental and Telephones.

But today he had time. As he strolled through the terminal, he realized that the place had been completely transformed since his student days. Back then, Bradley had been the dreary final stop on the Allegheny Airlines puddle-jumper from St. Louis. Today, it was shiny and modern and largely indistinguishable from its counterparts around the nation.

But not completely indistinguishable. His wanderings brought him to a row of tall enclosed phone booths—the retro type with wooden sides and folding glass doors. Something about them, something more than just their quaintness, caught his attention. As he stared at the hinged doors, searching for the connection, an image—a long forgotten image—bobbed to the surface of his memory:

Andi.

Standing in one of those phone booths.

Talking with her mother.

And Lou waiting. Standing in just about the same place he was standing now.

The rest came back, like color bleeding into a black-and-white still. Ten years ago. June of 1984. His tenth reunion. They'd flown to Hartford. Just the two of them. No gathering of the James Gang for that reunion. Billy still in Nicaragua, Ray still in the drug trade, Gordie off at some film festival pitching scripts to distracted producers. Katie just a toddler—fourteen months old. Staying with Andi's parents for the weekend. It was the first time Andi had been away from her baby overnight. That call home would be the first of many calls home that weekend.

Reunion headquarters in 1984 had been one of the houses on fraternity hill. Their tiny room was at the top of a creaking staircase on the fourth floor overlooking the back veranda. They'd come back from a coed tennis tournament on the second afternoon to find a cocktail party in full swing on the veranda. He went to fetch two cups of beer from the tap. Returned to find Andi trapped near the French doors by Bryce Wharton, their goofy class secretary, in full flirtation mode, his shrill guffaws sounding like donkey's brays. Andi's face flushed from tennis. A sheen of perspiration on her forehead and upper lip. He'd paused to watch—to admire his beautiful wife and her cheerleader legs in that short tennis skirt.

Bryce Wharton finally excused himself, headed over to the crowd to trawl for tidbits for his Class Notes column in the alumni magazine. Lou approached with the beers. Andi's gaze met his. She raised her eyebrows, nodded toward the stairway beyond the French doors. He grinned. Set the two beers on the ledge. Hurried up the stairs behind her, entranced by the view. Inside the room, they quickly undressed, staring at each other. The walls were thin. Two women in earnest conversation in the next room. Andi naked, tanned, beautiful, put a finger to her lips as she leaned back on the bed. She was sweaty and musky and honeyed and exquisite. They made love on the narrow bed, silent, fierce—with laughter and loud voices wafting up from the veranda below.

Nine months later—to the day—Kenny was born.

◇◇◇

Lou turned from the phone booths and checked his watch. Still forty-five minutes before the kids' plane arrived.

He picked up a copy of *Sports Illustrated* at the newsstand— the one with heavyweight boxing champion Mike Tyson and his wife Robin Givens on the cover—got a cup of coffee at the Starbucks booth, and settled down in an empty seat near the gate where the flight from St. Louis was slated to arrive.

After they got back from dinner at the Rusty Scupper last night, he'd called Ray to explain his deposit theory for locating Sirena. Ray told him he'd place a trace on all charges by Frank or Reggie over the past several days.

That was last night. He still hadn't heard back when he left for the airport.

Lou's chair faced the main corridor. He started reading an article by Peter Gammons on the drop in the number of home runs that season. Across the way was another gate. Through the large windows he could see an American Airlines 767 pulling into position as the jetway swung out to meet it. A crowd was milling around the gate, waiting to greet the arriving passengers.

Lou looked up from the *Sports Illustrated* when the airline agent opened the door. A moment later the first passengers began emerging. He watched with mild interest. Odds were that this flight included one or two Barrett alumni returning for the reunion weekend. One of them might be from the Class of '74.

He recognized her immediately.

Donna Crawford was wearing an oversized blue turtleneck, a stonewashed denim skirt cut just above the knees, and leather sandals. As she adjusted the shoulder strap on her carry-on bag, she turned to hold out her hands to two young girls, both blonde, each with a stuffed backpack slung on her back. He guessed the older one was about eleven and the younger one maybe seven. They wore bright shorts and patterned T-shirts and white tennis shoes. The older one had on a Dodgers baseball cap turned backward, and the younger one was carrying a stuffed white rabbit. As Donna moved toward the corridor, holding each daughter by a hand, she looked up at the signs for directions to the baggage claim area.

Lou stood. "Donna?"

She turned toward the voice and then smiled with recognition. "Lou, what a nice surprise."

He came over and gave her a kiss on the cheek.

"Did you just get in, too?" she asked.

"I'm here to pick up my kids." He kneeled in front of her two girls. "And who are these cuties?"

Both girls turned their heads away bashfully.

Donna placed her hand on the older one's head. "This is Leah. And this is Sara. Girls, this is Mr. Solomon. He was a friend of Daddy's."

"Hi, Leah," Lou said. "Hi, Sara."

"Hello, Mr. Solomon," Leah said, her expression solemn.

Sara put her thumb in her mouth. Lou touched her gently on the cheek, and she smiled at him around her thumb.

As Lou stood, he suddenly felt uncomfortable, as if he'd barged in on this family uninvited—which, he realized, was exactly what he'd done.

"Here," he said, reaching for her bag, "let me carry that."

"Oh, Lou." Donna gave an embarrassed laugh. "It's not that heavy."

"All I have is this." He held up his magazine. "And you have two girls to worry about."

"Okay." She handed him the bag and turned to her daughters. "Come on, girls."

They started down the corridor toward the baggage area.

"How are you doing?" he asked.

"Better." She glanced at him and sighed. "One day at a time."

He nodded, trying to think of something appropriate to say.

Bruce Crawford had been the third member of Lou's class to die. Rob Sonderman had been the first, succumbing to brain cancer just four years after graduation. Then came Toby Henderson, dead of AIDS six years ago. All three were to be honored in a special memorial service during the reunion weekend.

They continued down the corridor in silence, looking back every few steps to check on the little girls, who were trailing right behind.

"Lou?"

He turned. She was staring at him.

"Your letter meant a lot to me."

Lou shrugged. "I remembered the card you sent me."

"I saved your letter," she said. "I read it again two nights ago, as I was getting ready to come out here."

He nodded.

When Lou first met her—at a mixer during the fall of his freshman year—she was Donna Hendricks of Hampton College. She met Bruce Crawford later that evening, and before the night was over Donna and Bruce had fallen utterly in love. Bruce lived on the same dorm floor as Lou. He was a big, brawny, good-natured blond from Minnesota who played lacrosse for Barrett and majored in geology (aka, rocks for jocks).

Bruce and Donna became BruceandDonna. Even senior year, after four years together, you'd find them in the student union, seated alone at a table and holding hands and gazing into each other's eyes, silent for what seemed to others an eternity. The mushy stuff was way over the top for Lou—and for everyone else, too. Gordie claimed it was only a matter of time before they'd burst into song. Ray prayed they would burst into flames.

He glanced over at Donna. Back in college she had been a classically pretty girl, with ash blond hair and pug nose and blue eyes. Now there were streaks of gray near the temples, lines around the eyes, a hint of sag in her neck. But to Lou she looked just as lovely as she did when they used to share a cup of hot cocoa along the sidelines at the freshman lacrosse games and cheered on Bruce. The important word was "pals." At first glance, Donna didn't look like the type of woman a guy could be pals with. She seemed decidedly "ladylike"—existing in a gossamer world of powder puffs and perfumes and soft music and nail polish and bath oils. But Lou soon learned that you can no more judge a woman than a book by its cover. Donna had played halfback on her high school varsity field hockey team and bore the leg scars to prove it. And there was nothing demure about the way she played touch football with them. Twenty years later, Lou could still remember how she looked going out for a pass in her turtleneck sweater and grass-stained jeans and long blonde hair stuffed under a Philadelphia Phillies baseball cap—sexy enough to make you regret that she was in love with your friend.

"Where are you staying?" Lou asked.

They were waiting for her luggage at the carousel.

"At one of the Hampton dorms. Bryant Hall, I think. How 'bout you?"

"Barrett Best Western. I've been sharing a room there for the last couple days with Billy McCormick and Gordie Cohen. I'm switching over to another room with the kids tonight."

"Gordie." She smiled fondly. "Bruce and I had dinner with him…oh, it must have been ten years ago. Right after we moved out there. Is he still in Hollywood?"

"He moved back to Chicago. He's in advertising now."

"What about that crazy friend of yours?" She giggled. "Your dishwasher partner?"

"Ray Gorman."

"Right. Is Ray coming back for the reunion?"

"He's landing here this afternoon. I'm picking him up, too. If you don't mind waiting, I'd be happy to give you and the girls a ride to Barrett."

She shook her head. "Thanks, but I have a car rented. This is my first time back. I want to take the girls over to Hampton. Show them where Mommy went to school. After the reunion—" she paused, eyes bright "—I'm thinking about going to the Berkshires."

"Really?"

"It's so beautiful this time of year. Bruce and I—" She paused, her spirits fading a little. "We spent our first anniversary up there."

"Where will you stay?"

She shrugged. "I have no idea. I didn't decide to go there until the plane ride out. Spur of the moment. The girls and I are just going to hop in the car, drive out there and find a place for a couple of nights. It shouldn't be hard this early in the season."

"That's a great idea."

Lou had been so focused on Sirena and June seventeenth that he'd given no thought to life on June eighteenth.

Donna studied him. "You and your kids are welcome to join the caravan. I'm sure there'll be plenty of vacancies in June."

The prospect of a couple of days unwinding in the Berkshire Mountains with his children was tempting.

His thoughts were jumbled.

She was staring down at the luggage carousel. After a moment she looked up at him. "You haven't remarried?"

He shook his head. "No."

She nodded, eyes distant.

"It's hard," she said quietly—more to herself than him.

"There it is, Mommy," Leah shouted. She was pointing at the suitcase sliding down the shoot to the carousel.

Lou walked with them to the car rental booth and then out to the curb beneath the rental car sign. As the Hertz bus pulled up, Donna turned to him and held out her hand.

"Thanks, Lou. It's wonderful to see you again."

He shook her hand.

"Listen," he said, clumsy again, "maybe we could get together for dinner. With our kids. Maybe, oh, tomorrow night?"

She gazed at him a moment and then nodded. "That would be nice."

After the Hertz bus pulled away, he walked back through the terminal, trying to make sense of these new feelings. It had been years since anything had stirred in that corner of his heart.

He thought back to the last time he'd seen Donna. And Bruce. It was at their wedding, which had been a week after graduation in Philadelphia. The newlyweds settled in Philadelphia, where she got a job as a legal secretary to help put Bruce through the Wharton School of Business. After that, they moved to New York City and Bruce joined Drexel Burnham's bond department, where he became one of Michael Milken's boys. He was transferred to Drexel's Los Angeles office. They bought a house in Beverly Hills. Life seemed good until the Milken scandal erupted. Two years ago, Bruce died of a massive overdose of sleeping pills in a hotel room in New York City, where'd he gone on a bond deal. In a rambling suicide note to Donna, he apologized for his weakness. A few weeks later, the Justice Department revealed that Bruce had been the principal target of an insider-trading investigation.

When Lou first heard of Bruce's death—it made the newspapers—he'd flashed back to that night freshman year when Bruce returned from the mixer and proclaimed in the dormitory hall that he was in love with a girl named Donna. It was love at first sight, Bruce declared. Although it earned him jeers and mockery from his dorm mates, Bruce stuck with his story.

Lou hadn't been among the taunters. He believed in love at first sight.

Lou paused to glance at the flight information on the arrival board, his thoughts drifting back to his first kiss with Andi.

Another lifetime, he told himself.

Chapter Forty-two

The plane from St. Louis arrived twenty minutes before Ray's plane, which gave Lou a chance to catch up on his children's lives. He bought them both a chocolate milk shake and settled back for all the stories.

After they'd given him their news, Katie asked, "What about the statue, Daddy?"

He told them the story—from Wrigley Field through the helicopter heist, leaving out only the bungee-cord seduction of Gordie.

"Those jerks," Kenny said, he faced flushed with anger.

"We're trying to get her back," Lou said.

"When's the deadline?" Katie asked.

"The day after tomorrow."

"That's not fair," Kenny said.

Lou nodded. "I know."

"Can we help you get her back?" Katie asked.

Lou ran his fingers gently through her hair. "First we have to find out where she is." He stood. "Come on, guys. Ray's flight ought to be landing soon. He's going to need our help."

◇◇◇

"Oh, my," Katie said as Ray appeared in the opening to the jetway.

He was in a wheelchair—his broken leg propped up on the leg rest, his broken arm in a sling, his other arm bandaged. He had two black eyes and bandages on the back of his head. An airline employee was pushing the wheelchair, and Brandi followed behind.

Lou came up to him. "Hey, buddy."

Ray glanced around. There were dozens of people looking at him while pretending not to. "Hey," he said, "how the hell was I supposed to know her husband played linebacker for the Steelers?"

Two elderly women exchanged shocked expressions.

Katie and Kenny kept Ray company near the exit doors while Lou and Brandi went to get the van. By the time Lou drove up to the exit, his two kids were laughing hysterically at something Ray had said.

On the drive back to Barrett they talked about everything but Sirena. Billy was waiting outside the motel entrance when Lou drove up. He helped them get Ray set up in the room, which was on the second floor near the elevator. The motel had moved each of them to a new room along the same side of the second floor.

When Katie and Kenny saw the pool, they were more interested in swimming than eating. The rest of the group agreed to meet poolside in half an hour and order pizzas. Gordie was gone when they had returned from the airport. According to Billy, he was having dinner with Sally Jacobs, the new love of his life, but promised to come back afterward.

While Lou's kids splashed in the water and the rest of them munched on pizza, Ray turned to the business at hand.

"Two days ago," he said, "there was a five-hundred-dollar charge to Reggie's Visa card. The payee is Hawthorn Aviation Corporation."

"Which is what?" Lou asked.

"Not sure. Its offices are at Hawthorn Airport, which is about ten miles west of that inn where they're staying."

He handed Lou a map of western Massachusetts. The airport was circled in orange marker.

Ray said, "I'm guessing they're going to do it by helicopter."

Lou looked over at Billy. "Gordie's due back when?"

"Eight."

Lou checked his watch. It was almost seven-thirty. He stood up.

"Can you guys watch the kids a second?" he asked them.

"Sure," Brandi said. "Where are you going?"

"I'm going to call out there. See how late that airport is open tonight."

When he returned, Ray asked, "Well?"

"Hawthorn Aviation is closed for the night," Lou said, "but the airport's open 'til ten. If you and Brandi are willing to babysit, we can go out there as soon as Gordie gets back."

Chapter Forty-three

"But I need to talk to the pilot tonight," Gordie told the bearded mechanic. "It's extremely important. There's been a change in plans. I need to give him the new schedule and explain it to him."

Gordie was in the main hangar at Hawthorn Airport. On the drive to the airport they'd decided it was best to approach an airport employee, since chances were good that Frank and Reggie had made strict confidentiality a condition of their deal with Hawthorn Aviation. While an employee of Hawthorn Airport might not know the details of the deal with Hawthorn Aviation, he nevertheless might know of arrangements Hawthorn Aviation had made with the airport, especially any flight plans that had been filed.

The burly mechanic frowned. "Well, sir, it could be Bob or Rocky or Clint. I know all three are booked on the seventeenth." He gestured toward the dark offices of Hawthorn Aviation Corporation. "If you come back tomorrow around nine I'm sure they'll be able to tell you which one it is."

"That's the problem." Gordie grimaced. "I'm not going to be around tomorrow. I've got to talk to the pilot tonight. He needs to know the change."

"Jeez, buddy, I don't know." He scratched his beard as he pondered the issue. "Where are your friends flying?"

"Just around western Massachusetts. The charter is probably no more than a half day."

The mechanic pursed his lips. "I suppose I could check the maintenance schedules."

Gordie followed him to a metal desk in the corner of the hangar. The mechanic lifted a clipboard off the desktop and slowly paged through it.

He looked up at Gordie. "You say just flying around western Mass?"

Gordie nodded.

"How many in the party?"

"I think three, but one of them weighs at least two hundred pounds."

The mechanic scratched his beard as he studied the schedules. "Well," he finally said, "that pretty much narrows it to Rocky. Looks like Clint's taking a load to Albany, and he's out all day. Bob's overnight to Canada with one passenger, so it ain't him. It don't say here where Rocky's going, but it looks like a big load, and we got the plane due back by sundown."

"Then Rocky's the one," Gordie said.

◇◇◇

"How far is South Hadley?" Billy asked.

Gordie checked the map. "About a half-hour drive."

"Should we call first?" Billy asked.

"No," Lou shook his head. "If Rocky's the one, we can assume he's been sworn to secrecy. If we give him advance warning, he won't see us."

"What makes you think he'll see us anyway?" Billy asked.

Lou pulled out of the airport parking lot. He paused at the exit and glanced over at Billy. "We've got about thirty minutes to come up with a good reason."

Chapter Forty-four

It was almost ten o'clock when they pulled in front of 7111 Cornell Avenue in South Hadley, Massachusetts.

Gordie peered through the van window. "Lights are on. That's good."

Lou opened the car door. He looked back at Billy. "Grab the beer."

They rang the doorbell. After almost a minute, a scrawny little guy opened the door. He was dressed in black—black T-shirt, black jeans, black boots. Even the unlit cheroot clenched in the corner of his mouth was black. He had a black Fu Manchu mustache and narrow black eyebrows that joined at the bridge of his hawkish nose.

He took the cheroot from his mouth and spit out a piece of tobacco. "Yeah?"

He said it more as a snarl than a question.

"Rocky?" Lou said.

The guy wore his long black hair pulled back in a ponytail. He put the cheroot back in his mouth and shook his head.

Lou smiled politely. "Is Rocky there?"

The guy sized him up. "What you want Rocky for?"

"It's about Mr. Pelham and Mr. Burke," Lou answered. "There's been a change in procedures for the seventeenth. We need to talk to Rocky."

The guy studied them. His face was lined, and there were gray hairs in his mustache. Lou guessed he was in his late forties.

"Wait here," the guy said, and closed the door.

Lou looked back at his two companions.

Gordie shook his head. "Delightful chap, eh? I should think that he and Reggie got along famously. Best of chums, no doubt."

Several minutes passed before the scrawny guy opened the door again. Standing next to him was a pale, sullen woman in tight jeans and faded chambray shirt, the sleeves rolled up, exposing an ornate red cross tattooed on the back of her right arm. She had straight brown hair that looked as if she cut it herself with a weed wacker. A cigarette dangled from her lips.

"Yeah?" she said.

"We're here to see Rocky," Lou said.

She took a deep drag on her cigarette and exhaled twin streams of smoke through her nostrils. "I'm Rocky."

Lou forced a smile. "I'm Lou."

She squinted at him through a wavering line of tobacco smoke. "Who the fuck sent you?"

Lou said. "We're here to make you a business proposal."

"Business proposal?" She snorted. "You lied to my old man. I don't talk business with no bullshitters." She started to close the door.

"Oh, really?" Lou said. "That's tough talk for someone doing business with thieves."

She paused, the door halfway closed, and scowled at Lou. "What you talking about?"

"Your customers. Reggie Pelham and Frank Burke," Lou said. "They're thieves."

"I ain't no preacher." She took a last deep drag of her cigarette and flicked the butt past Lou onto the front lawn. "It's just business."

"Same here. We'll top their deal."

She shook her head. "I don't go in for that crap."

As she closed the door Gordie shouted, "Not even for fifty grand?"

Lou turned to Gordie and smiled. He held up both hands, fingers crossed.

A moment later, Rocky opened the door. The scrawny guy was at her side.

She squinted at Gordie. "Say what?"

"Fifty grand."

Lou could tell she had her guard way up. She couldn't figure out Gordie's angle and didn't want to say anything that might make her look foolish.

"You said earlier that it was just business," Gordie said in an affable manner. "I know business, ma'am, and I know that anyone who passes up the chance to earn I'm guessing at least ten times more than she would under a prior agreement—especially a prior agreement with thieves—just isn't going to ever get far in the world of business. That's the sort of behavior you'd expect from a sucker, ma'am, and you sure don't seem like a sucker to me."

"Fifty grand?" she repeated.

Gordie nodded. "Yes, ma'am."

The scrawny guy thrust his chin forward, his head bobbing defiantly. "Yeah? Where is it?"

"Well, sir," Gordie said calmly, "we don't have it quite yet. It's prize money, you see. That's where Rocky comes in."

The scrawny guy snorted and reached to close the door. "I knew this was bullshit."

Gordie held up his hands. "Hold on, pal. My buddy Billy here has with him two six-packs of fine Massachusetts beer. Why not settle back, have a few brews with us, and listen to our proposition? When we're through, if your lady friend doesn't want to earn fifty large for two perfectly legal hours of flying, that's fine. No problem. We'll say good-bye and be on our way. No hard feelings."

Gordie shifted his gaze back to Rocky and gave her a pleasant smile. "Way I see it, ma'am, you got nothing to lose and plenty to gain. What do you say we sit down and talk some business over a few cold ones?"

Rocky turned toward her boyfriend, whose brain seemed to have gone into vapor lock. He didn't move or change his expression.

She turned to Gordie and gestured toward the grocery bag in Billy's hands. "What kind of beer?"

"Sam Adams."

Gordie turned toward Billy, who reached into the bag and pulled out one of the six packs to show her.

She frowned.

They waited.

She lit another cigarette with her lighter.

Her boyfriend stood watching her, waiting.

She stared at the floor and exhaled the smoke through her nostrils. After a moment, she looked up at Gordie.

"What the fuck," she said. "I'm thirsty. Come on in and let me hear this bullshit proposition."

Part 5: Redemption

I see my light come shining,
From the west unto the east.
Any day now, any day now,
I shall be released.
                    —Bob Dylan

Chapter Forty-five

According to the printed program, the Reunion of the Class of 1974 would officially begin at noon on June sixteenth with a luncheon for class members and their families under the big tent on the front lawn of Pembroke House. To make sure they'd be under that tent by noon, Brandi agreed to watch Lou's kids as Lou, Gordie, and Billy worked their way down a shopping list that was, by any measure, bizarre. Billy, in the familiar role of navigator, had been up at dawn to map out their route.

First stop was a seedy strip mall on the outskirts of Linden, twenty miles up the road from Barrett. At 9:05 a.m., Gordie walked into Naughty Nicole's Lingerie. At 9:26 a.m., he walked out with a plastic bag and a leer.

Next stop was Arnold Bros. Lawn & Garden in Vernon. At 9:57 a.m., all three of them walked in. Thirty minutes later, Lou backed the van into position by the store's pickup door. Gordie and Billy came out carrying a small tube of super glue, a can of red paint, and a paintbrush. Behind them came a store employee pushing a flatbed cart with a large object wrapped in several Hefty bags.

Third stop was Dr. Whammy's House of Novelties, located in a strip mall four miles outside Hawthorn. At 10:46 a.m., Billy hopped out of the van. Fourteen minutes later he climbed back in, held up a small bag, and announced, "This was their last one."

Final stop was Booker's Lock 'N Key in downtown Hawthorn. At 11:17 a.m., Lou strolled in with three crisp one-hundred-dollar bills. Thirty-two minutes later he exited without those bills. As he approached the van, he flashed Gordie and Billy the thumbs-up sign.

At 12:21 p.m., the shopping spree complete, Lou settled into his seat between Kenny and Katie at one of the long tables under the large yellow-striped tent on the front lawn of Pembroke House. Gordie was at their table, too, along with Ray and Brandi, and a few other classmates and wives and children. Billy's chair was empty. He'd borrowed Lou's van and was driving down to the airport. Dorothy had surprised him last night with the announcement that she and their son were flying up there in the morning. Lou had never seen Billy so elated.

Lou was determined to enjoy this part of the reunion—to focus on his kids and the festivities, to be just another guy cruising through his reunion weekend with a grin on his face and a beer in his hand and two kids in tow. The effort added a surreal edge to the reunion experience. Thoughts of what they'd done that morning and what awaited them tomorrow kept intruding—and all the while, wherever he looked, whatever he did, more memories of Andi appeared, as if the journey back to Barrett had jarred open a passageway into his past.

He spotted Donna and her two girls a few tables over. They were seated with several of Bruce's fraternity brothers and their families. When she looked his way he waved. She smiled and waved back. He was looking forward to having dinner with her that night.

The luncheon speaker was the dean of the students, who'd been the assistant dean when they were freshmen. He welcomed them back with a warm, humorous speech. Following him to the podium were several members of their reunion committee, each with a brief speech about the weekend's events. Throughout the speeches, their goofy class secretary Bryce Wharton worked the crowd, moving from table to table, pumping hands, sliding his eyeglasses back up his nose with his finger, scribbling notes onto what looked like a steno pad. Lunch concluded with a clever audiovisual presentation about their class by one of their classmates who was now head of public relations for a major oil company.

The list of the afternoon's events ranged from a seminar on coping with midlife career changes to a mixed-doubles tennis tournament on the Chilmark courts to a panel discussion on enhancing emotional intimacy in marital relationships to a lecture by Bryce Wharton (in his Northwestern Mutual persona) on "Life Insurance for the Millennium." Ray, Brandi, and Gordie opted for the Bloody Mary party over at the Class of '74's reunion tent. Lou and his children opted for the family softball tournament down on Clark Field. Before separating, they agreed to meet back at the motel by six to review the plan.

After the softball game, Lou and the kids hiked back up the hill from the ball fields, sweaty and victorious. Katie had scored the winning run for their team, and Kenny had made a key defensive play at third base that saved a run.

Lou led them toward the big red tent in the center of the quad, where the refreshments included kegs of beer, coolers filled with iced soft drinks, and bowls of pretzels and nuts and popcorn. After he got Katie and Kenny settled at a table with cans of root beer and plates of munchies, he went back for a beer.

As he was leaning over the keg to fill his cup, he heard his name called. He looked back toward the voice. Straightening, he turned to face Frank Burke.

"Lou," Frank said with a triumphant smile, "you and your boys gave us one hell of a run for the money."

Lou took a sip of his beer. "We did more than that. We found her."

"That you did, and it was a damn fine accomplishment. Can't take that away from you."

"Actually, Frank, that's exactly what you did."

"Now, now, Lou." Frank chuckled. "That's what this challenge is all about. No one owns her. She doesn't belong to any of us, no matter how much care and attention we lavish on her. She belongs to our school, to our shared academic tradition."

Lou took a sip of his beer and said nothing.

Frank chuckled. "Think of her as the trophy wife from hell. Come to think of it, she's about as big a cunt as my ex, and just as cold." His expression became serious. "I know it seems a bitter pill to swallow, but in a few weeks you're going to realize the full dimension of what Reggie and I pulled off."

"Tell that to Ray. You bastards almost killed him."

Frank held up his hands, grinning.

"Let's be fair, Lou. We didn't do anything to Ray. He pulled that stunt all on his own. That was not what you'd describe as a stellar display of good judgment on his part."

Lou gazed at Frank as he took another sip of beer.

"I know you guys are pissed," Frank said. "But just remember—there are no rules in this game. Never have been. That's the whole point. Anything goes. Anything. Whatever happens happens."

Lou gazed at Frank. After a moment, he said, "Whatever happens happens, eh?"

"Precisely. Like Tom Hanks said in that movie about girls playing ball. There's no crying in baseball. Same with Sirena, Lou. Suck it up."

Lou turned and strolled back to his children.

SCENE 65: FRONT-END, PART III {3rd Draft}:

CUT TO:

INT. DISHWASHER AREA - NIGHT

Lou is working front-end, Ray on back-end. They're smooth and fast and efficient—every bit as good as Buzz and Charlie were.

> RAY
> (unloading a steaming tray of clean plates)
> I can't believe she dumped me.

> LOU
> Hey, you want to go over to Hampton tonight? Gordie told me there's a mixer at Franklin Hall.

> RAY
> Fuck mixers, man. Fuck women.
> Fuck all.

The Graycoat sticks his head through the pass-through window.

> GRAYCOAT
> Boiler's down. No hot water. Don't run anything through but trays until we get the boiler back up.

The Graycoat leaves.

> RAY
> What's that asshole want now?

> LOU
> Boiler's down. No hot water.

                    RAY

Jesus, what a night. Everything's fucked
up.

                    LOU
                 (smiling)
Hey, Ray.

                    RAY

What?

                    LOU
             (turning to face him)
No hot water.

                    RAY

I heard.

                    LOU

Come on, man. Your dream.

                    RAY
           (smiling and leaning back)
Oh, yeah.

INT. DISHWASHER AREA - A FEW MINUTES LATER

A mob of students has squeezed into the small area.
Others crowd around the pass-through window, peering in.

                    LOU

Ready, Captain?

CLOSE ON RAY

He is seated on an empty rack facing the front-end of
the dishwasher. His feet are resting on another rack in
front of him, which is poised at the entrance. Ray nods.

Lou pushes Ray forward far enough so that both racks
are engaged on the conveyor belt. The two racks inch

forward. Ray's feet slowly enter the front end of the dishwasher.

> LOU
> (to the crowd)
> We have liftoff.

The crowd CHEERS as Ray's legs disappear into the dishwasher. Lou grabs another rack and slides it in place behind the one Ray is sitting on.

Ray lies back on the rack. Lou hands him the dish towel. Ray places it over his face. The conveyor belt keeps moving. Ray is now up to his waist inside the machine.

> LOU
> (leaning in close)
> You have any trouble, start banging. I'll
> turn it off and pull you out.

Ray nods. He's now in the machine up to his chest. He reaches blindly for Lou and pulls him down close.

> RAY
> Christ, water's ice cold. My balls shrank.

Ray is in the machine up to his neck. With a final, blind wave, he disappears into the machine and the crowd ROARS. Lou moves to the back end.

CLOSE ON LOU

as he nervously watches the canvas flaps at the back end.

And finally—

> VOICE IN CROWD
> His feet!

ANGLE ON BACK END

Emerging through the flaps are Ray's tennis shoes, soaking wet. LOU waits until Ray's knees are visible and then, unable to hold off any longer, he reaches in and pulls the next rack out. Ray comes sliding out, still on his back on the racks.

CLOSE ON RAY

Motionless, face covered by the towel, arms crossed over his chest. Water pours off him.

> VOICE IN CROWD
> Is he okay?

Ray whips off the towel and sits up. The crowd CHEERS. Ray hops down, soaking wet. He's the man of the hour, and loving every minute as people pound him on the back and slap high fives.

ANGLE ON LOU

who is off to the side, smiling at his pal's glory.

Chapter Forty-six

Lou glanced at the clock radio on the nightstand.

3:25 a.m.

After the first hour he thought it might be the coffee. He'd asked for decaffeinated, but with all the people and commotion at the table the waitress could have gotten things confused on the refills. If so, it was a small price to pay for a wonderful evening. Ray and Brandi had been there, as had Billy and Dorothy and little Sandino. Gordie arrived with his date, Professor Sally Jacobs. They seemed to be getting along nicely. Best of all was his end of the table, with his kids and Donna Crawford and her two daughters. Several times during dinner their eyes met, and each time the tumult around them seemed to vanish. It had been instantly comfortable—the two of them surrounded by the four children—and thus instantly unsettling.

Don't overwhelm her, he'd warned himself after dinner. *And don't overwhelm yourself.*

"She's really nice," Katie told him afterward.

"I like her, Dad," Kenny had said as Lou tucked him in bed. "She's pretty."

That's when he'd mentioned the possibility of adding on a few days to the vacation to spend it with Donna and her daughters in the Berkshires. Both kids said that sounded fine.

Not too fast, he reminded himself.

He glanced again at the clock.

It couldn't be the coffee. The caffeine would have worn off long before three-thirty in the morning.

No, this was about tomorrow. For the last two hours he'd been sorting through the details—so many steps, and so many of them critical ones that could go wrong in so many ways and ruin their plans.

It would be over in less than ten hours, he told himself. Whatever was going to be would be. In less than ten hours, they'd be victors or they'd be spectators.

He turned in bed again and fluffed his pillow.

Spectator.

He lay back on the pillow and stared at the dark ceiling.

He'd been a spectator for too long.

There was a restlessness inside him, a vague unease. It had been building ever since they pulled out of Chicago in the wee hours with Sirena in the back of the van. From the moment he turned onto Lake Shore Drive, his journey east had been seeded with memories of Andi.

Even little things triggered memories—like that telephone booth at the airport.

Or the stirred coffee at the restaurant tonight. He'd been watching Donna stir sugar into her coffee when he suddenly remembered that Andi never took sugar with her coffee. Just milk.

Milk but no sugar—the sort of thing that you knew without realizing you knew it, a fact absorbed as part of the stream of life. Like how Andi used to spread strawberry jam on her toasted English muffin with a spoon. Or the tilt of her head when she put in an earring. All of that—all of those little moments—had come rushing back at the restaurant that night, amid all the voices and the laughter and the clanging of dishes, as he'd watched Donna stir her coffee.

He glanced at the clock.

3:37 a.m.

He sat up. Kenny was asleep next to him in the double bed. Katie was breathing deeply in the other bed.

He got out of bed and walked barefoot across the carpeted floor to the dresser. Slipping on his jeans, he felt around the dresser top until he located the room key.

Stepping into the night air, the first thing he heard was the sound of frogs. Peepers. Hundreds of them. He closed the door gently and stepped over to the metal railing along the second floor landing. Leaning against the railing, he tried to pinpoint the location. They were out there somewhere in the dark, probably ringing a pond, chanting prayers to their frog gods.

"Noisy little fuckers."

Startled, Lou turned. Seated in his wheelchair three doors down was Ray.

Lou walked over. "Can't sleep?"

"Don't know why. All I do tomorrow is ride shotgun."

"Not so." He leaned back against the railing and smiled at Ray. "You're still the captain of this crew."

"Not anymore, *Captain*."

Lou shook his head. "I'm just the stand-in."

"You're in charge here. You've always been, man. I'm just the shit disturber."

"*Just?* I'd say that's a title to be proud of."

"Maybe." Ray stared into the darkness. "I just hope that redneck pilot holds up her end of the bargain."

"Gordie's pledged—or I guess now we've all pledged—fifty thousand reasons for her to deliver."

Ray shrugged. "We'll see."

After a moment, Lou said, "You're a genius."

Ray frowned. "What's that mean?"

Lou bowed in an exaggerated show of respect. "No matter what happens tomorrow, whether we pull it off or not, this was a wonderful idea."

"Just don't fuck it up, Solomon."

Another voice said, "Don't fuck what up?"

They turned. Gordie was walking down the landing toward them. He was wearing boxer shorts and carrying a boombox.

"You, too?" Lou asked.

Gordie nodded. "Been rolling around for hours."

"With Sally?" Ray asked.

"Very funny, Gimp. For your information, you nosy bastard, *Professor* Jacobs went home right after dinner."

"Shows excellent judgment," Ray said.

Gordie sat down on the landing, back to the railing, and pulled up the radio antenna.

"Couldn't sleep," he said. "Finally decided to come out here and listen to some tunes." He turned on the radio and moved the dial until he came to Van Morrison singing "Moondance."

Lou leaned back and closed his eyes. "Perfect song."

"Well, well, well," Ray said, "look who else is here."

They turned to see Bronco Billy coming down the walkway. He had a red plaid robe over his pajamas. He grinned self-consciously. "Hi, guys."

Lou was seated next to Gordie. He rested his back against the railing and looked up at Billy. "None of us could sleep."

Billy smiled as he put his hands in the deep pockets of his robe. "We look like that scene in *Henry V.*"

"What scene?" Ray asked.

"You remember," Billy said. "We read it in Professor Ryal's class? The night before the battle? The scene in the English camp at Agincourt, everyone waiting for the morning."

"Don't get carried away with that literary crap," Ray said. "All the world is definitely not a stage. Just keep your eye on the prize and don't fuck up."

"Hey, Major Kong," Gordie said, "we've been doing okay since you took your three-and-a-half gainer off the high board into Sherwood Forest."

Ray smiled. "Keep it that way tomorrow, Shorty."

There was a slight breeze. The final notes of "Moondance" faded into the peeping of the frogs and the grinding of the crickets. A moment of radio silence, and then the familiar opening guitar chords to "Sweet Baby James." In the darkness, James Taylor's plaintive voice:

There is a young cowboy, he lives on the range,
His horse and his cattle are his only companions.

"Ah," Gordie said. "Great song."

Lou closed his eyes, caught off guard, snatched back in time to the little coffeehouse in Woodstock, Vermont, back to the table near the rear of the crowded room with its rattle of china and buzz of voices and occasional gurgle and hiss of the espresso machine. They were holding hands. This was the mini-vacation they'd promised themselves, the romantic weekend away from the kids.

Her pregnancy had expedited their plans. They both knew that within a month she wouldn't feel like going up the stairs, much less halfway across the country. Her first two pregnancies had been rough ones, and high risk—so much so that her gynecologist warned against a third. He'd wanted to tie her tubes after the second delivery, but she wasn't yet ready for that final step. Andi had wanted a big family. One of her fantasies, going all the way back to their penniless days in Cambridge, was to cruise around the neighborhood in a golf cart picking up her six children one by one by one to bring them home for dinner.

But the doctor kept pressuring her. Around the time of Kenny's second birthday she finally relented. If she couldn't have them herself, she told Lou, they'd adopt, and she'd still get that golf cart. They agreed that Lou would get a vasectomy. And he intended to go through with it, no question. But there always seemed to be a scheduling conflict—a deposition or a motion or a client meeting. Over a six-month period he'd rescheduled the appointment five times.

And then she got pregnant. It was unplanned, and entirely Lou's fault, though she never said so. Abortion was out of the question for her.

"We'll get through it," she told him, "because we know what's coming at the end."

That night in the coffeehouse in Woodstock he'd gazed at his beautiful wife. Her cheeks were red from the Vermont winter air, her dark hair hanging in thick ringlets to her shoulders.

Andi had winced.

"What?" he'd asked, concerned.

She shook her head. "Another cramp. I started spotting again this morning." She stood up and took a deep breath. "I'll be back."

It was at that very moment—as he watched her walk to the bathroom—that James Taylor's "Sweet Baby James" came over the sound system:

There is a young cowboy, he lives on the range,

She'd turned at the bathroom door, remembering—remembering that song and that coffeehouse back at Wellesley. She found his eyes across the room and smiled at him before she went inside the bathroom.

Her last smile.

He'd listened to the song as he waited for her to return from the bathroom, and as he did his thoughts had drifted back to that night at the coffeehouse at Wellesley, the night they'd come back together.

Won't you let me go down in my dreams?

The waitress had interrupted his reverie, asking whether they wanted anything else. He'd ordered two more cups of hot cider, hoping Andi would return from the bathroom before the song ended.

The cider arrived. He realized the song had ended. He checked his watch. How long had it been? Twenty minutes? A tinge of panic.

He'd walked over to the women's restroom and knocked on the door. Called her name. No answer. He found a waitress and asked her to check inside to see if his wife was okay. She went in and came out a moment later, frantic.

"I'll call an ambulance," she said.

Andi was on the tile floor inside—her eyes glassy, her mouth slack. He cradled her in his arms as they waited for the ambulance. He hugged her against his chest, rocking her against him, kissing her forehead, telling her that she'd be okay, telling her how much he loved her. Over and over again, hugging and kissing and rocking as he waited and waited and the blood continued to seep out, spreading in a red pool on the tiles. She was cold and her breathing was shallow when the paramedics arrived.

He rode in the ambulance with her, holding her hands under the blanket, rubbing them, trying to make her warm, telling her everything would be okay, telling her he loved her, telling her he was sorry, and praying all the while, praying, praying.

They took her from him at the hospital—rolled her down the hall and around the corner and out of his life. As he waited those long hours, pacing the halls, his mind kept returning to the night she got pregnant, to the Jacksons' poolside party the prior August. Maybe it was the alcohol, or the St. Louis heat, or the way Andi had looked in that clingy white dress, or a combination of them all, but when she went inside to the bathroom Lou had followed her in.

"Louis," she'd giggled in surprise when he slipped into the bathroom behind her.

He kissed her hard. "Come on," he whispered, pulling up the back of her dress, grasping her marvelous tush.

"Here?" she whispered between kisses. "Now?"

"Yes."

"But I don't have my diaphragm."

He unzipped his pants. "Don't worry."

She giggled again. "Oh, my goodness. Someone's sure ready."

It could have been even worse, a nurse told him near dawn.

He'd stared at her in disbelief.

Fortunately, the nurse continued, *your wife went into shock so quickly that we knew it might be the blood. We were able to stop the other blood—the blood she was supposed to get—before it reached the other patient.*

He'd just stared at her, struggling to parse her words. *Could have been even worse?*

The nurses lips were moving, but all he heard that morning was Andi's giggle and her whisper, *But I don't have my diaphragm.*

"Hey?" Gordie said. "You okay, Lou?"

He was rubbing his eyes, his head down. He tried to say something, but he couldn't. He shook his head, biting his lower lip.

Billy found a handkerchief in the pocket of his robe and pressed it into Lou's hand. After awhile, Lou raised his head. He tried to look at his friends.

"Andi?" Billy asked softly.

Lou nodded, pressing his clenched fist against his lips, struggling for control. He took a deep breath.

"The hardest part," he finally said, "was telling my kids."

He squeezed his eyes closed and tilted his head back toward the night sky.

"I took their mother away for a weekend and brought her home in a coffin."

Billy was kneeling beside Lou. He put a hand on Lou's shoulder and gave him a squeeze.

The eastern sky was edging toward gray. The frog chorus began to fade. Lou sat there, his back against the railing, head down.

He heard the creak of the wheelchair approaching. He looked up.

Ray had a sad smile. "You're a good man, Lou. We got your back, pal."

Chapter Forty-seven

Lou pulled the cargo van into the stand of pines just to the south of the Hawthorn Airport runway. He turned off the engine and checked his watch. 7:46 a.m.

There were five of them—Lou, Ray, Gordie, Billy, and Floyd Booker, the locksmith. Each had a Styrofoam cup of coffee. There was a sack of fresh doughnuts to hold them over. Ray was belted into a captain's chair with his foot propped up, the wheelchair folded and stashed in back.

Lou opened his door. "I'll check things out."

He walked through the pine trees and across the grass to the edge of the runway. Beyond the runway he could see the two-lane blacktop road that led to the small airport. The road ran parallel to the runway. He turned back to study the pine trees. He could barely pick out their rental van through the trees. It would be invisible from the road or the airport.

He headed back to the van.

"How long will it take you, Floyd?" Gordie asked.

Floyd scratched the back of his neck as he considered the question. He was short and wiry and bald, with a pointy red nose, spiky gray eyebrows, and a neatly trimmed goatee that made him resemble a schnauzer.

"Shouldn't take but a minute," he said in his high-pitched Maine accent, "'less they got something on there I never seen before, and it's been a heckuva long time since I seen something I never seen before."

So they sipped their coffee and ate their doughnuts and waited.

At 8:15, a skinny mechanic slid open the large hangar door. Lou raised the binoculars. He could see Rocky inside the hangar in front of a single-engine biplane. She was peering around the bottom of the propeller and fiddling with something in the engine. The mechanic came over, and Rocky pointed at something. The mechanic bent down, peered at where she was pointing, stood, shook his head, and said something to her. She nodded. Then the two of them moved into position on either side of the lower wing and pushed the plane slowly onto the concrete apron outside the hangar.

Rocky had on black leather pants, a black leather jacket, black boots, and a navy Boston Red Sox baseball cap. The mechanic moved around to the propeller with a small toolbox, and Rocky returned to the hangar out of view.

At 8:51, while Gordie was out in front of the van taking a leak between two pine trees, he heard the heavy downshift of truck gears. He peered through the branches. A Brink's armored truck was rumbling along the road toward the airport. Following directly behind was a red Porsche convertible with the top down. Gordie squinted. He could make out Frank behind the wheel and Reggie in the passenger seat. He quickly zipped up and hurried back to the van.

The five of them watched from the van as the Brink's truck swung around the bend and out of view on its approach to the airport. It reappeared a moment later, moving slowly down the paved lane along the outer wall of the hangar, turned onto the concrete apron in front of the hangar, and pulled up to the biplane. The Porsche parked behind it.

Ray checked his watch. "So far so good."

From their cover in the pine trees, they had a side view of the truck and the Porsche. Reggie and Frank got of the Porsche and walked into the hangar. A moment later a uniformed guard stepped down from the passenger side of the Brink's truck, came around the front of the truck, and walked over to the plane.

Inside the hangar, they could see Frank and Reggie greeting Rocky.

"You sure about this pilot?" Ray asked.

Lou shrugged. "I'm not sure about anything. We signed the agreement last night and I gave her the check."

Frank, Reggie, and Rocky emerged from the hangar, Rocky in the middle. They walked over to the Brink's truck, and the uniformed Brink's guard joined them. Frank and Rocky spoke with the guard while Reggie trotted back to the Porsche. He returned a moment later carrying what looked like a big bolt of shiny gold fabric bound with rope. He stopped at the tail of the plane, and Frank and Rocky joined him back there. Frank helped unwind the rope, which appeared to be connected to the bolt of fabric. Rocky tied the rope to a metal hook on the bottom of the plane's tail.

"What's that?" Billy asked.

"A banner," Ray said.

The guard moved to the rear of the Brink's truck and rapped on the door. The door opened from the inside and another guard poked his head out. From his angle in the van, Lou couldn't see what else was in the truck.

Rocky walked toward the front of the biplane as the two guards talked with Frank and Reggie at the rear of the truck. On her way to the cockpit, Rocky pulled open the cargo door on the side of the plane. She walked around the front of the plane to the other side, stepped up onto the lower wing, and climbed into the cockpit.

A moment later the engine coughed and the propeller lurched through a half-rotation. It stopped for a moment, jerked through a full rotation, slowed again, and then the engine caught, immediately transforming the blades into a blurred circle. The engine coughed, vented several bursts of dark gray smoke, and then roared.

The two guards had climbed into the rear of the truck and were sliding a large gray strongbox onto the elevator ramp at the edge of the truck. The strongbox was at least six feet high and four feet wide. Once it was on the ramp, the two guards lowered it to the ground.

"That has to be her." Lou handed the binoculars to the locksmith. "Check it out, Floyd."

The guards slid the strongbox onto a large dolly. As they started to tilt it back, Reggie came over and had them stop. He knelt by the container and inserted a key into the large steel lock that hung from the latch on the hinged front panel. He opened the lock, slipped it off, and swung open the door of the strongbox. Although Lou couldn't make out what was inside the container from that distance, it was clear that Reggie was satisfied with what he saw. He closed the front of the strongbox, slipped the lock through the latch, and clicked it shut.

"Well?" Ray asked Floyd Booker.

The locksmith lowered the binoculars and nodded solemnly. "Don't think that one should be a problem, boys."

The guards rolled the strongbox over to the side of the plane and then, with Frank's help, slowly lifted it into the cargo hold. Frank closed the cargo door and checked to make sure it was firmly shut. Then he backed away from the plane and gave Rocky the thumbs-up signal. The engine revved higher, and the plane started to move forward.

Frank scanned the airport road as Reggie watched the biplane taxi slowly past the hangar toward the runway, its wings vibrating. The plane turned into position at that end of the runway. The engine whined louder. The plane was shuddering now, straining against the brakes. Rocky pushed the engine speed one notch higher and then released the brakes.

The plane started rolling down the runway, picking up speed. The bolt of gold cloth attached to the tail bounced along and unrolled until it trailed flat behind, skimming along the concrete.

Halfway down the runway the plane's wheels lifted off the ground.

After the plane cleared the trees across the highway, Rocky banked it back toward Frank and Reggie in a big, easy turn. They waved as the plane passed over the runway, climbing into the sky. The banner had fully unfurled. It was gold, with bold red letters spelling out the message:

WELCOME HOME, SIRENA!

Rocky dipped the wings in a salute and then banked the plane south. Down below, Reggie and Frank slapped each other high fives.

Ray said, "Enjoy the moment, you preppie motherfuckers."

They watched Reggie and Frank shake hands with the Brink's guards and get back in the Porsche. A moment later, there was a squeal of rubber as the Porsche pulled away. The guards got back in the Brink's truck, turned it around in front of the hangar, and drove off.

As soon as the truck disappeared around the bend in the road, Ray said, "Hit it."

Lou started the engine and backed the van out of the stand of pines and onto the road. Shifting to Drive, he accelerated down the road and turned into the airport entrance, scattering gravel under the wheels. Pulling the van around the hangar and onto the concrete apron, he stopped in almost the same spot the Brink's truck had parked.

Gordie was the first one out. Shading his eyes, he scanned the sky. Billy got out next, went around to the back of the van, and opened the rear doors to work on the final preparations. Ray waited in the van.

Lou and the locksmith joined Gordie on the runway.

"Where the hell is she?" Gordie asked.

Lou scanned the sky, straining his ears for the sound of the plane.

"How's the time?" Gordie asked.

Lou checked his watch.

10:05 a.m.

Rocky was supposed to fly over Remington Field at Barrett College at exactly eleven o'clock. While the plane could get there in less than twenty minutes, it would take them thirty-five minutes to drive there.

Over the field by 11:00. Touch down at 11:05. Out of there by 11:15. That was the schedule. That was the deal.

"We've got fifteen minutes," Lou said.

"Come on, Rocky," Gordie grumbled.

"Gordie," Billy called from back of the van. "I need some help with this thing."

"Hold your horses," Gordie said. He shaded his eyes as he surveyed the sky. "First we need the damn plane. If that skanky bitch double-crossed us, I swear—"

"Quiet," Lou said.

Lou pointed at a small dot near the horizon. "There?"

Gordie squinted in the direction of the faint buzzing. As the dot grew larger, they could make out the two wings and then the banner.

Gordie sighed. "Thank fucking God."

He turned toward Billy. "Coming, Bronco."

Lou watched the biplane bank into position and descend toward the runway, the wings tilting side to side, the banner fluttering at the slower speed. The plane landed, slowed to taxi speed, and puttered over to where Lou stood.

He turned to the locksmith. "You ready, Floyd?"

"Yep."

Lou walked with him toward the plane and yanked open the cargo door.

He turned to the locksmith and checked his watch. "Let's do it. We're cutting this close."

Chapter Forty-eight

Twenty-three miles southeast of Hawthorn Airport, the Barrett College sesquicentennial celebration is getting underway with all the pomp and circumstance befitting a distinguished New England college founded before the Civil War, ranked every year at or near the top of the *U.S. News and World Report* list of best liberal arts colleges, and whose alumni include one U.S. President, two Justices of the U.S. Supreme Court, and four Nobel Prize recipients.

It is a glorious day for a glorious birthday party. The sky is blue, the flowers are in bloom, and the birds are singing. The college band plays "Oh Gallant Barrett" at a stately pace as the Board of Trustees and honored guests walk in slow procession through the ornate cast-iron gates of Remington Field, down the cinder track alongside the football field, and onto the freshly mowed grass, where rows of chairs face the packed stands. Following the trustees and honored guests come the president and the deans and the members of the faculty, all clad in the special caps, tams, hoods, robes, and embellishments of their professional societies.

The murmuring in the stands rises as the crowd recognizes the men and women scheduled to receive honorary degrees today. There's John Updike over there—that gray-haired fellow readjusting his burgundy mortarboard as he takes his seat in the front row on the dais. And isn't that Henry Kissinger—the third one from the left? Who's the black woman he's talking to? My

God, it's Toni Morrison. And that woman there, the one pausing to nod at the pack of photographers and cameramen—why,
that's Justice Sandra Day O'Connor.

Proud sons of Barrett—and daughters, too—fill the stands.
All ages, including many future sons and daughters of Barrett.
Most are seated by class, and many of the classes hold up banners
and signs. There's the Class of '64, looking prosperous, well-fed,
and in their prime. And over there, the Class of '54—a gaggle
of board directors and CEOs and senior partners of major law
firms. And down near the front, squinting under their sun visors
and leaning forward on their canes, are John Andrew Davis IV
and Theodore Adams Worthington—the two surviving members of the Class of '16, both of whom had joined the American
Expeditionary Force right after graduation and served together
under General John Joseph Pershing. Each man wears on his
lapel the medal of valor he received for his role in the Battle of
Château-Thierry.

And then there are the members of the press. Lots and lots
of members of the press. Far more and far more varied than one
might ordinarily expect to attend the sesquicentennial of a fine
old college, even with its lineup of distinguished honorees. There
are plenty of other fine old academic institutions celebrating
special anniversaries this June and conferring honorary degrees
on notable jurists and artists and public servants. And while
the presence of a Supreme Court justice and President Nixon's
Secretary of State might be expected to lure the *New York Times*
and the *Washington Post* up to New England on this sunny day, it
is safe to assume that the film crews from *Entertainment Tonight*
and several news networks and the journalists and photographers
from *People* and *Vanity Fair* and *Newsweek* are not here today
crowding onto the cinder track just to catch a glimpse of the
author of *Rabbit, Run*.

The sesquicentennial speeches are a bracing mix of clichés.
They allude to "bold plans of action" for the future and "blessed
remembrances" of the past. Some of the speakers focus on the
challenges facing Barrett College as it "stands on the threshold

of a new millennium." Others charm the crowd with anecdotes from the college's first century and a half. In due time, honorary degrees are awarded, and those honored accept their degrees to polite rounds of applause.

But through it all, through the speeches and the music and the good cheer, every pair of eyes in the stands—young and old alike—keeps straying from the speaker behind the podium to the fifty-yard marker on the far sideline. That's where the Shield armored truck is parked. Everyone knows why it is here, and everyone knows to the dollar what is waiting inside.

The truck had been parked in position when the early birds started filing into the stadium at 9:30 that morning. They had watched from the stands as one television crew after another set up in front of the Shield truck to tape a short stand-up. It makes a striking framing shot. Indeed, the live feed from the CNN film crew has the truck in the background with the dais in the foreground. And speaking of CNN, isn't that Wolf Blitzer—the guy with the white beard and microphone over on the sidelines?

As the speakers drone on, the armored truck bears silent witness to two other anniversaries on this date. One hundred years ago to the day, Sirena arrived at the college. Indeed, she had been presented to the college president as part of the school's fiftieth anniversary celebration in 1894. So, too, this is the thirty-fifth year—to the day—of her final departure. Even for those with no interest in numerology, the numbers—150, 50, and 35—align this morning in near occult formation.

For those in the stands who have followed the recent buildup, who have read the articles in *People* and *Newsweek* or watched the half-hour feature on CNN last night, there are two others present today even more distracting than the armored truck on the fifty-yard line. They are Silicon Valley billionaire Robert Godwin ('59), and Susanna Harkness, great-granddaughter of the sculptor Augustus Cromwell, whose most famous work disappeared thirty-five years ago. Godwin, through his foundation, and Harkness, through her family's trust, represent the twenty-five million-dollar pledge—twenty-three million dollars of endowment funds for the college, two million for her rescuers. More precisely, twenty-three million in *potential* endowment money. The pledge is payable only if Sirena returns before today's ceremonies end.

Beginning two days ago, as the alumni started arriving for the big weekend, the air began to fill with news and rumors of the various Sirena quests. There has been more than enough speculation to keep that gray-and-black Shield Security Systems truck in everyone's field of vision throughout the morning's ceremonies.

Which means that the crowd is fully primed when the show finally begins.

Right on schedule.

Henry Kissinger has just finished thanking the Board of Trustees for his honorary doctorate. As he heads back to his chair under the cover of polite applause, the biplane comes into view in the sky above the hills to the west.

What initially catches the crowd's attention is its altitude. It seems to be flying unusually low. But what really gets them buzzing is the flight path. Although the plane is still at least a mile away, it is starting to look like the damn thing is going to fly directly over Remington Field. Then it banks to the west (to your left if you are sitting in the stands).

"There's a banner!" someone shouts.

And sure enough, there is a banner. When the biplane first appeared on the horizon, flying head-on toward the stands, the banner was hidden from view. But now you can see its red letters on a gold background. Too far away to read, though, and getting farther by the second. A wave of disappointment passes through the crowd. Probably some car dealer hired it to fly an advertisement around western Massachusetts, like the one last Sunday:

MACKLIND FORD—BEST DEAL AROUND!

Just as the crowd starts to lose interest, just as several generations of sons and daughters of Barrett begin to shift their attention to the next speaker at the podium, the biplane veers sharply around.

Whoa!

It's now heading due south, directly toward the field. All eyes in the stands—and all cameras and videocams on the cinder track—lift toward the left to follow the plane.

The banner becomes legible.

"Oh my God!" someone shouts.

Others join in. And then everyone—in the stands, on the field, on the dais—is standing. Down on the cinder track, the cameras are clicking away and the videocam crews are tracking the plane's flight.

The plane comes in low, passing over the goalposts and down the middle of the football field in front of the stands, barely a hundred feet above the grass, its engine whining. The bold red words on the bright gold banner are visible to all:

WELCOME HOME, SIRENA!

Good Lord!

Holy shit!

People cheer and clap and stomp and whistle and shout as the biplane zooms past. It banks east as it passes over the goalposts and climbs into the sky in a wide arc, heading back north for another flyby.

"LADIES AND GENTLEMEN!" a voice booms over the loudspeakers—a new voice. "LOYAL SONS AND DAUGHTERS OF BARRETT!"

All eyes shift from the biplane to the dais.

The speaker stands at the podium. He is a tall man with brown hair. Next to him is a shorter, stockier fellow. Both are wearing bright-colored sports jackets—the speaker's is kelly green, his sidekick's a canary yellow.

The speaker removes the microphone from its holder and walks toward the front of the dais.

"My name is Frank Burke," he says. "This is Reggie Pelham. We are loyal members of the Class of Seventy-four."

A proud roar goes up from a section of the crowd behind the Class of '74 banner.

"Reggie!" someone shouts.

"Yo, Frank!"

On the cinder track in front of the dais, the photographers snap away and the videocam operators jostle for position.

Frank gestures toward the approaching biplane.

"On behalf of the distinguished members of the great Class of Nineteen Seventy-four, please join us in a special salute to... THE LONG LOST GODDESS OF BARRETT!"

The crowd shouts and cheers as the plane does another flyby, this time just fifty feet above the football field, its engine roaring.

Microphone in hand, Frank strolls across the dais, the cameras and videocams tracking his movements.

"Thirty-five years ago she vanished," he says, clearly relishing this moment in the spotlight. "For thirty-five years we've wondered if she'd left us for good. For thirty-five years we've wondered if we'd ever see her again. But during all those lonely years, during those decades of separation, we knew in our hearts that she was still our goddess. Ours and no one else's. Well, my friends"—he pauses with a big grin, allowing the shouts and whistles and cheers to build again—"Reggie and I are pleased to announce that thirty-five years of separation IS ABOUT TO COME TO AN END!"

The crowd roars.

"Yes, ladies and gentlemen, loyal sons and daughters of Barrett"—he turns toward the field as the biplane approaches—"Today marks a special birthday. Our beautiful Sirena turns one hundred today. And guess what? SHE'S COME HOME TO PARTY!"

The crowd explodes with cheers and whistles.

Frank replaces the microphone in its holder and jumps down from the dais to join Reggie on the grass. He gestures toward three men in overalls who had stepped out on the cinder track while he was addressing the crowd. One of the men is rolling a dolly.

Frank and Reggie stride onto the football field, followed by the photographers and videocam operators and reporters.

What happens next will play as one long tracking shot that night on CNN, Fox News, and NBC Nightly News:

The plane comes in low over the north goalposts. It touches down at the fifteen-yard line and taxies to a stop at mid-field, the engine still running, the propeller a blur.

Frank steps forward and, with a flourish, yanks open the cargo door. He moves aside to give everyone in the stands—and every photographer and cameraman on the field—an unobstructed view of the tall metal container inside.

The three men in overalls move through the crowd of journalists to the plane, slide the container out of the cargo hold, and lower it onto the dolly. Frank and Reggie lead the way back to the dais as the workers roll the dolly across the field, the press trailing behind. The cheering of the crowd grows louder as they approach.

Meanwhile, the biplane turns and taxies back to the north end zone. Then it turns around to face the field, its engine revving high, and starts rolling forward, bouncing along the grass as it picks up speed. Just as the three men in overalls lift the container onto the dais, the biplane takes off and banks west, ignored by the crowd.

All eyes are now on the dais. No one notices the beige cargo van that has pulled to the edge of the end zone on the north side of the football field.

Frank and Reggie climb onto the dais. They stand on either side of the strongbox, waving at the cheering spectators, posing for pictures. As the applause continues, Reggie removes the key from his pocket and opens the lock on the large container. Then he slips the lock off and, with a dramatic flair, tosses it to the ground. The crowd roars.

Frank has the microphone again.

"It's Sirena's 100th birthday, people. Join us in a stirring round of Happy Birthday."

Frank pauses, raises his hand like a conductor, and starts them off:

"Happy birthday to you—"

Reggie opens the latch as the crowd joins in the song—
"—HAPPY BIRTHDAY TO YOU—"

Reggie looks up at Frank, who winks and gives him the thumbs-up sign.

"—HAPPY BIRTHDAY DEAR SIRENA—"

Reggie yanks open the door with a flamboyant pirouette that ends with him stepping back to allow the workmen to slide her out—

"—HAPPY birth—"

The chorus dwindles into silence, except for a few children's voices that continue on for another measure or so before stopping.

It is a stunned silence.

An eerie, incredulous silence, the hush broken only by the whirs and snaps of the cameras.

From somewhere in the crowd comes the cry, "You sick bastards!"

Frank turns toward the open container.

At least a dozen photographers catch that moment, including both of the ones on assignment from *People*. The best of those shots will be featured in the cover story with the following tag line: "Unveiling the Groucho Madonna."

For there, inside the container, sits not the legendary Sirena but a concrete Madonna. Not the singer but the mother of Jesus. Yes, one of those tacky lawn-ornament Madonnas. And no ordinary tacky lawn ornament, either. Oh, no. This concrete Madonna is wearing a Groucho Marx mask—that plastic eyeglass-nose-mustache contraption. She is also wearing a rigid cone-shaped black brassiere straight out of a 1950s porno flick. The center of each brassiere cup is cut out, exposing concrete nipples painted cherry red.

As the writer for *Vanity Fair* would later observe, "All that was missing from the bizarre tableau was a lawn jockey in a leather jockstrap and matching whip."

Chapter Forty-nine

"Now," Ray said.

Lou shifted into Drive and eased the cargo van forward onto the end zone and then the playing field. Boos and catcalls were still pouring down from the stands. No one had yet noticed the van.

As they passed the twenty-yard line, Gordie reached over to honk the horn. He kept his hand on the horn as Lou drove toward midfield.

"Who's that?" someone in the stands called out.

"Who are those guys?"

"Oh, Jesus, now what?"

"Are they drunk?"

When the van reached the midfield stripe, Lou turned it toward the stands and drove slowly down the center aisle between the rows of seated dignitaries, past the dais, and out onto the cinder track as the reporters and photographers moved aside. He swung the van all the way around and pulled it up, stopping with the front bumper almost touching the dais, just to the left of the Groucho Madonna. The rear of the van faced the crowd, which by now was murmuring and buzzing with a mixture of perplexity and suspicion.

Just what in the hell is going on now?

Lou put the transmission in Park, turned off the engine, and got out on the driver's side. Gordie got out on the front passenger side. Billy slid open the side door, stepped down, turned back to lift out the wheelchair, set it on the grass, and unfolded it. Then the three of them carried Ray out of the van and onto the wheelchair.

The crowd in the stands watched in puzzled, expectant silence.

Lou wheeled Ray over toward the dais. Gordie and Billy walked around to the rear of the van and took up positions side by side facing the stands. Lou climbed onto the dais, walked over to Frank Burke, and yanked the microphone out of his hand. Frank glared at him. Lou turned, went back to the edge of the platform, climbed down, and held the microphone toward Ray.

Ray shook his head. "You do it."

"Take it," Lou said. "This one is yours."

Ray considered him for a moment and then smiled. He took the microphone and squinted at the crowd in the stands.

"Hi, folks," he said. "Ray Gorman here. Class of '74. These are my freshman roommates. This is Lou Solomon. That's Gordie Cohen over there. And Billy McCormick. We call him Bronco."

Lou scanned the crowd. He spotted Katie and Kenny. They were standing next to Brandi and waving. He grinned and nodded at them.

"Frank and Reggie put on quite a show, eh?" Ray said. He turned slightly to give them a wink.

Hisses and boos from the crowd.

Frank and Reggie were still up on the stage. Frank stared at Ray. Reggie's eyes were down, as if he were looking for a trap door.

"Great bit, fellows." The acid in Ray's voice was detectible all the way to the top row of the stands.

Ray turned back to the crowd. "We don't have an air show, folks but we're still awfully glad to be here. You see—" he paused "—we found someone special on our trip to Barrett, and we decided to bring her home."

Lou could feel the surge of excitement through the stands.

"Believe it or not," Ray said, "we found her hanging out inside the scoreboard at Wrigley Field." He shook his head. "Thirty-five years of Cubs games, poor thing. So we rescued her."

Lou nodded at Gordie and Billy. Gordie unlatched one door and Billy unlatched the other. As the photographers and video-cams moved into position, the two men flung open the doors, reached in to slide the statue to the edge of the open back, and turned toward the crowd.

It was a wonderful scene—so wonderful, in fact, that it made the front page of the next morning's *Boston Globe*: Gordie and Billy flanking the famous statue, Lou and Ray to the side, all four men grinning, Sirena gazing into the distance.

As the applause and cheers continued and the cameras clicked and whirred, people started coming down out of the stands. First in singles, then in pairs, then in whole groups. They came down and walked over to the van to stare at Sirena. One of the first ones, an elderly man with a Class of '27 ribbon attached to his straw boater, put out a hand and touched her. Behind him a line began to form, and within minutes it stretched past the end zone—young and old, men and women, patiently waiting for their chance to touch the Siren of Barrett.

Lou moved off to the side and watched the reporters and photographers surge toward Ray, shouting questions at him.

It's Ray's moment, he said to himself, and he was glad.

He searched the crowd for his children. Just as he spotted them coming down the stairs with Brandi, someone grabbed him roughly by the arm. He turned to find himself eye to eye with Frank Burke.

"You fucking bastard."

Lou glanced down at his arm. "You want to take that hand off me?"

Frank's face was flushed red with anger, the vein in his right temple throbbing. "Enjoy it while you can."

Lou gazed at him calmly. "Is that supposed to be a threat?"

"You better believe it, asshole. You stole her."

"No, Frank. You stole her. We just took her back."

"You set us up, you cheating bastard."

"Cheating? Remember what you told me yesterday, Frank?

There's no crying in baseball. Same with Sirena. Suck it up. Those are your words, Frank, not mine. Live by 'em, die by 'em."

Frank shook his head. "You and your pals are going to pay big-time for this cheap trick. I'm going to find a lawyer and—"

"—Find one? You're looking at one, Frank."

Lou moved closer, their faces now less than a foot apart. His voice was low, barely above a whisper. "If I were you, Frank, I'd say a prayer every night until the statute of limitations runs out on Gordie's claims for assault and intentional infliction of emotional distress for what you had that hooker do to him. Trust me, Frank, if he ever gets you in front of a Cook County jury, they'll shove your head so far up your ass that every time you fart your lips'll quiver. Now get out of my sight."

Lou turned to find his children.

"Hey, fuckhead!"

Lou turned just in time to see Frank's punch coming. It was a big roundhouse swing, thrown with the sluggish windup of a man who'd never been in a fistfight in his life. Lou easily ducked the punch and came straight up with his right fist. The uppercut smashed into Frank's chin, snapping back his head. His legs wobbled as he stared wide-eyed at Lou, trying to keep his head steady, his body listing to the right. Then his eyes rolled up and he crumpled to the grass.

There was a smattering of applause.

Some guy hollered "Way to go, dude!"

Lou looked down at his right hand. The knuckles were throbbing.

"Daddy!" Kenny shouted as he ran up. He hugged Lou around the stomach.

Katie was grinning as she approached. "Awesome, Dad."

Chapter Fifty

Ray popped the tab on another beer. "All things considered, Reggie was cool about it."

"Oh?" Lou said.

"After the TV guys cleared out, he came over and shook my hand. Told me it was a great bit."

Gordie said "Even told me he was sorry about the motel scene."

Ray took a sip of beer. "Maybe there's hope for that preppy douche bag."

"Don't get mushy in your old age," Lou said.

None of them wanted this moment to end. It was, at last, an isle of tranquility at the end of one of the wildest days of their lives. Following the Remington Field craziness was a seemingly endless round of interviews, and then it was off to Braxton Hall for Sirena's official homecoming, where she would bide her time, surrounded by armed guards, until a state-of-the-art security system could be installed. After that, the four of them, along with Lou's kids, Billy's family, and Brandi Wine, had been guests of honor at a luncheon at the president's mansion. Then a press conference, more interviews, and a late afternoon private meeting with Rocky the pilot and her boyfriend. From there it was off to the Class of '74 reunion banquet under the tent. Throughout the dinner, classmates came over to pump their hands and slap them on the back. Neither Frank nor Reggie showed up. Then it was back to Remington Field for the sesquicentennial fireworks extravaganza.

An hour after the final rocket exploded, the four of them met in the lobby of the Barrett Inn. The original plan had been to have a few farewell rounds of beer in the bar, but a noisy function in the ballroom made conversation impossible, so they bought a bucket of iced Rolling Rocks from the bartender, went outside, grabbed three chairs off the back veranda, and carried them onto the lawn behind the inn. They arranged the chairs and Ray's wheelchair in a semicircle facing the veranda, put the bucket of beer and two bowls of pretzels on the grass in the middle, and settled in.

That was an hour ago. It was now nearly eleven-thirty, and what had started as a raucous gathering of four former roommates had grown subdued. And a little melancholy. They knew that this was their last night together for a long, long time. Billy and family were flying back to Chicago in the morning, Gordie following at noon, and Ray and Brandi later that afternoon to San Diego. Although they promised to do it again real soon, they all knew that "soon" could mean twenty more years. Each had his own life, his own gravitational field.

They also knew that these had been ten days together that could never be duplicated. There wouldn't be—couldn't ever be—a sequel. Charles Lindbergh might dream of a second Atlantic crossing, Neil Armstrong a return to the moon—but you could never recapture the magic of that first time. If and when they came together again—maybe for their fortieth in 2014, assuming they were all still above ground by then—it would never be more than a reunion.

"You know," Billy said, his voice faltering, "this was wonderful."

Lou smiled in the darkness.

Ray reached for another Rolling Rock. "How's the Great American Screenplay, Gordie?"

"Are you still working on that?" Billy asked.

Gordie shrugged. "I'm thinking maybe it's time to move on."

"You mean drop it?" Lou asked.

"Nah. I mean shift the focus. Make it more, uh, contemporary."

"Do me a favor, Gordie," Ray said.

"What?"

"Don't breathe a word to Brandi."

"Why not?"

"She'll try to get you to write a part for her."

"So?"

"So? You do that, man, and I'm screwed."

"You?" Billy said. "Why?"

Ray took a sip of beer and reached for the pretzels. "About six months ago, she read this article in *Forbes* about motion pictures being great tax shelters. Ever since then she's been bugging me to pour some money into one of those sinkholes."

"She's looking out for you," Billy said.

"Bronco," Ray said, "I need another tax shelter like I need another asshole. Brandi's looking out for Brandi. She wants to be in pictures."

"Well, she's smart," Billy said, "and really pretty. She'd be super in a movie."

They were quiet for a while, each lost in his own thoughts.

The sounds of a rock band came from the ballroom of the Barrett Inn.

"What's going on in there?" Billy asked.

"A wedding?" Gordie said.

No one answered.

After a moment, Lou said, "Twenty years is a long time."

"Seems like yesterday," Gordie said.

"Not really," Lou said. "We were kids back then."

"We're still kids," Gordie said.

Lou looked over at him. "No, Gordie. By the time you turn forty, you've been through too much to be a kid anymore."

They sipped their beers in the dark.

Suddenly there were lights and voices and laughter. Lou looked up as the hotel doors swung open, illuminating the veranda. High school boys and girls were streaming through the doors—the boys in tuxedos, the girls in full-length gowns.

A prom, Lou realized, rising from his chair.

June. Prom season.

Lou walked to the edge of the veranda, to the edge of darkness. The light from the veranda lit his face.

In the middle of the throng of kids was a girl in a white prom dress. A stunningly beautiful girl with dark, curly hair. She was gazing up at the stars. So lovely—and so young.

She took a deep breath and sighed with pleasure. A tall boy in a dark tuxedo came up and put his arm around her waist. She looked up at him and smiled. After a moment, the two of them turned back toward the doors and disappeared inside.

There were tears in Lou's eyes.

From the "Class Notes" section of the BARRETT COLLEGE ALUMNI MAGAZINE (Fall 1996):

CLASS OF '74
Submitted by
Bryce Wharton
(Class Secretary)

Hard to believe that more than two years have come and gone since our Big Two Zero. That insight flashed through your humble scrivener's brain a fortnight back when I attended the Left Coast nuptials of **Lou Solomon** in sunny Santa Barbara. Lou married **Donna Crawford** (Hampton '74), who looked even more winsome than in days of yore. After the "I do's" and the heartfelt toasts, Lou and his two scions, and Donna and her two heir-lettes, headed off for a one-month holiday (you heard me right fellas: thirty days and thirty nights!) in the Tuscan region of Italy, where they've rented a villa (complete with vineyard) on a hill overlooking Florence. Sounds like *la dolce vita* to me.

Rumor has it that Lou received welcome news from the Missouri Supreme Court just days before the ceremony. Something about a paralyzed widow he represents finally getting her just desserts on appeal, assuming that $3 million plus change qualifies as dessert! I'll have one of those banana splits, too, Your Honor.

The other three caballeros in the infamous James Gang were at the matrimonial. Only Sirena was missing—missing from the wedding party, that is! Don't get any funny ideas, Frank and Reggie. Just joshing, amigos. (Ha! Ha! Ha!)

Your ink-stained wretch remembered to bring his dog-eared copy of *People* to the wedding. **William "Bronco" McCormick** graciously consented to affix his John Hancock to the picture of the Gang on page 67. Bill attended with his lovely bride **Dorothy** and their charming legatee, Sandy. Bill was too modest to divulge what Dorothy was ready to proclaim from the rooftops: our own Bronco was named one of ten Illinois Teachers of the Year. ¡Muchos kudos, Señor Beel!

During the wedding reception, your intrepid reporter wheedled a few scooplets out of **Gordie Cohen**. Seems Gordo ankled his advertising job and resettled in (are your ready for this?) the lovely town of Barrett, Massachusetts. These days he shares living quarters with none other than Barrett College English Professor **Sally Jacobs**, Hampton '74, who yours truly once had the pleasure of escorting to a T.D. toga party. (Note to Prof. Sally: Where did you go that night, dahling? I still have your cup of Tropical Passion Punch.) Gordo is hard at work on a screenplay and—*drum roll, Maestro*—the Gordster may finally see his name up there in lights on the silver screen, thanks to a deep-pocketed investor.

The aforementioned deep pocket belongs to **Ray Gorman**, the mall maharajah and Hombre Mejor at Lou's nuptials. I am pleased to report that Ray had no problem "standing up" for Lou at the wedding. (Heh, Heh, Heh!) Ray was his inimitably irascible self when your servile scribe asked him to confirm that there was a cameo role in Gordie's movie for Ray's favorite little mermaid, **Brandi Wine**. Although my query triggered a few piquant suggestions—including one anatomical tour de force beyond the modest gymnastic capabilities of yours truly—let the record show that Ray did not deny the rumor. Save me an aisle seat, Raymundo, and make sure my popcorn is hot and buttered!

After the excitement of the Solomon wedding, it was back to my humble abode, where Mr. Postman has delivered missives from many of you. Keep those cards and letters coming in, folks.

We start the evening news with word from **Robbie Carlson**, who pens from the misty clime of Seattle of his promotion to...

Title: THE SIRENA QUEST }

                               }

Draft: 4th Revised   }

                               }

Author: Gordon Cohen   }

                               }

Scene: 49   }

                                     DISSOLVE TO:

EXT. THE BACK VERANDA AT THE BARRETT INN—NIGHT

ANGLE ON LOU

The four of them are seated in a semicircle, sipping beers in the quiet darkness. Suddenly bright lights and VOICES and LAUGHTER. Lou looks up as the hotel doors swing open. The light from inside brightens the veranda.

NEW ANGLE - THE VERANDA

High school boys and girls are streaming through the doors and onto the veranda. The boys are in tuxedos, the girls in full-length gowns. Prom night.

ANGLE ON LOU

as he rises from his chair and moves to the edge of the veranda, to the edge of darkness. The light from the veranda illuminates his face, his eyes wide with wonder.

NEW ANGLE

In the middle of the crowd is a girl in a prom dress so white it seems to glow.

CLOSE ON GIRL

She is stunning. So beautiful, and so young. She has dark, curly hair. Lou watches, spellbound. She gazes up at the night sky with a smile, takes a deep breath, and sighs with pleasure.

NEW ANGLE

Lou is standing, staring.

WIDER

His three friends are seated on their lawn chairs behind him, watching him.

> BILLY
> You remember prom night?

> RAY
> Sure. Drank a fifth of Jim Beam, booted on the side of my car, and passed out in the backseat.

> GORDIE
> (singing to the tune of
> "Mrs. Robinson")
> Where have you gone, Robin Silverman?

> RAY
> Yeah. Where did she go?

CLOSER ON LOU

as he stares at the high school kids.

> GORDIE
> The band took a break and she told me she was going to powder her nose. She

left.

                    RAY
    Left?

                    GORDIE
    AWOL. Gone. As in dumped me.

                    BILLY
    That's terrible.

                    GORDIE
    Welcome to my life.

CLOSE UP

of the girl in the white prom dress. A dark-haired boy
in a white tuxedo puts his arm around her waist. She
looks up at him and smiles.

ANGLE ON LOU

His eyes are shimmering.

LOU'S POINT OF VIEW

The girl in the white prom dress and the boy in the
white tuxedo turn toward the camera, smiling.

The image freezes. The color fades to black and white.
We are now staring at the prom photo of Lou and Andi
from his 1970 high school yearbook.

And on the soundtrack Neil Young is singing "Sugar
Mountain":

            ...though you're thinking that
            You're leaving there too soon.

FADE OUT

To receive a free catalog of Poisoned Pen Press titles, please provide your name and address through one of the following ways:

Phone: 1-800-421-3976
Facsimile: 1-480-949-1707
Email: info@poisonedpenpress.com
Website: www.poisonedpenpress.com

Poisoned Pen Press
6962 E. First Ave. Ste 103
Scottsdale, AZ 85251